The American Café

The American Café

Sara Sue Hoklotubbe

THE UNIVERSITY OF ARIZONA PRESS

TUCSON

The University of Arizona Press
© 2011 Sara Sue Hoklotubbe
All rights reserved

www.uapress.arizona.edu

Library of Congress Cataloging-in-Publication Data

Hoklotubbe, Sara Sue, 1952–
  The American café / Sara Sue Hoklotubbe.
    p. cm.
  ISBN 978-0-8165-2922-3 (pbk. : alk. paper)
  1. Restaurateurs—Fiction. 2. Restaurateurs—Crimes against—Fiction.
3. Family secrets—Fiction. 4. Cherokee women—Fiction. 5. Oklahoma—
Fiction. I. Title.
  PS3608.O4828A44 2011
  813'.6—dc22
                                    2010046946

This is a work of fiction. Names, characters, and incidents are products of the author's imagination and are not to be construed as real. Any resemblance to actual events or persons, living or dead, is entirely coincidental.

Manufactured in the United States of America on acid-free, archival-quality paper containing a minimum of 30 percent post-consumer waste and processed chlorine free.

16 15 14 13 12 11   6 5 4 3 2 1

For Eddie,

my source of joy and inspiration,

with love

Acknowledgments

Grateful appreciation goes to Gloria McCarty for her help with the Muscogee Creek language and her kind words of encouragement; and to Dennis Sixkiller and Wynema Smith for sharing their knowledge of Cherokee language and culture. Any errors in Native language are entirely mine. I am thankful for Judith Lee Soriano, who so generously lent her expertise to my manuscript; Pam Daoust, whose friendship and writing advice are beyond measure; Brandi Barnett, Linda Boyden, and Martha Bryant, who kindly gave of their time to lend fresh eyes to my work and make helpful suggestions; Mary Ellen Cooper, who inspired me to write mysteries and then left this earth before I had a chance to say good-bye; the Cherokee Nation Adult Choir and the Etchieson Indian Church Choir in Tahlequah, Oklahoma, who taught me to sing Cherokee hymns; my aunt Vera Youngblood Robertson, who is now baking bread in heaven, for her unconditional love, secret recipes, and principles of generosity; Patti Hartmann, acquiring editor, who believed in me enough to give me a second chance; the entire staff at the University of Arizona Press; and of course, Eddie, my loving husband, without whose constant cheerleading and loving support this book would never have been written.

Prologue

Goldie Ray knew she didn't have long to live, but she wasn't going to sit around and mope about it. Instead, she poured a second cup of coffee, stirred in a double helping of cream and sugar, and let the screen door bounce shut behind her as she made her way onto the back porch. The heady fragrance of a nearby honeysuckle bush enveloped her as she lowered herself into an old wicker chair, propped her feet on an empty flowerpot, and balanced the antique cup and saucer on her knee. She closed her eyes, inhaled, and smiled. What a beautiful day.

As she sipped from the gold-rimmed cup, she savored the taste of the fresh coffee. Holding the cup close, she used her thumbnail to outline the design of the fragile yellow rose painted on the side. The world looked different to her now as she had suddenly come to appreciate life's smaller joys. Natural, she supposed, when staring at one's own mortality.

A nuthatch landed on the feeder, picked at the seeds, then fluttered into the Oklahoma sky. Two hummingbirds zoomed through the air above her head and then disappeared. Goldie set her cup and saucer on the floor, walked to one of two hummingbird feeders hanging from the porch ceiling, and examined it. Satisfied that the flow of the ruby-red water remained unobstructed, she picked up her coffee and returned to her chair.

The way Goldie understood it, the wall of her heart had a weak spot that could explode any time—an unpredictable aneurysm. The young heart doctor with deplorable bedside manners had painted a hopeless picture, estimating a less than favorable chance of surviving surgery at her age. However, without it, he had said, her heart would give out soon. She would simply collapse and die.

Doctors don't know everything.

Goldie believed if it was her time to go, she'd simply go. She planned neither to waste money on an unpromising surgical procedure, nor spend her last days debilitated, lying in a hospital bed the way her father had done. Instead, she would opt for the unorthodox philosophy of living life to the fullest—to the very end.

Goldie didn't plan to tell anyone, including her sister Emma, about her plight. No one needed to know. She had already taken care of everything. She had prepaid her funeral years ago, and her one and only bank account didn't have enough money in it to worry about. She had deeded her house to the only living person she cared about and had sold her beloved café. And finally, when Emma arrived, they would release the ugly secret harbored for entirely too long. Then Goldie could relax and enjoy what little time she had left.

Her daily rituals hadn't changed for more than thirty-six years, but from this day forward someone else's hands would knead and punch pounds of yeast dough to yield dozens of pull-apart rolls. Some other person would roll out the pie crusts and sweeten the fruit filling to another's taste. Today she would sit on her porch and watch the sun peek over the trees, drink strong coffee, and delight in the melodies of the birds.

The restaurant had consumed Goldie's life for so long that the newfound freedom offered up by empty days seemed strange. She could hardly wait for Emma to show up. They would celebrate with a feast and bottle of pink champagne set aside for this special occasion. Then they would be off on an adventure. She had always wanted to see the Smoky Mountains, and that's where they would go. Goldie had made her peace with God. Now all she wanted to do was make up for lost time with her older sister.

Goldie took another sip. She liked Sadie, the Cherokee woman who had purchased the café. When they met, they connected as if they'd known each other their entire lives. Goldie shook her head and thought about how Sadie had made an offer to buy the café.

It all happened so fast.

It was as if the young woman had somehow known exactly what she needed.

Maybe she is an angel sent by God.

Sadie said she would come by and visit this morning. When she did, Goldie planned to share some of her secret recipes, something she wouldn't have done for just anyone. Goldie held the warm cup to her face and smiled again.

It feels right, and that's important.

Thoughts about Sadie ended abruptly with a deafening blast. A powerful thud in the middle of Goldie's back propelled her forward with excruciating pain. She tumbled in slow, uncontrollable, and soundless motion as the yellow rose on her delicate cup hit the porch and broke into three pieces, splashing coffee across the wooden floor. For a split second she saw birds flying in all directions, squirrels fleeing the grassy yard for the safety of high tree branches.

God, help me!

She felt a nail in the wooden boards of the porch tear her face as the early morning sunshine pierced the air around her. Dimly, she sensed the flight of a hummingbird as it zipped into the dead air, hovered nearby, chirped furiously, and flew away.

Who is it?

She tried to turn her head to glimpse who or what had done this to her, but she could no longer see. A blinding white light came toward her, engulfed her, and swallowed her pain.

Why?

In the distance, she heard someone speak of being sorry just before her spirit rose from the earth. For an instant, she felt forgiveness toward her assailant as she floated on eagles' wings, saw the face of the one she loved, and was gone.

The American Café

1

On July 23, 2003, a few days after celebrating her thirty-sixth birthday, Sadie Walela began a new chapter in her life. It had been one year to the day since she sat in a country cemetery mourning the loss of a little girl named Soda Pop and lamenting the course of her own life. When she later received an unexpected windfall from a life insurance policy, she used most of the money to fund a foundation for kids like Soda Pop who couldn't afford health care and set aside the rest to finance her new adventure.

She had always wanted to own a café, a desire instilled in her as a child from the stories of the café her great-aunt had owned during World War II. Sadie pulled a photo out of her pocket and gazed at the image of her great-aunt Vera in a white apron standing on the sidewalk in front of a large plate-glass window, the name "The American Café" painted in ornate, red-and-white letters behind her.

Both Vera and the café had passed on by the time Sadie was born, but everyone said Sadie resembled Vera in appearance and personality, so she kept the worn recipe books and her great-aunt's handwritten instructions for all of her culinary delights in hopes of following in her great-aunt's footsteps. That day had finally arrived.

Sadie had decided to carry on her aunt's legacy of the American Café and hoped the painter would be able to reproduce the red-and-white letters on the front window. She slid the photo back into her pocket. Now she had to figure out what to do with the permanent menu fixed high on the wall.

She walked to the middle of the empty café, placed her hands on her hips, and stared at the menu. "Let's see," she mumbled. "Liver and onions, meatloaf, fried chicken, chicken-fried steak, and catfish." She rubbed her chin and continued talking to herself. "What would we do without southern comfort food? I think we can do without liver and onions, but meatloaf might be okay since I've got Vera's meatloaf recipe. We should have ham and beans." She tapped her foot on the floor, weighing her options.

Then on the other hand, she thought, why not start out with a variety of custom-made burgers served with a choice of onion rings, regular fries, or her favorite: sweet potato fries. Everybody loves hamburgers. Standing on her tiptoes, she pried at the bottom corner of the menu, trying to loosen its ancient grip on the old brick wall.

A man's voice came from the corner of the room. "You must be the new owner."

Startled, she jerked her hand away from the menu and stumbled backward. Her heart raced when she looked toward the stranger, his face obscured in the early morning shadows. A ray of light filtered through the plate-glass window behind him.

"Geez, you about gave me a heart attack," she said. "Are you the painter my uncle called?"

The man calmly removed his hat and placed it on the stool next to him. His face remained hidden in the shadows. "You're not going to change the menu, are you?"

Sadie slowly exhaled. Her eyes had finally adjusted to the glare of the window, and she could tell her visitor appeared to be an Indian man in his early sixties. He had a slight build, gray hair, and an infectious smile. He looked like someone the neighborhood kids would gather around to tug at his pant legs until he gave them each a piece of candy or lucky coin.

As she walked toward him, she smoothed a wisp of shiny black hair from her face and offered her hand. "I'm Sadie Walela," she said.

"*Eto-Catuce.*" He took her hand. "But you can call me Red." His clear eyes reminded Sadie of the sky on a moonless night.

"Say it again," she requested. "That's not Cherokee, is it?"

"*Edo Chah-doo-chee.*" He emphasized the pronunciation for her and then added, "Muscogee Creek." The wrinkles deepened in his weathered face and his eyes flashed as he grinned. "You're taking over the place? What are you going to paint?"

"Yes, I need the new name painted on the front window." Sadie fished for the photo in her pocket.

"What's the new name?"

Sadie laid the photo on the counter in front of him. "The American Café. Can you do it just like it is in the picture?"

"Not me. I don't paint."

She could feel the warmth rising to her cheeks. "You're not here to paint the window, are you?"

"Nope. Just anxious for the café to open back up. Why did you name it the American Café? Why not the Indian Café? Or, how about the Cherokee Café?" His face took on a mischievous grin. "This is Cherokee country, and you look like you might be Cherokee."

Sadie replaced the photo in her pocket. "If you're not the painter, then who are you?"

"Told you already," he said. "Red."

Red seemed an unlikely name for an Indian. "You guessed right," she said. "I'm Cherokee. Where'd you get a name like Red?"

He nodded. "*Eto-Catuce* means Red Stick in Creek."

"Oh, okay. Nice to meet you, Red. I named it the American Café in honor of an ancestor." Dismissing the man, she returned to the middle of the café and began to eye the menu again. "Thanks for stopping by," she said, "but I'm not quite open for business yet." She hoped he would take the hint and leave.

"You want me to make the coffee?" he asked. "People are going to be here soon." No sooner had he finished his statement than the front door opened and three men in worn overalls entered. They each nodded silent greetings to Red, took their seats, placed their arms on the counter, and looked at Sadie.

"Are one of you guys the painter?" she asked.

The men exchanged puzzled looks and all three shook their heads.

"Well, then, I'm sorry, but I'm not serving food. The café's not open. The only reason the door is unlocked is because I'm expecting a painter."

The man in the middle spoke first. "That's okay, Miss," he said. "We heard you were here and came by to see what you looked like. Figured we could run a pot of coffee if nothing else. Goldie always lets us make our own coffee."

The man next to him removed his cap blazoned with the Farmer's Co-op emblem and nodded at Sadie. "I'd be proud to do the honors."

Sadie didn't know what to say. This was only her second trip to the café since she had closed on the deal. She had made this trip to do some cleaning and meet the painter. She certainly hadn't counted on so many folks taking such an overly friendly interest in her project. She shrugged her shoulders, not troubling to hide her irritation at the distraction these determined customers were creating. "I don't even know if I have coffee."

The second man slid around the end of the counter and pulled out a box of coffee packets from an underneath shelf. With a toothy grin he said, "Yes, ma'am, we've got coffee. May I?" He held open the palms of his hands. "They're clean. I just washed up before we came."

"Well, I guess." Sadie reluctantly nodded.

He pulled a packet of coffee from the box and placed it strategically in the strainer, then hit the red button on the front of the brewer and waited. Moments later, steaming coffee spewed into the waiting pot. The man returned to his seat and the conversation resumed.

The man in the middle spoke again. "My name is Virgil Wilson," he said. "These are my two boys, Barney and Junior. Moved here from Arkansas and bought the old sawmill at the edge of town last year."

"Sadie Walela," she said and offered her hand.

"Walela." Virgil shook her hand, then repeated her name as if trying to get the pronunciation just right. "What kind a name's that?"

"Cherokee. Means hummingbird in Cherokee."

"She's pretty as a hummingbird, too, isn't she?" Red winked at her and grinned.

Virgil smiled and nodded. "We're on our morning break and thought we'd stop by on the outside chance you might be open."

Sadie looked at the teapot-shaped clock on the wall. If the old timepiece was right, it was barely past seven o'clock. "You must have started pretty early if it's already time for a break."

"Yes, ma'am. We like to start splitting logs around five-thirty before it gets too hot, so by now we're ready for chow. We've been eating down at the Home Café since Goldie closed, but they can't cook anything like Goldie. Can you cook?"

"Well of course I can cook. It runs in my blood." She glanced at the menu. "I'm not sure about keeping those particular items on the menu, but we'll see." She raised her finger for emphasis. "I'm a quick study and Goldie promised to go over everything with me."

The coffeepot squeaked as it finished its cycle, and Sadie pulled four cups from a nearby shelf, placed them on the counter, and started pouring.

Carefully, she served the hot liquid to the three sawmill workers, then carried one cup to the end of the counter to Red, who had been quietly taking everything in.

"*Wado.*" Red grinned as he spoke the Cherokee word of thanks. "May I have a saucer?"

"*Howa.*" She answered without thinking, then stopped and turned toward him. "Hey, I thought you said you're a Creek."

He winked. "Multilingual."

Sadie rolled her eyes, then retrieved a saucer for him while the men at the counter swallowed their coffee so fast she wondered if it was even hot.

Red placed the saucer under his cup and carefully spilled coffee into it. He set his cup on the counter, raised the saucer to his lips and slurped, then repeated the ritual.

Before long, Virgil stopped talking and stood, signaling the end of the break for his workers. As he reached into his pocket and dropped several bills onto the counter, the door to the café burst open and a woman stormed inside.

Gray hair escaped from the bun on top of her head and floated in the air around her pink wrinkled face. She wore a sweat-stained, long-sleeved blouse and a long skirt that fell to the top of her boots. With squinty eyes and tight lips, she raised her left hand and stuck out a bony finger. "I know who you are, young lady, and I'm not going to let you reopen this godforsaken den of sin. You hear me?"

Perplexed by the woman's words, Sadie raised her chin and looked at her. "I'm sorry, I don't think we've met."

"Oh, get out of here, you old goat," Virgil blared from behind Sadie.

"I've got me a gun," the woman threatened. "It works real good and I know how to use it. If you don't believe me, just ask Goldie Ray."

"What are you talking about, old woman?" asked Virgil.

The woman raised her other hand and exposed a sawed-off shotgun from the folds of her long skirt. All three men at the counter dove at her simultaneously. As she aimed at Sadie, Red rounded the end of the counter with incredible speed and pushed Sadie to the floor.

Before the woman could pull the trigger, Virgil jerked the shotgun from her hands and Barney pinned her elbows to her waist. The wiry woman squirmed and kicked. Raising her knees, she managed to land the heel of her right boot slightly above Junior's left eye. He backed up, lost his balance, and fell on his rear next to the stool he had been sitting on moments earlier.

"Hold still, old woman," Virgil yelled.

Junior, regaining his senses, grabbed her feet and held them together. She cried out, stopped struggling, and fell limp.

By then, Sadie had pushed Red away, jumped to her feet, and rounded the end of the counter to rush headlong into the middle of the fracas. She grabbed the gun away from Virgil, freeing his hands so he could help the others.

"Who in hell let her out of the loony bin, anyway?" Junior pulled himself to his feet.

"Oh, our great state probably deemed her cured and sent her home so they wouldn't have to spend any more money to feed her." Virgil turned his head, trying to pull his face away from the woman's flighty hair. "What's wrong with you, Pearl? Are you going to behave if we let you go?"

Pearl nodded and the two men slowly loosened their grasp. She stood up and straightened her blouse. Her bun, barely attached, had fallen onto the back of her head.

Sadie broke open the chamber of the confiscated shotgun and looked around at everyone there. "It isn't even loaded." She placed the gun on the counter and approached the woman. "Who are you, and why did you do that? If that gun had been loaded, you could have killed someone. And why did you call this place a den of sin?"

The woman didn't answer, only frowned and stuck her nose in the air.

"If you want to call the police, we'll wait," said Virgil. "But it might take old George a while to get here. I heard he's got a new girlfriend. And Pearl's just a little off, that's all."

Sadie's eyes widened at Virgil's take on the situation.

"I thought he hired a new police officer," said Junior.

"She's never hurt anyone before," offered Red.

Sadie thought for a moment. "No, I'm all right. No harm done, I guess."

"Just consider yourself warned." Pearl pulled away from Virgil. "Let me go. I've got to go to the bathroom." With that pronouncement she walked to the bathroom near the kitchen and slammed the door shut behind her.

"We'll wait and make sure she's gone," Virgil picked up the weathered ball cap that Pearl had knocked off his head earlier, "then you can lock up when we leave." He slapped the cap on his knee and placed it on his head.

"Thanks." Sadie smiled at her new friends.

Everyone stood staring at the restroom door until Red finally walked over and knocked. No answer. He tried the doorknob. It wouldn't budge. Turning to Sadie, he asked, "Where's the key for this door?"

"I have no idea, but there must be one around here somewhere." She looked around, returned to the counter, and started opening drawers.

Red ran his finger above the door facing and retrieved a clump of dirt and a tarnished key. "Here it is," he called to Sadie. The others watched as Red unlocked the door and pushed it open. Even though the small window didn't look big enough to offer the woman an escape route, she was gone.

Virgil walked over to the window, slid it closed, and turned the rusty lock. "If it's okay with you, I'll drop off Pearl's gun at the police station."

"Okay." Sadie placed her hands on her hips. "But that woman had better realize she can't go around threatening people like that."

"You boys go on back to the mill." Virgil nodded toward the door. "We've got work to do."

As the three men left the restaurant, the front door closed behind them and Sadie stood staring into space. Finally, she looked at Red, who had returned to his seat at the end of the counter. "Wow. What was that all about?"

"Oh, that's Pearl Mobley. She's harmless."

Sadie pushed a lock of hair out of her eyes. "I'm glad you think so."

"I'll take some more of that good coffee if there's any left. Mine spilled all over the place."

"That's okay. I'll clean it up." She walked back to the coffeepot, picked it up and filled his cup, then poured one for herself before returning the pot to the burner. She grabbed a pile of napkins and wiped up the spilled coffee, then began to empty packets of sugar and powdered creamer into her cup.

The door opened and a slim Hispanic man walked in sporting a wide smile and a paint-splattered shirt with "Hector" embroidered above the left pocket. Sadie relayed to Hector exactly how she wanted her front windows painted and gave him a card with her name and number on it in case he had any questions when she wasn't around. He stuffed her card in his shirt pocket and stared at the photograph. Nodding, he said it would be no problem. In a few short minutes he measured the window and set off to purchase the red and white paint he would need for the job.

Sadie locked the front door and returned to the counter, then emptied the remaining coffee into Red's cup and switched off the coffee maker.

"Why did you buy this café anyway?" asked Red.

She slowly stirred her coffee and gazed out the window. "I've always wanted to own my own restaurant and I got tired of working for other people. It seemed like a good idea at the time, but after this morning, I'm not so sure."

The front door rattled. Sadie saw Barney feverishly trying to get in, so she hurried to the door and opened it for him.

He struggled to catch his breath. "That old witch killed Goldie. They just found her at her house shot to death. Isn't that what the crazy old loon said? Something about Goldie? She'll be after you next."

"Goldie?" Sadie's heart sank. "What are you saying?"

"You better watch out until the law can pick up that old bat. They never should have let her out of the crazy house and we never should have let her get away." He turned and disappeared down the sidewalk before Sadie could say another word.

"It can't be." Sadie stared at the street and rubbed her hand across her forehead. "I just talked to Goldie last night. She was excited about her decision to retire. She and her sister are going to travel. In fact, I stopped by to see Goldie this morning, but she didn't answer the door." Sadie gasped when she realized she and the killer may have crossed paths. "I thought you said Pearl was harmless." She turned toward the corner where Red had been sitting, but the man and his hat had disappeared.

2

Sadie found herself alone, feeling scared and vulnerable in this new place. She didn't know anyone in Liberty other than the folks who had made themselves at home in her café that morning. They seemed nice enough, but the thought of Goldie being found dead unnerved her. She decided to lock up and go back home. Hector had already said he didn't know how long it would take for him to return, and she didn't need to be there while he worked. She would have to trust him.

She locked the doors of the café and climbed into her car for the forty-five minute drive home to Eucha. As she backed the Explorer out of the parking space in front of the café, she lowered the windows to allow the July heat to rush in, hoping it would chase the chill of death from her soul. The morning events had transported her to another time and place she wished she could forget.

Even the music on the radio could not compete with the memories of the deadly bank robbery she had survived on April Fools' Day two years earlier. She couldn't stop the harrowing scenes from pushing back into her mind, forming a mental video that replayed in an endless loop, sending shivers through her body.

Now some lunatic woman had aimed a shotgun at her, and she assumed the only reason it hadn't discharged and blown her to bits was because the woman had already emptied it into Goldie.

Sadie's first impulse had been to rush to Goldie's house to see if maybe it was all just a bad joke. But she couldn't bring herself to turn the steering wheel in that direction, so she continued to drive north.

Nothing made sense. Why would Pearl want to murder a good woman like Goldie? And why was Pearl so angry about the reopening of the café? Sadie didn't want to be drawn into another murder investigation, but she couldn't sit idly by and have her new business ruined, either.

The familiar Oklahoma landscape flew by Sadie's open window. The foothills of the Ozarks, covered with a healthy variety of oak, birch, maple, and sycamore trees rooted in rocky red dirt scarcely registered in her mind. The curves disappeared before her as she thought about how she had ended up owning a café in Liberty, Oklahoma, in the first place.

The decision to buy the café had not been quite as impulsive as some of her friends had thought. Twelve years working at the Mercury Savings Bank had taught her a lot of things. For one, her life was too short to spend trying to please an elitist bank board, most of whom had no idea how to go about handling an irate customer, much less what to do when a teller couldn't balance his, or her, cash drawer. She was also quite certain none of them had ever faced the wrong end of a Smith and Wesson in the hands of a crazed robber.

She craved a job that made her want to get up and go to work in the morning. She wanted to feel the pleasure she saw in her great-aunt's face in those old, grainy black-and-white photographs. Finding the newspaper ad about a restaurant for sale in Liberty, Oklahoma, seemed the answer to a lot of prayers.

Instead of calling the number in the paper, Sadie had gone unannounced to see the Liberty Diner in operation. It was easy enough to find, on the main road in the middle of the small town. The brick building looked empty, which didn't seem like a good omen to Sadie until she noticed, according to the information painted on the window, it was almost closing time.

She went inside and took a seat on one of the red vinyl-covered stools at the counter just as a woman burst through the kitchen door carrying a tray of cups.

"Afternoon," the woman greeted Sadie as she deposited the coffee mugs on a shelf behind the counter.

"Am I too late to get something cool to drink?" asked Sadie.

"No, no. Not at all." The woman introduced herself as Goldie Ray, beaming a welcoming smile as she filled a glass with ice water and slid it, along with a laminated menu, in front of Sadie. "I'm out of the special for today, but I can fix any of the sandwiches listed there. Or I've got one piece of apple pie left and one lonely sticky bun."

Sadie couldn't resist the homemade cinnamon roll, so she ordered it with a glass of milk.

Goldie served Sadie, then helped herself to the final piece of pie. "Mind if I join you?" she asked. "I'm bushed."

"Please, do."

Goldie moved around the counter and sat on a nearby stool.

Sadie imagined the charming woman to be in her fifties. She was short and round with curly auburn hair that framed her friendly face with strands of gray clumped at each temple. When Sadie looked closer, she could see the weariness in the woman's green eyes. Before long, the two were chatting as if they'd known each other all their lives, and then the conversation abruptly turned to retirement.

"I would give anything if I could find someone to take this café off my hands," said Goldie. "I could really use the time off. My health . . . well, I could use the money to pay off some medical bills."

Before she knew it, Sadie had made an offer and the two women negotiated a deal. Less than a month later, they both sat in an office with Tom Duncan, the manager of the newly opened Liberty branch of the First Merc State Bank, signing papers to transfer ownership of the café to Sadie.

Sadie and Tom had worked together in Sycamore Springs, and Sadie relished the feeling of being on the customer side of the desk for a change. Relaxed and happy, she chatted with Tom about the huge conglomerate that had taken over the Mercury Savings Bank, renamed it the First Merc State Bank, and started opening branches all over northeast Oklahoma.

"You know I think you're crazy, Sadie," Tom had teased. "Thelma in the personnel department is always asking about you. She said they would take you back in a heartbeat."

Sadie smiled, thinking about how Thelma had begged Sadie to come back to work for them. Eventually, Sadie agreed to help, but only in the case of a dire emergency. Returning to the bank would be a choice of last resort for Sadie, especially now that her new entrepreneurial adventure had reached fruition.

Sadie remembered watching from a distance as the teller handed Goldie two cashier's checks and quickly counted a rather large pile of currency onto the counter. Goldie wiped a tear off her cheek with the back of her hand and then carefully placed the money in her purse. She walked out of the bank that day with a spring in her step.

Sadie's thoughts catapulted back to the present when a powerful red-tailed hawk left its perch in a tall pine tree and sailed across the road in front of her car. She gasped and slammed on the brakes as the magnificent bird mercilessly clasped a small rodent with its talons and in an instant flew off into the sky. With her car at a complete stop, Sadie gripped the steering wheel and stared at the road, her foot aching from the pressure against the brake pedal.

"Life and death, the circle of life," she murmured. Why did death have to be so painful?

She drove on at a slower speed, noticing the small houses nestled in the woods along the road. They were modest, typical Indian homes built by the Bureau of Indian Affairs—a brick rectangle with a carport at one end. She wondered about the inhabitants and if any of them had ever traveled to Liberty and ate at Goldie's Liberty Diner. She found herself wishing she could go back in time and get to know Goldie. But now that would never happen.

Pearl crawled through the bathroom window of the café, fell to the ground, and found herself in the alley behind the restaurant. Dusting herself off, she got up and walked quickly to the end of the alley. There, she looked both ways before heading toward a line of trees where the street suddenly ended.

When she reached the trees, Pearl continued into the wooded area until she found a secluded spot. She dropped next to a large tree and leaned against it. Her jumbled thoughts made her weary. She would have to sit and think for a while before she would know what to do next.

Before long, she spotted a jagged rock in a nearby clearing. She rose, walked into the sunshine, picked up the rock, and heaved it toward a sapling. It snapped the small tree in half. She retrieved the rock and tested its weight again in her hand. It would do nicely.

She sat back down and waited. After her mind cleared, she walked back toward town carrying her new weapon.

3

Police officer Lance Smith put the phone down, pushed the brim of his khaki-colored western hat away from his forehead, and rubbed his brow. "This is no way to end your first week on the job, Smith," he mumbled as he repositioned his hat. He picked up the phone again and dialed Maggie Whitekiller's number. She answered on the second ring.

A full-blood Cherokee who served as the dispatcher for the small police department when no one was around to answer the phone, Maggie knew everyone in town. She worked from her home and seemed to be on call twenty-four hours a day, seven days a week. It was a job Lance didn't think many people would take for minimum wage, but for Maggie it gave her an income and allowed her to stay at home and care for her two-year-old grandson while her daughter worked long hours at the Wal-Mart Super Center in Tahlequah.

"Maggie, this is Lance. I'll be out of the office for a little while."

"Okay, Lance. But you don't have to call me. It will automatically ring here if you don't answer by the third ring."

"Just making sure." Lance wanted to ask her what happened if she was in the shower, or needed to go to the store, or a dozen other things that came to mind. Then he decided he didn't really want to know the answer to any of those questions.

"I'll radio if anyone needs you," she said.

Lance thanked her, hung up, and mumbled to himself again while he looked for the all-important handheld radio. He missed the more sophisticated transmitters, attached to an officer's shoulder and always within easy reach, used by the Cherokee marshals. He finished his coffee in one long gulp and tossed the Styrofoam cup into the metal trash can. Suddenly, the door opened and a middle-aged man entered carrying a sawed-off shotgun.

Lance instinctively removed the tie-down from over the hammer of his Smith and Wesson .357 and rested his hand in front of his holster. He stood and walked around his desk. "Can I help you?"

The man transferred the shotgun to his left hand, careful to keep the gun barrel pointed toward the floor. "Virgil Wilson," he said, extending his hand. "I was looking for George, but by the looks of things you must be the new man we've heard about."

"Smith," Lance responded, and the two men shook. "What can I do for you?"

"The boys and I were down at the old Liberty Diner a while ago and ran into a little episode with Pearl Mobley." He removed his ball cap and ran his hand across his balding head. "You'll get to know all the locals before long, but in the meantime we thought it'd work out better if she wasn't pointing this thing at folks, loaded or not, and I decided to drop it off here for George to worry about. I guess it would be your problem now."

Lance listened with interest, his right hand still resting near his belt. When Virgil offered the shotgun, Lance accepted it, checked to make sure it was unloaded, and placed it on his desk.

"You say this Mobley woman was pointing this thing at someone?" Lance asked.

"Yeah, but it wasn't loaded."

"Where's the woman now?"

"Pearl? Don't rightly know." Virgil rubbed his chin. "She tricked us and run off."

"Did you want to file charges?"

"No, I don't think so. You'll have to talk to the new owner of the café." Virgil stopped for a moment and then continued. "Pearl's a little off, that's all. She ain't never hurt nobody."

"I see. I'll talk to George about it when he gets in."

"Say, I heard you used to work with Charlie McCord up in Sycamore Springs."

Lance grinned. "Taught me everything I know."

Virgil affirmed with a nod. The two men shook hands again, and Virgil left. Lance took a pen and small spiral-bound notebook out of his shirt pocket and began to write. He tore off the sheet of paper and stuck it under the trigger of the shotgun for later reference. After securing the gun in the weapons safe, he headed toward the door.

Talking about Charlie brought back a flood of memories for Lance. At the age of forty-nine, taking the job in Liberty had given him the sense he had come full circle. He had grown up in Kenwood, a few miles north of Liberty, near Lake Eucha. One night, at the age of seventeen, he convinced his inebriated father to sign papers so he could join the U.S. Marines. He thought it was his one-way ticket out of a dead-end town and an escape from two alcoholic parents who took turns beating him on a regular basis.

Instead, on the eve of his eighteenth birthday, he walked off of a plane in DaNang to a world filled with deadly horror. After spending the worst thirteen months of his life sloshing through rice paddies and dodging bullets in Southeast Asia, he decided Oklahoma wasn't nearly as bad as he once thought. Since then, he had also come to the conclusion there must have been better ways of separating himself from abusive parents than joining the military and volunteering for combat duty.

Still wearing his military uniform, Lance arrived home from Vietnam by way of a Greyhound bus that dropped him off in front of Bobcat's Watering Hole, a bar in Sycamore Springs. In an effort to forget what he had just experienced in Vietnam and cope with his sudden reentry into American society, he ordered shots of tequila one right after the other until his eyes would no longer focus on the bartender, or anything else.

By the time the bar closed he had lost the ability to walk on his own, so the bartender and the waitress together helped the stout young Cherokee out onto the sidewalk, left him there, and locked the door. He came to when a black-and-white police cruiser slowed to a stop and shined a spotlight in the middle of his face.

When he regained his senses, he was sitting across the table from a big man in a gray uniform at an all-night diner drinking coffee. He wondered if he looked as bad as he felt and reasoned that keeping his mouth shut at that juncture was probably his best bet. Finally, the officer started talking and, for the first time in his life, Lance thought he was hearing fatherly advice. Strangely enough, those words of wisdom were coming from a white guy not much older than himself. He really hated that. But by the end of the officer's shift, Lance Smith had agreed to meet him the next day for lunch and talk about applying for a job at the police department. That was a long time ago, but he had never forgotten the favor from Sergeant Charlie McCord, the man who had taken him under his wing and put him on the right path in life.

True to his word, Lance applied to the Sycamore Springs Police Academy, graduated with honors, and received his certification from CLEET, the Council on Law Enforcement Education and Training, to become a police officer in the state of Oklahoma. His ability to handle a weapon came from his experience in the Marines, and the rest came naturally. He put in a lot of good years working under and alongside McCord on the Sycamore Springs Police Department. But he eventually lost his ability to stomach the bureaucratic politics and decided at the age of forty-eight to leave the force and go to work as a marshal for the Cherokee Nation in Tahlequah. That job lasted less than a year before he was ready to move on.

One day he noticed a blind ad in the local newspaper for the position of "a law enforcement specialist." On a whim, he answered it. The job turned out to be for the second-in-command on a two-man force in Liberty, Oklahoma, a small community twelve miles north of Tahlequah. That was three weeks ago.

Now he had been on the job for only one week and already had a dead body. The police chief, George Stump, had phoned in the report a few minutes before Virgil Wilson's visit. According to Stump, an old woman by the name of Goldie Ray had been shot to death on her back porch only a few blocks from the four-way stop that marked the main intersection of Liberty.

At least it isn't going to be a boring job. Wonder if Virgil's shotgun has something to do with the murder.

Lance locked the door to his office, a habit for which George Stump had been chiding him. No one in Liberty locks their doors, the chief had said, especially not the police department. But Lance ignored his superior's advice and locked it anyway.

If we can have dead bodies, we can have thieves.

As he opened his car door, he heard the unmistakable sound of a Harley-Davidson motorcycle roaring down the street. A middle-aged man with a weather-worn face rode a full-dressed Harley hog down Main Street, a U.S. flag perched above the back fender. The rider, dressed in jeans and a tank top, wore mirrored sunglasses and a red-white-and-blue bandana tied around his head. Riding without a helmet already labeled the guy as questionable in Lance's mind. The rider obviously hadn't seen as many heads cracked open on the pavement as he had.

As the rider downshifted and slid through the stop sign without so much as a tap of the brakes, Lance saw what he thought was the scabbard of a long gun sticking up next to the man. *This character definitely needs more scrutiny*. He turned his cruiser in the same direction the rider had gone and picked up the radio transmitter.

"Deputy Dawg, come in," called Lance.

The radio handle had originated a few days earlier when Stump traded two old police cars for a used vehicle from the county sheriff. The front left fender still sported the word "deputy" in capital letters, and Stump had decided the cost of a new paint job simply wasn't worth the money, especially since everyone in Liberty already knew he was the chief of police. The speakers crackled a couple of times before Lance heard a reply.

"Stump here."

Lance knew George Stump had been the one and only officer of the law in Liberty since the last head cop had fallen victim to a heart attack. The former chief had died almost two years ago while sitting at his desk eating a greasy hamburger and double order of cheese-fries. Finally, the mayor decided to bestow the title of chief on Stump, who gladly accepted the boost in prestige and reflected it in his face, his stance, and his attitude. It was a good thing to go out on top, he had said, since he was only a year shy of giving it all up and living on Social Security.

"Chief, I'm going to be delayed a few minutes," said Lance. "I've got a suspicious-looking character in my sights, and I'm getting ready to check him out."

"Okay," replied Stump. "Meet me here when you're through. The doc just got here."

"Do you have any suspects?"

"Not yet. One of the neighbors reported seeing a red vehicle. One of those SUV's."

"Do you want me to notify the state boys?"

"Negative," said Stump. "It would take the Oklahoma State Bureau of Investigation three days to get here. If we need any help, I'll call the county sheriff."

"Okay, Chief. I'll be on my way shortly."

"Stump, out."

Lance found the motorcycle with Arkansas plates parked in front of the American Café. The rider had removed his glasses and was in the process of stowing them in one of the large saddlebags positioned over the back wheel of the bike. He had secured the long gun in what appeared to be a special-made hard case above the saddlebag.

The stranger, ignoring the policeman, walked up to the café, rattled the front door, and stepped back. Obviously perturbed when he found it locked, he returned to his Harley. Lance parked next to the bike and got out of his car.

"Say, buddy," said Lance. "I don't suppose you realize that you failed to stop at that stop sign back there."

"Oh." The rider looked down the street. "Sorry, 'bout that, but there wasn't another car for miles."

"Is that a loaded weapon you've got there?"

"No, sir. Never ride with a loaded weapon. That's my motto."

"Well, how about we double-check and see if you're living up to your motto today?"

The rider unlocked the case, pulled out a long gun in a suede cover, and handed it to Lance. Lance unzipped the gun cover, exposing a 20-gauge Remington single-barreled shotgun. He opened the chamber and saw that it was empty.

"Where are the loads for it?" asked Lance.

"Not carrying any."

"Oh? And where would you be headed carrying a shotgun with no loads?"

"Look officer, I don't want to get off on the wrong foot here, but you must be new in town. I come to Liberty at least once a week to check on my mother. I like to be prepared for hunting season, so I keep a lot of my guns at her place. This is just one more for the collection." The rider stepped forward and offered his hand to Lance. "Name's John Mobley. My mother lives north of town, out past the sawmill, at the bottom of the big hill."

"You Mobleys seem to be getting around this morning."

"Huh?"

"You got a license and registration?"

The rider grimaced and shook his head as he pulled a billfold from a compartment near the handlebars and produced an Arkansas driver's license. He dug for a moment longer and handed the registration papers to Lance.

Lance leaned the shotgun against his car while he studied the license and papers for a moment. "When did you get into town, John?"

"Just rode in. Thought I'd get a bite to eat before I headed out to the house. My mother can't cook worth a darn. But I guess the café's closed."

Lance handed the documents and shotgun back to the rider. "Just keep it legal, John, and we won't have any problems. And try to obey the stop signs if you can, even if there isn't much traffic."

"Thanks," John said and nodded.

"Have a good day, now."

Lance waited for John Mobley to ride off before he got into his car, then he picked up the transmitter. "Deputy Dawg, come in." The speakers sputtered.

"Stump here. Smith, I'd appreciate it if you'd address me with more respect over the airwaves."

"Yes, sir. I'm on my way." He dropped the microphone on the car seat and headed for the crime scene of the day.

Thirty-five miles north of Liberty, a red vehicle pulled up next to a ledge overlooking a deserted lake. The driver got out, looked at the water below, and flung a long, slender cardboard box as far as possible, then watched as it fell short of the water, dumping its contents on the rocks. Seeing that nothing could be done, the driver cursed and got back into the vehicle, then drove around the north side of the lake before turning south again toward the Cherokee Turnpike.

4

Lance drove the short distance to the murder victim's house. He could see George Stump walking toward the backyard, camera in hand. Lance pulled his cruiser between the ambulance and Stump's car, barely missing the young ambulance driver leaning against the vehicle smoking a cigarette. Lance got out and offered a few words of advice to the young man before moving on. "Those cancer sticks will kill you," he said.

The young man grinned, obviously unaffected by Lance's warning. "They're in the back," he offered, pointing with his chin.

Lance walked around the outside of the small frame home to the back porch. Stump's camera flashed again and again as another man, whom Lance presumed to be Doc Brown, pointed at the corpse. Stump stopped taking photographs, took a handkerchief from his pocket, and held it near his left ear.

"What happened?" asked Lance.

Stump dabbed at his face. "Darned bumblebee stung me."

"Oh." Lance looked at the doctor. "I meant with the victim."

Stump made the proper introductions, then stuffed his handkerchief in his shirt pocket and began to update Lance on the situation. "It looks like someone just walked right up behind the poor old woman and let her have it in the back, with a shotgun no less."

Lance frowned. "I've seen two 20-gauge shotguns this morning. First one came off of a woman named Mobley down at the café, and the second one was in the possession of her son. You suppose the perpetrator goes by Mobley?"

"You mean Crazy Pearl Mobley?" Stump's laugh turned into a snort. "I doubt it. And John's a drunk. Been that way since he came home from Iraq."

The doctor ignored the two lawmen's conversation and continued with his inspection of the body.

Lance returned his attention to the victim. "How long?" he asked.

"Not very," the doctor said without looking up. "In the last couple of hours, I'd say."

"Did you find the empty shotgun shell?" Lance turned and scanned the area. "We might be able to match it back to a murder weapon."

Stump shook his head. "Negative. They must have taken it with them."

Lance stepped onto the porch, knelt next to the doctor, and studied the corpse. He retrieved the spiral-bound notebook from his shirt pocket and made several notes. After a few minutes, he stood and walked to the back door of the house. "Do you need me to search the house?"

"No. I've already done that. Looks like all the damage is out here."

"What about the neighbors?" asked Lance. "Surely someone saw or heard something."

"Maggie said an anonymous caller reported hearing gunfire. She couldn't tell if it was a man or a woman. No one was home across the street. Another neighbor said she heard the shot but didn't think anything about it since the old man down the street is always shooting at something or another."

"Do we have a better description of the vehicle other than 'red'?"

"SUV. That's about it."

Lance adjusted his hat and watched as the doctor pulled off his latex gloves, wadded them into a ball, and stuck them into his coat pocket.

"You can go ahead and remove the body if you're through, Doc," Stump said. "Can you let me know when the lab determines the size of the buckshot?"

The doctor nodded in agreement.

"Are we going to fingerprint the victim here?" asked Lance. "Or do you want us to do that at your office?"

The doctor glanced first at Lance and then at Stump with a puzzled look on his face. Stump stared blankly at the corpse.

Lance elaborated for the doctor's sake. "When we try to determine if the killer left any fingerprints, we have to be able to eliminate those of the victim."

"Oh." The doctor shrugged. "Makes me no difference."

"We'll get them at your office then," said Stump. "Let's get her out of here before it gets too hot."

The doctor nodded again and walked back toward the ambulance. A few moments later he returned with a gurney, a body bag, and his helper. While the two worked with the body, Lance and Stump stood in the yard and watched. "Who was this woman?" asked Lance.

"Goldie Ray. She owned a little café downtown for as long as I can remember. Heard she sold it not more than a few days ago. She made the best cinnamon rolls you ever sunk your teeth into."

"You think it was connected to the sale of her business?"

"Could've been, I guess. Wouldn't make much sense, though."

"Married?"

"Old maid. Never married and never had any kids."

"Think it might have been someone she knew?"

Stump looked off into the distance. "Nah, I doubt it. I can't imagine anyone who knew Goldie wanting to hurt her."

Lance removed his hat, scratched his head and replaced it. "So you don't think she had any enemies to speak of?"

"Goldie? Enemies?" Stump shook his head. "No way." He turned and spit into the yard. "Couldn't have been anyone from around here. Must have been a drifter, or someone trying to steal something."

Lance walked over to the back door that stood ajar. "But you said there wasn't any sign of a break-in or a struggle. Thieves are cowards. They don't normally shoot people."

Stump laughed. "Where'd you learn that bit of wisdom, Smith? At the Cherokee Nation?"

Lance held his tongue for a moment and took a deep breath before he spoke. "Just picked it up along the way, I guess. You don't mind if I take a look around, do you?"

"Be my guest. I could've missed something, but I doubt it."

Lance used his elbow to push the back door open and entered the house. Stump followed. Once inside, Lance continued his search for anything that looked out of place. He scanned the floor, table, and countertops, then raised the lid on the trash and glanced inside. Just as he switched off the coffeepot, the radio receivers on the two lawmen's belts squawked simultaneously. "It's Maggie," said Stump as he spoke into his transmitter. "Go ahead."

"Chief, I got a call reporting a break-in at the old Liberty Diner. Someone broke out the front window."

"Anyone hurt?"

"They hung up before I could get any information."

Stump groaned. "Okay, Maggie. We'll take care of it." Stump clicked off his transmitter as he and Lance left through the back door and walked toward their vehicles. "I'm going to secure the area and dust for prints," said Stump. "You check out the café, then meet me back here. It's probably just a bunch of kids causing trouble."

Lance ran to his cruiser, hit his lights and siren, and pulled away from the curb as the doctor and his cigarette-dangling helper loaded the gurney holding Goldie Ray's remains into the ambulance. There would be no lights or siren for Goldie. Too late for both.

Across the street, a small crowd gathered under a tall blackjack tree. Three older women stood whispering to each other, and a young mother stood wringing her hands while her two children scuffled over a skateboard.

Not far away, Red crouched behind a honeysuckle-covered fence. He watched until Lance's vehicle and the ambulance turned the corner at the end of the street before he emerged onto the crumbling sidewalk. He tipped his hat politely to the women and watched while Stump strung yellow crime-scene tape from Goldie's front gate to the big maple tree on the south side of her house.

Red had known Stump all his life and didn't particularly like him. Stump had accused him of stealing a horse over twenty years ago, and when the real thief returned the animal a week later, Stump hadn't even bothered to apologize for the false accusation. Nothing consequential had actually come from the incident, except Red hadn't had much to say to Stump since then.

Red sauntered up the street. When he got to the house on the corner, he turned and walked behind a thick hedge and waited to see if Stump had seen him.

Stump showed no interest. Instead, he went back inside Goldie's house, only to reemerge several minutes later carrying a brown paper sack. He put it in his police car and returned to the front porch, where he began to work with a fingerprint kit around the door.

Red turned and walked back to Goldie's house, careful not to attract Stump's attention. He ducked under the yellow tape and quietly entered through the back gate, behind the detached garage, not far from the back porch. The fragrance of honeysuckle hung in the air, mingled with the smell of death. He could see where Goldie's life had been shattered like a delicate piece of crystal, her blood spilled like fine red wine.

"I'm sorry, Goldie," he whispered.

Steering clear of the porch, he moved on. He could see footprints in the yard that had already been carelessly intermixed with others. He stood at the end of the porch and looked down and to the right at an old whiskey barrel. It contained an unlikely hodgepodge of blooming plants—pink and red lantana, orange and yellow zinnias, and several clumps of purple and red moss rose. The foliage filled the container and cascaded down the side into a tangled bed of purple coneflowers.

Red bent over and carefully parted the leaves, and in doing so disturbed a very busy bumblebee which made a straight line for his head. But instead of swatting at the insect, he stood perfectly still and spoke softly.

"Forgive my intrusion, my friend, but I must find something, and I think it might be among your flowers."

The bee hovered for an instant and then, as if it understood what the old man was saying, flew straight up and away. Red resumed his search, pushing the mass of flowers from side to side. Nothing. After a few minutes, the bee returned and the two made a truce. "Okay," Red whispered. "You win."

If his estimate was right, the shell casing from the shotgun would have become a projectile and landed somewhere near the blooming plants. He stood up and visually searched around the barrel. Goldie's grass had been cut short recently, leaving the small area between her flower gardens looking like the green indoor-outdoor carpet sold at Masters Hardware Store in Tahlequah. Again, nothing. He walked to a small shed in the corner of the yard filled with Goldie's gardening tools. The door hung at a precarious tilt, permanently stuck in an open position. Carefully, he poked his head inside. The contents were neatly organized, everything in its place.

As Red walked back into the yard he heard the front door close and assumed Stump had entered the house. Careful not to be seen, Red hurried back toward the garage. A hummingbird suddenly whirred to a nearby feeder, drank red sugar-water for a second, hovered, and then fled. As he neared the barrel of flowers again, he noticed the bumblebee take flight. He decided to try one more time.

He bent over and painstakingly felt between the dense foliage with both hands. This time, when he brought his outstretched fingers together, he felt a lump. No longer trying to save the plants, he pulled the entangled leaves apart. There, balanced among the vivid blooms, rested the prize: a red shotgun shell casing. He pulled it out and held it up for inspection before shoving it into his pants pocket. He glanced around. When he was sure Stump had not seen him, he left in the same direction he had come.

When Lance Smith pulled his police car in front of the Liberty Diner and killed the siren, he could see a man sitting on the sidewalk, his shirt covered in blood.

"Dispatch, come in. I'm at the Liberty Diner. The front window is broken and there's a man down. Send an ambulance, and see if you can find out who bought this café and get them down here."

5

Sadie turned off the highway, crossed the cattle guard, and drove up the lane toward her house. She could see her Uncle Eli riding toward the barn on Joe, her paint-horse stallion. Her wolf-dog, Sonny, trailed nearby. She parked next to her old blue truck, jumped out, and hurried through the gate. Sonny met her with a yelp and a wagging tail, and she returned his greeting by scratching his head. Eli raised his chin acknowledging his niece.

" *'Siyo*," said Sadie. "What are you guys up to?"

Eli dismounted and began to loosen Joe's saddle. "I wanted to double-check your fence line on the north side." Eli pulled the saddle and blanket off Joe's back and carried it into the barn while Sadie patted Joe's neck and rubbed his cheek. When Eli returned he was grinning like a mischievous youngster. "Joe said he wanted to go along."

She knew her uncle loved to ride her stallion, and she felt guilty for not having time to ride him more herself. Standing at Joe's shoulders, she placed her hands on his mane and back and jumped up onto him, balancing herself on her belly until she could throw her right leg over and right herself on top of the gentle creature. Eli shook his head, handed her the reins, and knelt to pet Sonny while she and Joe took a slow walk around the corral. Sadie leaned forward, stroked Joe's neck and whispered into his ear, then slipped off his back.

"Go ahead and let him go," she said. "I'll brush him in a little while."

Eli pulled the bridle off over Joe's ears, opened the gate, and watched Joe walk toward a nearby shade tree in the adjoining pasture. He removed his sweat-stained straw hat and wiped his brow with his forearm. "How's the new business adventure coming?"

Sadie frowned and shook her head. "Don't ask."

Eli grunted and placed his hat back on his head. "Well, let's not stand out in the sun to talk about it." Without saying another word, Eli struck out toward a well-worn path that connected Sadie's place with her aunt and uncle's adjoining land.

"I think I'd rather drive," she called after him.

Without a glance, he held up a hand to let her know he'd heard her and continued walking.

Sonny barked, looked at Eli, back at Sadie, and barked again.

"Oh, okay." She pulled the keys from her pocket and opened the door to her old farm truck. Sonny jumped into his regular spot on the seat next to the window. She turned the key and pumped the accelerator, encouraging the old engine to life. Within minutes they were jostling through the pasture. They caught up to Eli, and Sadie slowed so he could jump on to the truck's tailgate and ride the rest of the way.

When they rolled to a stop, Eli slid off and walked around to Sadie's window. She pushed the truck door open with her shoulder and Sonny bounded onto the ground behind her.

"Come on in the house," said Eli. "Mary's got the air conditioner cranked up. We'll have a bite to eat."

Sadie's aunt and uncle had treated her like their own daughter since her dad had died over ten years earlier. Sadie's mother had remarried and moved away. She and Sadie eventually became estranged. They had never gotten along, mostly because Sadie could never please her mother no matter how hard she tried. Sadie identified with her father's Cherokee heritage and never felt like she fit in with her mother's Anglo family. It was a constant strain between them.

Sadie missed the relationship she imagined most mothers and daughters had, but she didn't miss her own mother. In contrast, Sadie's aunt Mary Walela loved her niece with an unconditional love and Sadie relished their bond.

Mary's life seemed to revolve around whatever was happening in the kitchen. She had a large Black Diamond watermelon balanced on the counter, going at it with a knife when Sadie and Eli came through the kitchen door. It cracked and fell open revealing a juicy red center.

"Oh, you caught me." Mary grabbed a nearby towel and wiped her hands. "You know whoever cuts the melon gets to eat the heart." She scooped out a chunk and handed it to Sadie.

"This is delicious," Sadie said as she leaned over the sink and slurped the juicy meat. "Where'd you find the Black Diamond?"

"The neighbor's niece stopped in Rush Springs and picked up a backseat full on her drive in from out of state. They were kind to share, so enjoy." Mary wiped her brow with her forearm. "You two look hot. Sit down and I'll get you some iced tea."

Sadie washed her hands and then took over slicing the melon while Mary retrieved the drinks. Eli parked his hat on a nail by the back door and splashed water on his face and neck at the kitchen sink.

Mary threw a clean towel at Eli as she returned to the refrigerator to retrieve all the makings for sandwiches: a round stick of bologna, fresh-picked lettuce and tomatoes, and home-canned pickle relish.

Eli finished wiping his hands and face, then tossed the dish towel on the counter and grinned. "Ah, tube steak," he said, "Indian food."

Sadie loved the safety she felt in this home as they sat down to a table covered with a summer feast including freshly made deviled eggs and cucumber slices floating in vinegar-water. They waited while Mary blessed the food and then Eli dug in as if he hadn't eaten in a week. Sadie stared at her plate.

"Are you okay?" asked Mary.

Sadie took in a deep breath and exhaled. "I need to tell you about what happened this morning."

"How's that?" asked Mary. "Eli, could you pass the eggs?"

Eli slid the plate of deviled eggs toward Mary.

"Something happened to Goldie. They found her dead."

Mary sucked in air and almost choked on a cucumber. "Goldie who?"

"The woman I bought the café from."

Eli and Mary both stopped eating and stared wide-eyed at Sadie.

"What happened?" Eli flattened his sandwich with his hand so it would fit in his mouth and took a bite.

"I'm not sure." The words spilled out of Sadie as she began to recount the events of the morning. She included every detail about Red, the workers from the mill, and the "crazy woman" they called Pearl. "After I heard about Goldie, I just kind of freaked and drove home."

Mary's fork banged against her plate. "I knew you should have stayed closer to home. You know they're still looking for someone to run the drug store in Eucha." She wiped her mouth with the edge of her apron.

"Did you call the law?" asked Eli.

"What was I going to say? She didn't hurt anyone, and besides, I got the impression she wasn't exactly playing with a full deck."

"What are you going to do now?" Mary shoved her plate to the side and planted an elbow next to it.

"I don't know. I'd take Sonny with me, but I'm guessing the health department would frown on the restaurant having a wolf-dog as a mascot." She managed a reassuring smile for her aunt's sake. "I'll be okay. I can take care of myself."

Mary began spooning food onto Sadie's plate as if eating would make everything better. "Eli, isn't there something you can do?"

Eli leaned back in his chair. "You oughtn't to go down there by yourself, Sadie, until all this is settled. And, I wouldn't care what the health department thought about Sonny, at least until you're up and running." He pushed away from the table and stood. "You want me to go with you?"

"Thanks, Uncle, but I'm not going back until the morning and I think I'll be okay. The painter should be finished with the windows by then and I need to pay him. You may be right about taking Sonny, though, at least for the next couple of trips."

When they finished, Sadie helped her aunt clear the dishes.

"I don't think it's safe for you go back to that café," said Mary.

Sadie kissed her aunt on the forehead. "Don't worry," she said. "I'm sure everything will be fine."

She left through the back door and invited Sonny to ride next to her on the front seat again while she drove back through the pasture to her house. When she turned the corner next to the barn, she could see Joe drinking from the water tank. The stallion raised his head and nickered at the approaching truck. Sadie leaned toward Sonny and whispered, "If you're going with me tomorrow, you're gonna have to have a bath." Sonny ignored her, stuck his face out the open window, and barked.

Back inside the house, Sadie quickly changed into a worn pair of cutoffs and a tee shirt. As she walked toward the door, she noticed the red light blinking on her answering machine. She started to punch the button to hear her messages then changed her mind. "First things first," she said to herself and pulled the door closed behind her.

When she got to the barn she decided to straighten a few things. She spent the rest of the afternoon sweeping and rearranging in a barn that needed neither sweeping nor rearranging. The muscles in her hands, arms and back ached, and her sweat-drenched clothes clung to her body; her mind, too, was busy, working like an old-fashioned sewing machine. Finally, she retreated to the horse trough and scooped water onto her face. Joe stood in the shade of a nearby mulberry tree persistently swishing his tail at horseflies and shuffling his feet.

The water felt so good, she decided to share the blessing. She wasted no time hooking up the hose and fetching a bucket, soap, and sponge from the barn. The stallion shook his mane in opposition but stood perfectly still while she hosed him down and sloshed soapy water over his back. She rubbed his neck and legs, massaging his hard muscles. When she was through, she rinsed him all over with cool water. When she finished brushing his brown-and-white coat, his tail, and his mane, he looked ready to lead a parade.

Sonny watched the entire ordeal from the nearby shadows of the barn. When she looked toward him, he lowered his head in unhappy anticipation. "Okay, Sonny, you're next."

Sonny ducked his head, eyes squinted and ears flattened, as Sadie doused him with soapy water. While she bathed the wolf-dog, she carefully laid out her problems, withholding not one detail about the day's events. At one point, he took advantage of her close proximity and licked the end of her nose, bringing forth the first real laughter of the day. After she had rinsed him with the hose, he shook his entire body, starting at his nose and crescendoing to the tip of his tail. She tried to cover her face, and as soon as she loosened her grasp on his thick coat, he surged into a playful run around the barn.

As Sadie laughed, the tension began to drain from her shoulders. She held the hose over her head and let the cold water spill over her tired body, allowing her new resolve to surface. She would return to the café in the early morning and take Sonny with her.

When Sadie got back to the house and entered the screened-in back porch, she took advantage of her secluded surroundings and dropped her wet clothes and sneakers next to the door before hurrying into the house naked. She could hear the phone ring and the answering machine click on. Whoever it was would have to wait until she finished with her own warm bath.

After an extra long soak, Sadie wrapped herself in her robe and sat down on the sofa to listen to her messages. The first message was useless, just a lot of background noise and a hang-up. The second message came from a woman named Maggie wanting to know if she was the new owner of the Liberty Diner, and if so would she call as soon as possible.

When Sadie returned the call, she discovered Maggie worked for the Liberty Police Department and she was calling because there had been an "incident" at the café.

At first Sadie thought Virgil had changed his mind and made a report about the incident with Pearl Mobley. Then the words began to run together on the other end of the line. "Broken window . . . break-in . . . vandals . . . man was hurt." Then there was a long pause on the other end of the line while Maggie put Sadie on hold to answer another call. "Anyway," Maggie said when she returned to the line, "you need to stop by the police department as soon as you get to town."

"I'll be there in less than an hour." Sadie thanked Maggie, hung up, and began to dress. If someone was trying to scare her away, it wouldn't work. Her grandmother's words came to her. *Hi tsalagi.* You are a Cherokee, she had said, you are a Walela. Now Sadie prayed this Cherokee—this Walela—would not be as easy a target as Goldie had been.

6

As Lance got out of his car, the man on the curb rose to his feet, holding his left arm close to his side. "I'm okay, officer. I thought I should wait here for the lady."

"Oh, yeah? Then why are you bleeding all over the sidewalk?"

"When the window broke, I fell off the ladder and hit the brick planter." He grimaced. "I think I broke my arm."

Lance could now see that most of the "blood" on the man's shirt was actually red paint. "What's your name?"

"Hector Emanuel." Hector pulled a billfold from his back pocket and offered Lance his driver's license. "I'm a painter."

Lance glanced at his identification. "Okay, Hector, is there anyone else here with you? What happened?"

"No, my brother was here, but he went to call the lady." Hector repositioned his left arm. "She hired me this morning to paint a new name on the window. I just got all the old paint scraped off and was getting ready to start on the new name when all of a sudden someone threw a rock and broke the window. My ladder slipped, and I fell, and spilled all the paint. I guess I tried to break the fall with my arm."

"Who is this lady? The one who hired you."

"I had her name and number on a card, but I gave it to my brother to go call her and he isn't back yet."

"Did you see who threw the rock?"

"No. It caught me off guard. I didn't see anyone." He twisted his mouth.

"Just relax. An ambulance is on the way."

"Oh, please, no," he pleaded. "I cannot pay for an ambulance. My brother will be right back. No need. Really."

The same ambulance driver Lance had seen earlier at the murder scene drove up next to the curb and parked.

"Let's not worry about paying right now," said Lance. "We need to make sure you're okay."

As the paramedics stooped down to examine Hector, Lance began to survey the damage. He could see the large rock that had landed on the floor inside. He reached through the broken window, unlocked the door, and entered.

The café appeared to be empty. He moved methodically throughout the entire building including the kitchen, a small bathroom, a storage room, and an upstairs office. Both the rear door and window were secure.

As he returned to the sidewalk, one of the paramedics approached. "His arm may be broken. He doesn't want to go, but we're going to take him in to Tahlequah anyway. He hit his head on the sidewalk and might have a concussion."

Lance nodded in agreement, and in a few short minutes they were gone.

"Dispatch, come in. Have you had any luck finding the owner of this café?"

"No, I had to leave a message. I will let you know when I hear back."

Lance reported his findings to Maggie. "Is there someone we can call to put a piece of plywood over this window?"

"I'll call the manager down at the hardware store. He'll take care of it."

Lance thanked Maggie for her help, grateful that she seemed to know how to handle all the messy details directly from her kitchen table. He climbed into his cruiser and began to write a detailed report. In less than five minutes, two men drove up in a truck and started to cover the broken window.

Maggie's voice crackled on the radio. "This is dispatch. Chief, can you answer?"

Lance listened while Maggie asked Stump to respond to a call for a disturbance at one of Liberty's churches on the east end of town. When he agreed to take the call, Lance picked up his transmitter and interrupted. "If you're not through with the murder scene, I'm about to wrap this up here."

"Negative. I'm closer than you are."

Lance frowned. "Roger, Chief. Then you want me to swing by to keep the murder scene secure?"

"I took prints off both doors," said Stump. "That's about all I can do." His voice took on a condescending tone. "But if you'd like to lend your expertise, come on by."

Lance couldn't get used to small-town police work. If they didn't keep the crime scene secure until all the evidence was collected, there would be no way to solve the murder.

"Roger, Chief. Just lock the door and I'll swing by and get the key from you."

"Can't lock the door," Stump sneered. "Don't got a key."

Lance shook his head in disbelief. "I'm on my way."

When Stump arrived at the Liberty House of God Church, a crowd had already gathered. He grabbed his nightstick and worked his way around the people, up the steps of the church, and through one side of the double front door into the vestibule. From there he could hear loud voices inside. He turned the doorknob and slowly craned his head around the door to see what was happening.

On the floor at the front of the sanctuary, right in front of the pulpit, the town's crazy woman, Pearl Mobley, flopped first on one side and then on the other. She let out a shriek from time to time and muttered a stream of words, all unintelligible. An Indian man, whom Stump presumed to be the preacher, stood on one side of her, holding his hands toward the heavens, praying as loudly as he could. The janitor of the church stood on the other side of her with a look of fear on his face, as if he might take flight at any moment.

The chief stood in the doorway taking the whole thing in, unsure of what to do. He didn't want to act too fast and get mixed up in some religious ceremony.

Stump wasn't what one would call a churchgoing sort of guy. His daddy had convinced him a long time ago that most of the people in Liberty lived one life inside the walls of the church and another on the outside. Bigots, he had called them, and as long as Stump could remember, that had been his father's excuse for refusing to attend church, unwilling to sit on a pew next to those sinners. Taking his daddy's philosophy to heart, Stump usually volunteered to work on Sunday mornings, the quiet time for criminal activity.

The preacher finally noticed the chief and motioned for him to enter. Stump took off his hat, walked around the back of the pews and up the aisle close to the wall, and shook the preacher's hand.

"We got a call, Preacher," said Stump, holding his hat in his hand and gripping the nightstick under his elbow. "Do you need some help here?"

"Well, sir," said the preacher. "Mrs. Mobley's been here for over an hour, I guess. I can't understand a word she's saying, except for when she says something about Goldie Ray. I got word a while ago that something terrible happened to Mrs. Ray. I don't know anything about that, but I think maybe this lady here needs some help. Maybe you could call those doctors at that hospital over in Vinita."

About that time, Pearl stopped flailing her arms and looked at the ceiling.

The preacher kneeled beside Pearl and placed his hand on her shoulder. "Pearl, do you know what happened to Goldie?"

Pearl stood straight up. "Well, if she wasn't already dead I'd be happy to shoot her again." Then she dropped onto the front pew and wept.

Stump replaced his hat and nodded at the preacher. "Come on, Pearl," he said. "Everything's going to be all right." He took hold of Pearl's arm, and she reluctantly followed him down the aisle and out the front door.

The crowd that had gathered backed away from the steps when Pearl Mobley and Stump appeared. A few began to disperse while the others watched Stump guide Pearl into the back seat of his cruiser. He got in and pulled the vehicle into the street, then drove through town toward the police station with Pearl Mobley sitting tall in the back seat.

When Lance arrived at Goldie's house, he could see through the front window that Stump had left the fingerprint kit in the middle of the living room floor. He used his handkerchief to let himself in through the front door, wondering if he should take it upon himself to retake prints. Either that or maybe call the OSBI. But he figured, being the new man in town, he'd better keep a low profile.

Goldie's house was small and very orderly. Her eclectic collection of furniture was old but well cared for. A clock on the fireplace mantle ticked like a metronome, overwhelming the stillness. When he stepped into the living room, the worn wooden floor offered up an eerie creak, causing Lance to hesitate before continuing his examination of the room. Crocheted doilies covered every available surface, even the back and arms of the red velvet loveseat, which looked as if it had never been used. Lace curtains hung like a new petticoat behind the matching chair. An ornate upright piano stood against the wall between the two pieces of furniture, covered with family photographs and handmade Cherokee baskets.

Three doors led from the living room, not counting the one through which Lance had entered. He hadn't had a chance to see anything but the kitchen when he and Stump had been there earlier, so he made the rounds,, careful not to disturb anything.

In the bedroom, the messy bed bothered him. He wondered if perhaps the killer had been looking for something, but why disrupt only the bed? It could also mean that Goldie simply hadn't gotten around to straightening the sheets that morning, but this detail seemed out of place in a house kept in perfect order.

Lance used his handkerchief again to pull open the top dresser drawer which contained nothing unusual except for a small beaded suede pouch. The pouch was obviously old, yet in pristine condition. Lance didn't recognize the bead pattern as being Cherokee, but he knew instantly the intricate design had been applied by a skilled artisan.

He closed the drawer and moved on to the closet where he coaxed the closet door open with the toe of his boot. Goldie must have lived a simple life. The dresses were worn but clean, probably her work clothes. Two pairs of sneakers and a pair of dress shoes lined the floor of the small closet.

On a shelf above Goldie's clothes lay some kind of a long gun secured inside a beautifully beaded suede cover. Lance pulled the gun off the shelf and untied the leather strip releasing the flap over the butt of the gun. Careful not to touch the weapon, he let the beaded sheath fall away to reveal an old Remington .410, engraved with elaborate scrollwork surrounding Goldie's name. Lance stared at the masterpiece and its intricate work and searched for the obscured initials of the engraver. They were hard to make out, but one of the letters looked like a Y.

Knowing the gun was too small to have delivered the size of shot that killed Goldie, he replaced it in its case and retied the leather strip. Then he took a minute to admire the beadwork on the side of the suede case. It matched the work on the small pouch he'd seen in the dresser. Once again he detected two small initials: MY. He replaced the gun, pulled out his notebook, and made a note.

Although a dirty apron covered the bottom of the empty laundry basket, everything else was clean. Even the towels in the bathroom looked fresh and unused.

Lance made his way on through to the kitchen where the coffeepot still held the morning brew. He opened the refrigerator and wasn't surprised to find it fairly bare. He supposed if a person worked in a restaurant, she would have very little need to cook when she got home. He decided to check the trash again. When he raised the lid, he reacted with a groan. An aluminum pan had mysteriously appeared since he had checked the container earlier. He picked it up by the corner and looked closer. The brown sticky residue in the pan reeked of brown sugar and cinnamon. He placed it on the kitchen table and replaced the cover on the trash.

Moving on, he opened the back door. The spring on the screen door sang as he pushed it open and made his way onto the back porch. As he stepped he almost tripped, sideswiped by a bumblebee. He took off his hat and fanned at the insect. As the bee flew away, Lance noticed that the flowers in a whiskey barrel planter had been disturbed. He searched through the blooms. Nothing. He pilfered through the rest of the flower garden until he had a good mental picture of the scene, then returned to the porch.

Noticing where several pellets lay embedded in the porch, he pulled out his pocketknife and fished a couple out of the wooden floor. He rolled them between his thumb and forefinger, then pulled a piece of paper from the small spiral-bound notebook in his pocket and carefully folded them securely inside. He spent the rest of the afternoon lifting fingerprints from windows, doors, and various items in the kitchen and bedroom.

As he worked, his thoughts kept returning to Goldie Ray and why someone would want to kill an old woman. He had never met this woman, but he felt as if he knew her. She obviously had an appreciation for Indian baskets and beadwork, and that moved her up one notch in his book. In all his years of police work, he never seemed to get over the helpless victims. Crimes against them seemed so senseless.

With nothing left for him to do at the murder scene, he decided to return to the police station. After the short drive through the streets of Liberty, he parked in front of the police department and got out. As he climbed the steps, the lonely sound of someone singing greeted him at the door. It sounded like a tune he must have once known, but couldn't quite place. Stump, sound asleep on the couch in the lobby, didn't flinch an inch when Lance closed the door. Lance opened it again and let it slam. Stump almost rolled onto the floor before he caught himself.

"Damn, Smith," fumed Stump. "Can't you make some noise or something before you start slamming doors? You're going to give me a heart attack."

"Maybe you should do your sleeping at home then." Lance didn't try to hide his disgust as he dropped the fingerprint kit on Stump's desk.

"Can't leave." He moved into an upright position. "Got a prisoner."

"No kidding." Lance sounded sarcastic. "Who's the lucky tenant?"

"The crazy woman, Pearl Mobley."

"Pearl Mobley? Someone decided to file charges from the incident at the café this morning?"

"Nope."

"What then?"

"She killed Goldie Ray."

"Oh? I thought you said earlier you didn't think she was involved in the murder. What changed your mind?"

"She went nuts over at the church and confessed to the preacher. I heard everything she said."

Lance peered through the window in the door that led to the holding cells. He could see Pearl Mobley rocking back and forth on a cot, singing "Onward Christian Soldiers."

Suddenly Lance remembered the hymn, sung at the Kenwood Indian Baptist Church the last Sunday before he left for the Marine Corps. The preacher had insisted the young recruit stand at the front of the church while the congregation sang all four stanzas, followed by "Amazing Grace" in Cherokee.

Lance shook his head and hesitated before he spoke again. "Does she have a record? I mean, does she have a history or something?"

"Not really. She spent some time over in Vinita, you know, at the state mental hospital. Is that what you mean?"

"No, I mean has she ever been arrested for anything? Done anything violent?"

"Not that I know of."

"Then what makes you think she killed Goldie?"

"'Cause she said so."

7

"Time's up, sweetheart. Move it." The female police officer spoke with a growl that sounded as if it came from some sort of disgruntled animal. She stood with her feet shoulder-width apart, one hand on her nightstick and the other in front of her .38 Smith and Wesson.

Rosalee Singer placed the grimy receiver back on the wall phone and followed the woman back to the tiny jail cell in the basement of a building she thought must have been built around the turn of the century.

The Cherokee County Courthouse was indeed a landmark. The gray limestone building took up an entire block near the middle of Tahlequah. It housed the county sheriff and jail, as well as a myriad of county offices, courtrooms, and judges—a convenience for anyone entangled with the county bureaucracy.

Rosalee winced and her body stiffened when the door clanged shut behind her, leaving her alone once more in the cold, lonely cubicle. Realizing she was about to be shut off from the rest of humanity again, she yelled after the officer who was walking away. "He said he already wired the money. How am I going to find out what happened to it?"

The officer turned and frowned at Rosalee. "Don't worry, sweetheart. I'm sure someone will let you know." Then she turned on her heel and disappeared through the doorway at the end of the hall.

Rosalee leaned against the wall and slid into a heap on the floor. How in the world had she ended up here? "Oh, Logan, how could you leave me like this?" she wailed. She dropped her face into her hands and sobbed.

When she stopped crying, she thought of her friend, Logan Ross, who had literally saved her life. He had been a drummer for a local band, a baby-boomer trying to relive his youth by losing himself in forty-year-old rock songs. She loved his passion for life. The first time she met him he had been trying to coax a bass drum into the backseat of a Ford Mustang behind a bar on Highway 10 north of Tahlequah. As usual, she had drunk too much and wandered out the back door of the bar looking for a place to throw up. Just before she fell onto the shiny hood of his car, he abandoned the drum and ran to steady her on her feet. Then he walked her around the parking lot until she began to sober. He took her home, cleaned her up, and introduced her to Alcoholics Anonymous. It was the organization, he said, that had already saved his life and the lives of many of his friends.

That night changed her life. She had now been sober for more than six months, following all of the rules, doing all the right things. She attended AA three times a week, learned and lived by the guidelines. By the time her old gang had graduated to manufacturing their own methamphetamine, she had already moved away, hoping none of them would ever find her in northeastern Oklahoma. Even though they knew she had grown up there, they would never believe she could return to such an economically barren part of the country.

She had no idea she could ever care about anyone like Logan— especially since he was a Cherokee. It seemed everywhere she went she found herself surrounded by Indians of some sort. She had grown up around plenty of Native people, but her mother had forbidden her to have Indian friends. Indians were drunks, her mother told her, and lived off government handouts and welfare. Certainly not the kind of people Rosalee should ever hang around.

That had been years ago. An older and wiser Rosalee realized her philosophy of life did not necessarily need to reflect her mother's. She loved Logan and his gentle ways. He helped her face the day without a bottle in her hand and remained by her side no matter what time she needed him, day or night. That was, until the night a brawl broke out in the bar where his band performed every weekend. A stray bullet found the brawny Cherokee in the middle of the melee, where he was banging people in the head with his drumsticks trying to break up the fight.

Now it was all over. He was gone. Everything was ruined. They said he died quickly, but that didn't make it any easier for Rosalee. She drove her worn out red Jeep straight to the first liquor store she could find, tanked up on beer and vodka, and remembered nothing else until she hit the floor of the same cell in which she was now sitting, charged with "driving under the influence." The word "influence" seemed to be about right.

Perhaps mother was right. Maybe Indians are too wild.

Rosalee climbed onto the iron bed to wait and pushed her stringy bleached hair out of her sad, swollen eyes. Her throat felt like sandpaper, and her mouth tasted like bile. She wiped her runny nose on the back of her forearm, wishing more than anything she could remember where she'd been and what she'd done for the last two weeks. She swore to Logan's memory she would never end up like this again.

She didn't know if her brother would come through with the bail money or not. He promised he would on the phone, but depending on another drunk didn't leave her with very good odds.

Maybe he will feel sorry for me and send a little extra.

At least one good thing would come out of all of this. She would be sober by the time she got out of jail.

Two hours later, the woman officer reappeared at Rosalee's cell and the door banged open. "You're in luck, sweetheart. I guess someone really was on the other end of that phone line."

Rosalee jumped up and hurried down the hallway toward sunlight and freedom.

8

"Let's go, Sonny." Sadie opened the car door and the wolf-dog jumped into the backseat. When she pulled onto the highway, the clock on the dash registered 4:06 p.m. She should be in Liberty before five o'clock.

The red Ford Explorer hugged the curves as she drove across the Lake Eucha Dam and through the Spavinaw Hills State Game Refuge toward Kenwood where she turned south. After she crossed the overpass on the Cherokee Turnpike, she decided to take a shortcut, the back roads through Teresita. The landscape flew by as the winding curves straightened one after another in front of the vehicle.

This new adventure in Liberty was taking a turn she didn't like. Why would anyone want to be so hostile toward her? She didn't even know anyone in Liberty besides Tom Duncan at the bank, and she couldn't imagine him wanting to cause trouble for her. She had barely known Goldie, and now Goldie was dead.

She quickly turned onto the final shortcut to Liberty, a dirt road that would lead her up Billy Goat Hill. She rarely took this route because the county didn't maintain the road very well. But today she was in a hurry. After climbing the rocky rise, the road flattened and she made the turn that would take her into the north side of Liberty.

At the curve, her attention strayed to a herd of goats huddled near the fence. On any other day, she would have taken the time to stop and watch the nanny goats and their kids. They reminded her of Billy, the pet goat she'd had as a child. He was banished from the farm after he rammed Sadie's mother from behind, and Sadie had never forgiven her mother for giving him away.

Suddenly, Sadie noticed a man on the right edge of the road. She swerved, stomped on her brakes, and came to a stop only a few feet from him. It was Red. He walked up to her window and waited for her to lower it. Sonny moved to the edge of the seat and growled.

"*Eluwei*, Sonny. Quiet." The dog backed off but remained alert.

Sadie sat and stared at Red, waiting for the dust to clear and the pounding of her heart to subside. Then she hit the button on her armrest and lowered the window halfway.

"Hello," he said.

"What is wrong with you?" Anger lit up her voice. "Do you have some kind of a death wish?"

"Sorry," he said. "I didn't mean to startle you. I thought you saw me. Haven't you ever seen goats before?"

Sadie frowned and shifted the vehicle into park. "What are you doing all the way out here? And where exactly did you disappear to this morning?"

Red ignored both of her questions. "Are you on your way back to Liberty? I need a ride into town."

Sadie silently weighed the pros and cons for a moment, then reluctantly agreed. "Okay, but don't touch the dog. He'll take your hand off." She tapped the control to unlock the passenger-side door.

Red got in, pulled the door closed, and ignored Sonny. "Nice car," he said. "I gave up cars, you know. I've got two good feet and that's all I need. They get me where I need to go."

"Obviously. That's why you need a ride, right?" Sadie checked the rearview mirror, pushed the gearshift into drive, and drove forward.

"You know, our ancestors walked everywhere they went," he said, "and they were healthier than people are today."

"Well, my ancestors were smarter than yours. They rode horses."

Red looked around at the interior of the vehicle. "This is no horse." He pursed his lips and nodded. "Everybody's in a hurry."

"Everyone except you, I guess."

"If you're going back to Liberty to find out what happened at your café, I can tell you."

"Oh, yeah?" Sadie looked at her passenger. "And what exactly do you know?"

"Pearl just went a little berserk, that's all."

"A little berserk?" Sadie glanced at him again with eyes wide. "You call shooting someone in cold blood a 'little berserk'?"

"I didn't see her shoot Goldie, but I did see her heave a rock through your front window."

"Pearl threw a rock through my window?" Sadie slowed the vehicle and shot an angry look at Red. "That's just great. Did you tell the police?"

"No, I was busy, but someone else did."

"Busy?" Sadie's voice rose in pitch, and Sonny growled.

"*Eluwei*," Sadie commanded again.

"Nice dog," said Red as the vehicle rounded the last curve and Liberty came into view. "You can let me out at the edge of town."

"No, after we take a look at the café you're going to go with me to the police station and tell them what you just told me."

Red nodded. "Okay, good plan."

As Lance searched the storeroom for a trash sack, he decided the chief needed a lesson or two in tidiness. The trash can in the corner of the small kitchenette had overflowed and was beginning to stink. He found a trash bag and began filling it with the office refuse. As he dumped the kitchen trash, a brown paper sack fell onto the floor. It was stained on one side with a greasy brown substance. For a moment he wondered about Stump's eating habits but dismissed that thought and continued collecting trash in the outer office.

Each time he dumped the contents of an ashtray, the stench of stale cigarettes belched into the air and Lance grumbled. He missed the "clean air" policy he enjoyed while working at the Cherokee Nation.

The front door opened and Lance looked up. He took a step back as he felt his heart rise up in his chest. "Sadie," he blurted. "What in the world are you doing here?"

Lance had first met Sadie while working on a bank robbery in Sycamore Springs a couple of years before. He thought she was one of the strongest women he had ever met, not to mention intelligent and beautiful. Her long black hair and electric-blue eyes captivated him. If it hadn't been for the difference in their ages, he would have tried to get to know her better. He'd decided against it back then, but seeing her now made him wish he'd decided otherwise. He hoped it didn't show all over his face.

"Lance?" Sadie beamed. "I didn't expect to find you here."

Lance dropped the trash bag. "Hold on a moment." He quickly retreated to the bathroom, washed his hands, and then made his way to where she stood. "It's good to see you," he said as he offered his hand. "How have you been?"

"I'm well." She smiled. "How about you?"

"Can't complain." Lance turned his attention to the man standing quietly behind Sadie. Red introduced himself, Lance stepped forward, and the two men shook hands. "Have a seat." Lance pulled out a chair for Sadie. "What can I do for you two?" he asked.

"I bought the café down the street."

"Oh, no," Lance said with surprise. "Don't tell me you're the lady with the broken window."

"I'm afraid so. We just came from there. Maggie told me someone was hurt. Do you know who it was?"

"A painter took a fall from his ladder."

"Oh, no," Sadie gasped. "That's Hector. Is he all right?"

"I think so. They took him to Tahlequah to make sure."

Sadie turned to Red. "Red says he saw Pearl Mobley throw the rock that broke my window."

"Is that right?" Lance pulled the notebook from his pocket and began to take notes. "Tell me what happened," he said.

"Not much to tell. She walked up, threw a rock through the window, and kept walking down the sidewalk as if nothing had happened."

"Did you see the painter fall?"

"Yes, and he told me he was not hurt. He said he would call the police and Miss Walela, so I went on about my business."

Lance turned his attention to Sadie. "What's this I hear about this same woman threatening you this morning, Sadie?"

Sadie and Red took turns recounting the events of the morning, which brought the conversation around to Goldie's murder.

"Pearl seemed to be upset about the café reopening," Sadie said. "Do you think she might have killed Goldie?"

"We're still gathering information, so I don't know." Not wanting to get into a conversation about an ongoing investigation, Lance changed the subject. "What happened to your career in banking?"

"It's a long story. I'll have to tell you about it sometime. I still fill in for them on occasion, but as far as a career in banking . . . life's too short."

Red stood. "I don't want to intrude," he said. "It sounds as if you two have a lot of catching up to do. But I wanted to leave this." He dug into his pocket, fished out a red cylindrical item, and tossed it to Lance.

Lance caught the shell casing with his right hand and held it up for inspection. "What's this?"

"That is what the killer left behind."

"Red! You didn't tell me about this." Sadie sounded irritated.

Lance frowned at Red. "You want to explain?"

"I picked it out of Goldie's flower barrel this morning," he said, "while your police chief was busy taking . . . Let's just say he didn't notice."

About that time the radio gurgled with static and George Stump's voice came across the airwaves. Lance walked over to Stump's desk and picked up the transmitter. "Smith here." Lance held the transmitter to his chest and waited for a response.

"Smith, I'm en route to the bank, the one First Merc just opened up in the old First Liberty Bank building, so we can test the alarm system. So disregard the alarm if it goes off. It should only take a few minutes. I'll keep my radio on in case there's an emergency."

"Okay, Deputy Dawg . . . uhh, chief, sir, I'll be here if you get robbed." Lance held the transmitter for a moment, waiting for Stump to demand he stop referring to him as Deputy Dawg.

"Chief will suffice," said Stump. "Out."

Lance deposited the transmitter back on the corner of the desk and held up the shell casing again. "Okay, Red. Tell me again how you found this."

Red leaned against the wall. "A bee took me to it."

"A bee?" Sadie repeated Red's words.

"And when was that?" Lance thought of the bee he had dodged earlier at the murder scene.

"Right after your, uh, what do you call him, dog-man? Yeah, right after your dog-man carried a bag full of sticky buns out of Goldie's house."

The brown paper sack in the kitchen trash flashed into Lance's mind, and then the aluminum pan that had mysteriously appeared in the victim's trash can. He rubbed his face with his hand. "Why should I believe you?"

"You shouldn't. You should figure all these things out for yourself."

"I don't suppose you considered that you were trespassing on a closed crime scene, not to mention you've probably destroyed any viable fingerprints on this shell casing."

Red moved toward the front door. Sadie sat quietly.

"Where can I find you in case I have some questions?" asked Lance.

"Around," he said as he disappeared through the door.

Lance opened a drawer, withdrew a plastic bag and dropped in the shell casing. He tossed the bag on a stack of papers in his "in" tray.

"I'm sorry," Sadie said. "I didn't know he had the shell casing."

"Where did you hook up with that character, Sadie?"

"In the café this morning." Sadie pushed her hair behind her right ear. "When Pearl raised the gun, he jumped up and shoved me to the floor. If the gun had gone off, he could have taken credit for saving my life."

Lance made a note in his small notebook. "Yeah, and he could be covering his tracks by doing what he just did."

Sadie gasped. "Red couldn't possibly have killed Goldie. If he had, he'd be long gone by now."

Lance wondered if Sadie had forgotten about the bank robber who had not only killed her friend but also returned to the scene of the crime and hidden in plain sight while he stole her heart. "You never know," he said.

"What about Pearl Mobley? Are you going to look for her?" she asked.

"Don't have to."

"Why not?"

"Deputy Dawg hauled her in today after a little incident at a church." Sadie eyes widened.

"We'll keep her here until there's room for her at county jail," he said. "In fact, would you consider delivering some food for the prisoner?"

"Here?" Sadie looked surprised. "I'm not exactly up and running at the café, but I'm sure I can come up with something."

"Good. Nothing fancy." Lance grinned. "The city is on a budget."

"So, then, you think Pearl killed Goldie."

"I'm just a cop, Sadie. That's up to a judge and jury. Until then, as far as I'm concerned, everyone's still a suspect."

Sadie smiled. It was good to see her old friend again.

9

Emmalee Singer stepped off the Greyhound bus in front of Cronley's Service Station and waited for the bus driver to retrieve her bags. While he shuffled suitcases and boxes in the belly of the bus, she shielded her eyes from the intense early-morning sunshine and looked across the intersection and down the street.

She twisted her head from side to side trying to loosen the tightness that gripped her neck and snarled the muscles in her shoulders. Emmalee, or Emma as Goldie had always called her, had made the long trip from Carthage, Missouri, after her sister phoned and asked her to come. Goldie was selling the café and wanted to travel. The announcement devastated Emma. How could her sister turn the family business over to an outsider? Not to mention, the buyer was an Indian. It was unthinkable, and Goldie hadn't even asked for her opinion.

Even though Emma had married and moved away from Liberty over three decades earlier, she felt a strong attachment to the café. It once belonged to their great-grandparents, opened when they moved from Arkansas in the late 1800s into what was then Indian Territory, before Oklahoma became a state. Emma would gladly have taken over the café herself if only she'd known Goldie was so determined to get rid of it.

The two had traded harsh words on the telephone when Goldie suggested her sister might be too old to run the café. The words stung. Although Emma's next birthday would be her sixty-fourth, she reminded her sister that she walked three miles a day and considered herself as fit as anyone half her age. She continued to lash out at Goldie, calling her a spoiled brat. In the end, however, Emma had conceded that it was indeed her sister's café to do with as she wished.

Goldie planned to see the Smoky Mountains and had invited her sister to come along. A chance, she had said, for the two to reconnect with one another. Emma thought it was a ploy, Goldie's way of trying to make up for selling the café out from under her.

The door slammed behind her and Emma realized the bus driver had already deposited her three bags inside the gas station next to the front counter and bounded back onto the bus. Emma hurried to catch him before he closed the door.

"Thank you for such a safe trip, young man," she said and handed him a shiny new gold coin with the image of Sacagawea on it.

The driver tipped his hat, pulled the lever to shut the door, and steered the mighty vehicle toward the road, leaving Emma alone. She entered the station and looked through the door into the work area. "May I use your telephone?" she asked.

The attendant, busy installing a new pair of wiper blades on an old Buick, used one of the blades to point at a grubby phone on the wall and then returned to his work.

Emma pulled a tissue from her purse and used it to hold the receiver while she dialed. Before the phone on the other end began to ring she hung up and thought for a moment. Promising to be back soon, she made arrangements with the attendant to temporarily store her bags. Then she struck out walking up Main Street.

Sadie finished dumping the final dustpan full of broken glass into a cardboard box and carried it through the kitchen. Sonny lay just inside the back door where she had instructed him to stay. "Good boy," she said, as she left the box to dispose of later.

When the front door of the café rattled, Sonny growled. Sadie saw a small gray-haired woman peering through the glass with an air of desperation. "*Edoa*, Sonny. Stay," she commanded. "It's okay. She looks pretty harmless. If I need you, I'll let you know." She walked to the front door and unlocked it.

"Hello there," the woman said. "I'm looking for my sister, Goldie Ray. She was supposed to pick me up at the bus station this morning, but she must be running late. I thought she might be here. You're the new owner, aren't you?"

Sadie could feel the warmth rise to her face. This woman obviously didn't know about Goldie's death, and Sadie didn't want to be the one to break the bad news to her. "Hello," she said. "Yes, I'm the new owner, Sadie Walela."

"Oh, yes. My sister told me about your pretty name. You're Indian. Cherokee, I think she said." Emma gazed beyond Sadie toward the kitchen area. "Is she here?"

"Uh, yes, ma'am. Cherokee." Sadie allowed the door to swing open. "No, she's not here. But please come in and have a seat," Sadie stammered, "uh, and I'll call someone for you. Can I get you a cup of coffee or some ice water? I'm afraid that's all I have to offer right now."

"Oh, yes, coffee would be nice. Thank you." Emma sounded tired. "Why is the front window boarded up?"

"There was an accident with a rock yesterday. The glass man is coming tomorrow to fix it." Sadie poured a cup of coffee and took it along with a glass of water to a table near the center of the café. The woman stood looking at the walls of the café as if searching for something. Sadie motioned to the table where she had placed the coffee and water. "Would you like to sit here, uh, ma'am?"

"Oh, I'm so sorry," she said, walking toward the table. "I'm Emmalee Singer. You may call me Emma, if you'd like."

"Nice to meet you, Emma." Sadie pushed a small ceramic bowl filled with packets of powdered cream and sugar substitute toward the center of the table and returned to the counter. She picked up the phone and dialed. After a few seconds she spoke softly. "Lance, this is Sadie. I need your help. A woman is here looking for Goldie. It's her sister. Can you come down to the café and talk to her?" After a long pause she thanked him and hung up. For once in her life, she was without words.

When Lance arrived at the café, he noticed a red Ford Explorer sitting nearby and remembered the chief's comment about a red SUV being observed near Goldie's house on the morning of the murder. He sat for a moment contemplating the possibility of a killer returning to within blocks of the crime scene and parking in full sight. Although he had seen a lot of stupid criminals in his years of law enforcement, his sixth sense told him chances were slim to none that this was the same vehicle Stump had reported someone seeing. Nonetheless, he would check it out.

He returned his attention to the restaurant in front of him. This was the part of the job he never liked. As a police officer in Sycamore Springs, he had on more than one occasion had to deliver bad news to folks. It was just part of the job. Over the years he had managed to arm himself with the appearance of cold indifference. In reality he loathed delivering a death notice to a family member.

Sadie saw him coming, unlocked the door, and welcomed him in. Lance walked into the café and looked around. He could see an older woman sitting alone at one of the small tables.

"Lance," said Sadie, "this is Emma Singer, Goldie Ray's sister."

Lance stepped forward, removed his straw Stetson and faced Emma. "Hello," he said.

Emma rose from her chair with a sense of alarm. "Why are you here? Is something wrong?" she asked and then gasped. "Is it Goldie?" She looked scared as she walked toward the police officer.

"Yes, ma'am."

"She's not coming, is she?"

"No, ma'am, I'm afraid not."

"Where is she? Where is my sister?" Emma's voice began to strain. "Something awful has happened, hasn't it?" A distressed look came over her face as if she had already heard his unspoken words. "Oh, no. You're trying to tell me she's never coming, aren't you?"

Lance nodded. "Yes, ma'am."

"I don't believe you. What happened?" Her mouth tightened and her intense eyes began to blink.

"She was discovered at her home yesterday morning." Lance hesitated for a moment before continuing. "She was the victim of a gunshot wound."

"You mean someone murdered her?" Her mouth flew open, she grabbed her head, stood for a moment, then teetered on her feet. Both Lance and Sadie reached for her just before she started to fall. Lance held her easily with one hand while he pulled over a nearby chair. Sadie quickly dipped a napkin in a glass of water and dabbed at Emma's forehead. After a few moments, Emma opened her green eyes, now dulled. She sat up straight and looked around,then buried her face in her hands and began to moan.

Lance had no stomach for this part of the job. He could untangle wrecked vehicles, clean up murder scenes or move dead bodies, but emotional women unnerved him. He backed away from Emma, hoping Sadie's caretaker instincts would take over. To his relief, they did.

After several minutes, Emma wiped at her eyes and started asking questions, all of which Lance preferred to postpone answering.

"Who could have done this? Where was she?" asked Emma. "I want to see her."

Lance leaned over and patted Emma's shoulder. "The coroner will release her body later today. There's only one funeral home in town. Is that the one you'd like to use?"

Emma nodded.

"Is there someone we can call for you, ma'am?" he asked. "Do you have somewhere to stay?"

Emma spoke in a decisive voice. "I will stay at my sister's place."

"No ma'am, I'm afraid that's not possible," said Lance. "It's still considered a crime scene." He wanted to give himself a chance to go through the house one more time. Especially in light of the new evidence: Red's shell casing.

Emma stared blankly at Lance.

"You can stay with me, Emma," said Sadie, "until you get everything sorted out. That is, if you don't mind the ride to Eucha and back every day. Or if you want you can stay here at the café in the room above the kitchen. It's kind of a mess right now, but we can make do. It looks like it may have served as an apartment or an office at one time."

"Oh, my," said Emma. "I don't know."

"You can also stay in Tahlequah," offered Lance. "It's only twelve miles south of here."

"Oh, my," Emma repeated. "I guess I could take Goldie's car, but I don't really like to drive on these curvy roads around here."

"I don't mind taking you into Tahlequah," said Sadie. "I need to make a trip to Wal-Mart anyway."

Emma chewed on her lower lip. "You're sure it won't put you out any?"

"I'm sure."

Emma reluctantly accepted Sadie's offer with a nod.

Relieved that this part of the episode was about to end, Lance prepared to leave. He turned to Sadie and asked, "Uh, Sadie, could I speak with you for a moment?"

Sadie followed Lance out onto the sidewalk.

"Sadie, whose vehicle is this?" He nodded toward the red Explorer.

"It's mine. Why?"

"Oh." He smiled. "My mistake."

The door of the café opened and Emma emerged. "I just realized all my things are still at the bus stop," she said and took off walking in that direction.

"Whoa," said Lance.

"Wait, Emma."

Emma stopped walking when they both spoke.

"I'll get them for you," said Sadie. "Then we'll go to Tahlequah."

Emma looked at Lance. "When can I get into my sister's house?"

"I'll have it ready by tomorrow," he said.

She looked at Sadie. "Yes, that'll be fine."

Sadie hurried back into the café and reappeared a few seconds later with Sonny close behind. Pulling a set of keys out of her purse, she locked the door behind her. "We'll stop at Cronley's on the way and pick up your things," she said as she pointed the keyless remote at the Explorer and clicked it twice.

Lance helped Emma climb into the passenger's side of Sadie's vehicle, then walked to his cruiser. "You'll let me know if you need me, won't you?" he asked.

Sadie nodded as she opened the back door for Sonny to jump in. Then she climbed behind the wheel and waved as they drove off.

After collecting Emma's bags at Cronley's Service station, two women and one wolf-dog headed toward Highway 82, which would take them south to Tahlequah. Emma stared out the side window while Sadie made small talk.

"Where is home, Emma?"

"Carthage, Missouri." Emma returned her attention to Sadie. "I grew up around here when my folks ran the café, but I haven't been back in years. After our parents passed on, Goldie and I didn't keep in touch like we should have. Too busy. Or just didn't take the time. She had the café and I was working. We talked more in the last few weeks than we had in years. I couldn't believe she was selling the café. If she needed help she could've asked me. I know how to cook as well as she did." She looked at Sadie as if some new revelation had just occurred to her. "Do you think she knew something was going to happen to her?"

"Oh, no. I don't think so." Sadie maneuvered the Explorer through another set of hilly curves. "Goldie was incredibly happy last time I saw her. If she thought she was in danger, I think she would have said something."

"I'm the oldest." Emma looked down at her hands, then turned her face away. "I should have been here to take over," she murmured.

"You can't hold yourself responsible for what happened to Goldie."

"She never would let anyone take care of her." Emma's voice quickly turned angry. She pulled a tissue from her purse and blew her nose. "She was so blasted independent."

"I didn't know her very well. Did she have any other family? Kids?"

"Oh, no. It was just the two of us kids, and she never did get married. Her high school sweetheart ran off and joined the army. He was an Indian, you know." Sadie frowned at her passenger's condescending tone, but Emma didn't seem to notice. "And she never heard from him again. She kept saying he was MIA in the war, missing in action. I personally think he just took off. I don't think she ever knew what really happened to him." Emma stuffed the tissue back into her purse and gazed out the window again. "But after that," she said, "no one was ever good enough for Goldie."

Sadie turned off the highway into the parking lot of the Holiday Inn Express. "Is this okay?" she asked. "If not, there's a couple more south of town."

"This is fine."

Sadie pulled under the canopy in front of the door and turned off the engine. "I'll come back and get you any time you want."

"Could you have that police officer call so I can make arrangements for Goldie?"

"Yes, ma'am. Or I'll call you myself. Hold on and I'll help you with your bags." As Sonny watched from the backseat, Sadie jumped out of the car, pulled Emma's bags out of the back, and dragged them into the lobby. They approached the front desk where Sadie helped Emma check in, then helped carry the bags to her room, which was not far from the lobby. After

Emma appeared satisfied with everything, Sadie picked up a notepad from the nightstand, scribbled her phone number on the front page, and handed it to Emma. "Call me if you need anything."

10

The next morning, Sadie sat with her arms resting on top of the steering wheel, watching Emma stare at her sister's house. Goldie's car, a station wagon that had lost its luster decades ago, rested under the carport.

Sadie had driven from Eucha to Tahlequah in record time, picked up Emma and returned north to Liberty—and it was only 8:30 a.m. Emma had been so anxious to get into Goldie's house and now she sat frozen, gripping the Explorer's armrest. "The last time I talked to Goldie," she said, "we got into a terrible argument. I shouldn't have said the things I did. I feel awful." She looked at Sadie with sad eyes. "What am I supposed to do now?"

A feeling of helplessness grew in the pit of Sadie's stomach. "I don't know, Emma. But if you want to go back to the hotel, I'll take you."

Silence fell between the two women again before Emma finally spoke. "You've got more things to do than chauffeur me all over the county. Where were you going from here?"

"To the café," she said. "The man is coming to replace the broken glass today, and I've got to get things ready so I can open. You're welcome to come along."

"You wouldn't mind?" asked Emma. "I'm not sure I'm ready to be alone in that house yet." She raised her glasses and rubbed her eyes.

"I'd be glad to have your company, Emma, and besides, I'd love to have your input on some things at the café. I'll take you back to Tahlequah later today, and you can stay there as long as you want . . . until you decide what to do."

Emma's face brightened as Sadie gave the Explorer some gas and the two traveled down the street en route to the café. When they turned the last corner, Sadie grew concerned. She could see several vehicles parked near the restaurant. The plywood had already been replaced with a new plate-glass window, and lights shown from inside the café. People walked in and out of the front door.

"What the—?" Sadie made a u-turn in front of the café and stuck the nose of her vehicle into the last open space.

"Oh, dear me," exclaimed Emma. "This must be the people Goldie told me about. She called them—"

Emma's words hung in the air as Sadie jumped out of the car and swept through the front door of her new business. "Hey, what's going on in here?" she yelled.

Just as the door closed behind her, one of the sawmill workers emptied the last of a pot of coffee into Virgil Wilson's cup, then held the pot in mid-air as if toasting the new arrival. "Morning, Miss Sadie," he said. "Come on in. I'll have another pot ready in no time. Don't worry about a thing."

"What are you doing?" she demanded.

The door behind her opened and Emma firmly moved Sadie out of the way. "Come on over here and sit down, honey. I think I can explain."

Sadie marched behind the counter and surveyed the area to see if anything was missing. At Emma's continued urging, she finally climbed onto one of the red vinyl-covered stools next to her at the counter. The men had gathered around two small tables they had pushed together to create one long surface. Sadie thought they looked like charter members of the local overalls-and-white-tee-shirts club. Other than the sawmill workers, she didn't recognize anyone until she noticed Red sitting in his normal place at the end of the counter sipping coffee from a saucer.

Sadie felt as if she had entered a fourth dimension. Everyone around her seemed to be going about their business completely unaware of her presence until one of the men pushed coffee cups in front of her and Emma and started pouring coffee. A drop or two accidentally sloshed onto Sadie's hand and the reality of the hot liquid brought her mind back to the present.

"Ouch," she said as she wiped her hand on her jeans, then repeated, "What are you doing?"

The man had already slid around the end of the counter, delivering more steaming brew to the other men at the long table. He replaced the coffeepot on its burner and took his place next to Virgil. Sadie turned toward Emma, as if looking for something stable for her mind to latch onto.

" . . . and that's why they all have keys. Goldie called them her 'regulars.'"

"Regulars?" asked Sadie. "I'm sorry, Emma, I didn't hear you. Could you say that again?"

About that time, the entire group of men at the table got up, placed their dirty cups on an empty tray on the counter and headed for the door. But before they left, each man laid a couple of dollars in the middle of the table.

"See y'all tomorrow," exclaimed Virgil as he wiped the tables and counter. Then he scooped up the money the men had left and deposited it into a red can next to the coffeepot. Before Sadie knew it they were gone and she was left sitting at the counter next to Emma with a cup of coffee in her hand.

She turned toward Emma and asked again, "What were you saying? Who are those people, and how did they get into my café before it was open? And does the health department know about this?"

Red chuckled as he added his coffee cup to the tray and then carried the whole lot of them to the kitchen. Sadie could hear water running and assumed he was washing cups. She realized Emma had been talking and she still hadn't heard a word of it.

"Wait, wait, wait." Sadie got up from her seat, retrieved Red from the kitchen, and led him to the seat where she had been sitting. Then she walked behind the counter and looked at both of them. "Okay, now, one at a time. Explain this. Since both of you act like this is a normal happening here. And we'll start with you, mister. Out with it. How did you get into this restaurant?"

"I have a key."

"What do you mean you have a key? How did you get a key?"

"The same way everyone else did. Goldie gave it to me. There's a bunch more in that drawer over there."

Sadie slid open the drawer and found a key ring with six keys attached. "And why did Goldie give out keys to all these people?"

"To get in," he said in a matter-of-fact tone.

"Okay, I guess that means I'm going to have to find a locksmith to change the locks. How many people do you suppose can get into my café now without me knowing it?"

"I told you a while ago," said Emma. "They're the regulars." She emphasized the word "regulars" like it was the name of an important group of individuals.

"Regulars," Sadie repeated. "Okay, I'll bite. Who are all of the regulars?"

"They are the people who come here every day," said Emma. "Goldie told me all about it on the phone the other day. She gave them all keys so whoever arrives first can start the coffee."

"Why bother locking the café at all?" Sadie raised her voice.

Red grinned. "To keep out the riffraff."

Emma lowered her chin and shook her head. "It's the craziest thing I ever heard of, but that's Goldie for you. She'd trust anybody. She said sometimes they'd start showing up at 4:00 a.m. Goldie never got here until after six. But she liked the way it all worked out because she could make her pies, bread and what-have-you and not be bothered with the guys that just wanted to meet, drink coffee, and talk. You know, it's kind of a social thing."

Sadie looked at her watch. "It's almost nine o'clock. What are they doing here now?"

Red took over. "Everything's been all out of whack ever since Goldie closed down this darned place a couple of weeks ago. I guess that's when you bought it, right? They are just trying to get back to some semblance of order."

Sadie pushed her hair out of her face and looked out the freshly installed plate-glass window. "Why me?" She threw her hands into the air. "I can't have people just coming and going all the time. Especially when I'm not here."

"Why not?" asked Red.

"Because." She stamped her foot. *Okay, there must be something I'm supposed to be learning from this experience. I can hear my grandmother laughing at me right now.* Sadie looked up as if she could see her grandmother's spirit reaching down from heaven. *Patience is what she'd be saying.* Turning her attention back to Red and Emma, she declared, "I don't know what I was thinking when I bought this stupid café."

Emma was already standing. "It'll be fine, my dear," she said as she moved toward the kitchen and passed through the swinging doors that appeared to have been fashioned out of two used window shutters. "Come on," yelled Emma over the sound of clattering pans. "Let's get our hands dirty. Idle hands are the devil's workshop."

Red waved as he left through the front door.

When Sadie joined her new friend in the cramped kitchen, Emma had already slipped on a white apron and started pulling items off the shelf.

Sadie stood at the kitchen door and blinked twice. "What are you doing?"

"It looks to me like Goldie left you fully stocked with non-perishables," Emma said. "That'd be just like her, too." She chose a large bowl from under the counter and started scooping flour into it. "If I'm going to get you on your feet here, I'm going to have to see if I can remember how to whip up some of these old recipes." Emma lowered her nose and looked at Sadie over her glasses. "Some people might think I'm old, but I learned to cook in the same kitchen Goldie did. Let's see what we can come up with."

Sadie was taken aback by Emma's sudden transformation from a frail, grieving sister into an amazing kitchen machine. Before Sadie knew it, Emma had stirred up a ball of pliable dough, rolled it out on the floured countertop, and folded it into two pie pans. She trimmed the dough, then used her thumb and first finger to shape perfect ridges all the way around the edge.

As she worked on the pie crusts, she issued orders to Sadie. "See if you can find any red syrup. It should be in that pantry." She pointed with her head.

"Red syrup," Sadie repeated and then asked, "What is red syrup?"

Emma laughed. "Waffle syrup, honey. It'll say Griffin's on the label."

"Oh." Sadie opened the pantry doors and retrieved the syrup and other ingredients as Emma called them off.

"I hope you bought some eggs and milk and butter," said Emma. "If not, we're going to have to make a trip to the grocery store."

"Yes, ma'am," Sadie said, pulling items from the refrigerator. "Stocked up yesterday." Out of habit, she opened the carton of milk and performed the smell test. It passed. She placed the ingredients on the counter and watched as Emma haphazardly dumped and stirred them together in a large bowl.

"Emma, I don't know how to tell you this, but whatever you're making looks . . . awful."

"Oatmeal pie." Emma smiled. "You're going to love it. And so will the customers."

The mention of customers jarred Sadie. "I think I'd better see what else I can find in the way of groceries before we can think about serving customers." She opened the freezer and fished out a box of pre-shaped hamburger patties and placed them in the refrigerator. "Well, we can start off with hamburgers. I'm going to run to the store for buns and whatever else I can think of. I'll be back shortly."

Emma nodded as she placed two pies into the large oven.

When Sadie returned, the savory aroma of freshly baked pies almost overwhelmed her. She lowered an armful of brown paper sacks onto the counter and breathed deeply. Emma had been busy. Two oatmeal pies rested on a wire rack next to the oven, and Sadie thought they could easily be mistaken for pecan pies. Emma opened the oven and invited Sadie to peer inside. Three more double-crust pies looked as if they were almost ready.

"One apple, two cherry," beamed Emma.

For the first time, Sadie's chest began to fill with excitement. This is really going to work, she thought. "I don't know what to say, Emma. I didn't expect you to do all this."

"I know, neither did I, but you got to go with the flow, and this seems to be the direction the river is running."

Emma began to break out in giggles. As they laughed together, pent-up tension spilled into the air around them. Sadie wiped tears from her face and looked for something to write on. She opened a drawer and pulled out a pen and guest-check pad. "Okay," she said. "You tell me and I'll write it down."

"What?" Emma untied her apron and used it to wipe her face.

"The recipe for oatmeal pie."

"Oh. Well, honey, I start out with four eggs and stir in about a cup and a half of red syrup, a cup of coconut, and a stick of butter. Then I pour in about a cup of milk, real milk, not that watered down stuff, and a cup and a half of oats. That's the real oats, not the instant kind."

"That's all?"

"Yes, just put it all together in a bowl and stir it up. Then pour it in your pie shells. If you want to get fancy, you can line the bottom of the crust with pecans or walnuts. This makes two pies. Bake them about an hour at three-fifty or so, and you've got a crowd pleaser deluxe."

Sadie shook her head in amazement.

"I can do anything Goldie did." Emma smiled, turned her back, and muttered under her breath, "Only better."

11

The holding cell smelled like full-strength Lysol. Pearl hated the odor but decided it was better than the alternative. She didn't want to think about what had probably transpired inside this cage, but she was sure it could have smelled much worse. She would have to remember to say more prayers for the drunks of Cherokee County. A green cotton blanket covered a thin mattress on a narrow metal bed bolted to the wall. The bedding appeared to be clean, for which she was grateful.

This was the second day of Pearl's incarceration. Soon, she hoped, someone would come and take her back to the hospital with the white, shiny walls and bright lights. Pearl hated being in jail. She hated being anywhere. For that matter, she hated being alive. On more than one occasion, she'd simply prayed for death to deliver her from her miserable existence. However, much to her chagrin, that request had yet to be honored.

The door opened and Pearl stood up, ready to go. But instead of a limousine ride out of Liberty, it was George Stump delivering breakfast.

"Stand back, you old hag."

A wooden plank attached to the bars opposite the bed created a makeshift dining room table. Stump unlocked the door, carried in a metal folding chair, popped it open with one hand and plopped a tray of food down on the wooden ledge.

"I don't know exactly why you rate," said Stump, "but you got a visitor."

For the first time, Pearl noticed someone had come in behind the police chief. Pearl couldn't see too well, even with her glasses, but she could tell it was a woman.

"Who is it?"

"It's the woman from the café," he said. "She brought you this food and she wants to talk to you. So you be nice to her." Then Stump turned his attention to Sadie. "If you need anything, I'll be right out front. Okay?"

He slammed the cell door shut, then popped open another metal folding chair outside the cell for Sadie and retreated to his office. Sadie thanked him and took a seat.

"What do you want?" asked Pearl, swiping at strands of gray hair surrounding her face.

"Well, the police department is paying me to bring you food."

Pearl eyed her visitor. "So? What else do you want?"

"To be truthful, I'm not sure. I thought I might persuade you to explain why you dislike me so much. First of all, if your gun had been loaded, I would most likely be dead now. Secondly, you destroyed the front window of my restaurant, and in doing so, caused a man to fall off his ladder and get hurt."

Pearl looked at Sadie and then looked at the plate sitting inside the cell, covered with a red-and-white checkered dish towel.

"Go ahead and eat your food," said Sadie, "before it gets cold."

"You trying to poison me? That would be okay with me, you know."

"No, no," said Sadie. "I'd never do that."

Pearl uncovered the plate, took it back to her bed where she balanced the plate on her lap and began to devour scrambled eggs, bacon, biscuits, and sausage gravy. If it was poison, Pearl thought, it sure was tasty.

The two women sat in silence until Pearl finished her breakfast. She placed the plate back on the wooden plank but kept the dish towel in her hand. "Thank you," she said. "I'm sure you didn't have to make such a nice plate."

"Mrs. Mobley, is there something I did to you that I don't know about?"

Pearl stared at her. "What you got to say for yourself?"

"Say?" Sadie asked. "I don't know what you want me to say."

"You don't have to say nothing," Pearl sneered.

"Okay, how about a question then? Did you kill Goldie Ray?"

Pearl looked at the ceiling, contemplating Sadie's question while she nonchalantly stroked her slender neck. "She had it coming," she finally said.

"What do you mean?"

Pearl felt a surge of hatred rise within her as she spit out her words. "I mean, she was there."

"Goldie?" Sadie began to show interest in Pearl's words. "Goldie was where, Mrs. Mobley?"

"She was there when they had their way with me." Pearl shuffled over to the bed, sat down, and folded the dish towel on her lap.

"Please, wait. What are you talking about?" Sadie moved to the edge of her chair and touched the bars of the cell. "Who had their way with you, Mrs. Mobley?"

"See, there's where you're wrong. I'm not Mrs. Mobley."

"Oh." Sadie rolled her eyes and stood. "This is ridiculous. The police chief was right. Give me the plate."

Pearl retrieved the plate off the wooden ledge, walked to the cell door, and slid the plate through the bars to Sadie. When Sadie grasped the edge of the plate, Pearl stared at her for a moment before releasing it.

"I'm not Mrs. Mobley," continued Pearl. "I'm *Miss* Mobley. You got that? That means there ain't no Mr. Mobley. The name Mobley came from my folks, bless their souls." Pearl turned, walked to her bed, and sat. "That means that boy of mine is a bastard." Pearl slid onto the floor and began to weep quietly. "John is a bastard," she cried. After a few moments, she stopped crying and smiled at Sadie. "I had the sweetest little girl, too. But for some reason they took her away. Said I tried to kill her, but I didn't. They just took my little girl away."

"Who took your baby, Miss Mobley?"

"She was a mite prettier than John, too. Poor little thing. She never even cried." Pearl stared into space and began twirling the top button on her blouse.

Sadie shook her head. "What's all this got to do with Goldie?" she asked.

"She's the one. Took my girl."

"How did Goldie take your girl?"

Pearl tilted her head to one side. "I don't exactly know how she did that."

"Mrs. . . . Miss Mobley, none of this makes any sense."

Pearl looked away. "I'm tired," she said. Slowly climbing onto the bed, she wadded the dish towel, placed it under her head, and closed her eyes.

The door slammed behind Sadie as she walked back into the outer area where Stump sat with his feet resting on the corner of his desk. He smiled like a cartoon cat while he mashed his cigarette into an already overflowing ashtray. "Wasting your time talking to a crazy woman."

"Something about this doesn't smell right."

"It's the Lysol."

"No, I mean, do you really think she killed Goldie? She seems to be so confused."

"Hey, it's like I told Smith. If that's what she says, who am I to argue with her? Makes for less paperwork."

Sadie took her plate and left without saying another word.

12

Sadie stood at the back of the small church, trying to decide where to sit. The crowd had begun to assemble but the first four pews remained empty, reserved for the grieving family of the deceased. Unfortunately, she knew those pews would accommodate just one lonely sister, Emma Singer.

Earlier, she had left Emma at the funeral home to take care of the financial details of her sister's burial. Emma asked her not to wait, so Sadie had agreed to meet her at the church.

The small Indian church looked as if it had been built a hundred years ago. The furniture and fixtures showed signs of age not only in style but also in wear. The old upright piano sat near the front of the sanctuary near a side window, with two short benches nearby for the choir. Frosted windows provided privacy from the outside world yet allowed a soft light to shine through, creating a warm, welcome feeling.

The unopened casket stood in its place in front of the pulpit at the center of attention. Several sprays of fresh flowers lined each side, with two rows of blooming plants flanking the top step.

In the congregation, some fanned themselves with handheld paper fans, others spoke in whispers. Sadie noticed Red sitting alone at the end of a pew near the back. Staring blankly at the floor, he fingered the feather against the brim of the hat resting in his lap. A young woman played familiar hymns in soft tones on the antique piano while three ceiling fans stirred the stale air in the warm sanctuary.

Sadie rubbed her bare wrist and wondered about the time. She had taken her watch off the day she left her job at the bank in Sycamore Springs and never put it back on. Time, she had decided, was going to have to advance at her pace from now on instead of ruling her every movement as it had for so many years. Evidently, she hadn't quite mastered a total detachment from the timepiece.

She exited the sanctuary to wait for Emma. Outside, she pulled her hair behind her ears and then dug in her purse for a barrette to hold the long strands off her perspiring neck. Her search ended when a white Lincoln arrived and parked directly in front of the church. A young Indian man exited the driver's seat, opened the back door, and offered his hand to help steady Emma. She appeared frail against his athletic build as she stood, grasped his elbow, and walked toward the church. At the top of the steps, she motioned for Sadie to take her other hand. Sadie instinctively reached out to her newfound friend and gave her a gentle hug.

When Emma and Sadie entered the church everyone stood. Men in clean jeans and overalls, some clutching their caps in front of their chests, and women in their Sunday best stared straight ahead as the two women walked down the aisle toward the casket. Sadie could hear someone near the back of the church sobbing. Other than Red she recognized very few people, and although she was among a mostly Indian crowd, she felt like an outsider.

Goldie had no Indian blood, she had told Sadie, yet the church Goldie attended every Sunday, the church where her friends had gathered to say their last good-byes, was an Indian church. Goldie obviously had a lot of Indian friends and Sadie began to wish she'd known this extraordinary woman longer.

Once they were seated, six women gathered behind the pulpit and began to sing. Their voices blended in perfect harmony, filling the small sanctuary with the strains of "Amazing Grace" in Cherokee. The sound they created was so beautiful, Sadie wondered if these women were not mortals at all but angels sent down to sing on this unhappy occasion. Memories slowly rose within her, drawn to the surface by the music. The same hymn had been sung at her grandmother's funeral. Her eyes filled with tears. Suddenly she missed her Cherokee grandmother more than ever.

When the group finished singing, an older man began the service by reading Goldie's obituary. Then he launched into a plea for the lost souls in the congregation to get right with their Creator before they met a fate similar to that of Goldie.

Sadie's mind wandered, impervious to the preacher's words. She looked at her hand, still held in Emma's grip, and noticed the contrasting color of their skin—Emma's a pale ivory and hers a light brown. She thought about her own life. It, too, felt pale ivory at times and brown at others.

Returning from the maze of her thoughts at the sound of the piano, Sadie realized she had missed most of the service. The same young Indian who'd driven Emma to the church strode up the aisle and, after methodically rearranging flowers, opened the casket. The women began to sing as the crowd filed quietly past to catch one last glimpse of Goldie's earthly remains. Then the church was empty. Sadie and Emma found themselves alone with the casket.

"I'll wait for you outside," whispered Sadie.

"No, wait." Emma stood. "I'll just be a moment." Emma walked to the casket with what appeared to be renewed strength. She spoke softly and Sadie tried not to listen. " . . . a nice woman. Don't worry about the café. I'll take care of everything."

After a few minutes Emma returned to her seat. The driver came forward, closed the casket and motioned to the pallbearers. The two women followed as six men carried the casket toward the door, and Sadie felt a surge of relief once she felt the outside air.

After the short ride to the cemetery and a brief graveside service, the driver dropped the two ladies back at the church where Sadie helped Emma into the Explorer.

"Is there anywhere you want to go, Emma?" asked Sadie.

"Yes, yes there is," she said. "Would you take me to Goldie's house? I believe it's time."

"Are you sure?"

"Can't keep putting off the inevitable. I've got to sit down and figure out what I'm going to do."

"About what, Emma?"

"I put all my things in storage when I left Carthage," she said. "I didn't plan on going back for a while. Goldie wanted to travel and I told her I'd go with her. We were going to come back here and Goldie had asked me to stay with her for a while. But that's all changed now." A forlorn look came over her face. "The lease was up on my apartment and, well, I don't have anywhere to go."

"Maybe we should wait until tomorrow to tackle the house."

"No, I want to go there now." Emotion surged in Emma's voice.

Sadie drove the short distance to Goldie's house, parked in the driveway behind the old station wagon, and followed Emma to the front door.

"Why don't you come in with me, honey?" said Emma. "We can face this monster together."

Sadie smiled. "Okay."

Emma turned the doorknob and pushed the front door open. Sadie followed her into the quiet house. Emma put her purse down on the end of the sofa and Sadie followed suit. Together, they went from room to room. Finally, Emma sat down on the red love seat and began to sniff. "This is going to be harder than I thought."

Sadie sat beside her and put her arm around Emma's shoulders. "You don't have to do this today, you know."

"I know, but there's no reason to put it off or to sit around blubbering about it." Emma removed her glasses, wiped at her eyes, and put the glasses back on. "You see, I am eight years older than Goldie, but she was always in charge, telling everybody what to do. And heaven forbid if someone should tell her she couldn't do something. I don't know why she never married. I never understood that. I had already moved away when Goldie took over the café in sixty-seven. After that we grew apart."

"Nineteen sixty-seven?" asked Sadie. "She took over the café in sixty-seven?"

Emma nodded. "She was barely out of school. Nineteen, I think. I couldn't imagine why she wanted to hang around here and work herself to death in a restaurant. But she loved it, and Mom and Dad were thrilled."

"That was the year I was born. Sixty-seven."

"Summer of love."

Sadie frowned. "What do you mean, summer of love?"

"You know. Hippies. Flower children. Vietnam War protestors. They all got together in sixty-seven and called it the summer of love."

"Oh."

"Anyway, I was too old to take notice at the time. I was around twenty-seven or so and by then had been married for several years. I had my hands full taking care of a difficult husband and trying to raise three kids." Emma glanced at Sadie. "My youngest arrived that year."

Sadie realized she had assumed Emma was alone in the world. "So, where is everybody? Why aren't they here with you? Do they know about

Goldie? Why didn't they come to the funeral?" The questions tumbled out of Sadie's mouth before she could catch them.

"Well," said Emma. "I got rid of my husband twenty-four years ago after nineteen years of wedded misery. Just got fed up one day, packed my bags, and walked out. I've pretty much been on my own ever since. Anyway, he died almost ten years ago. I took early retirement last year from the county clerk's office." She looked at Sadie and smiled. "Got tired of the bureaucracy."

"I can understand that. What about the kids?"

"Oh, they're spread out from here to kingdom come. I hardly ever hear from them. Becky is the oldest. She's married to an oilman twice her age and lives in Saudi Arabia. I can't imagine why anyone would want to live there, can you?"

Sadie smiled.

"Jeff is the middle one. He lives in New York City and works for some insurance conglomerate. He's been married three times and travels all over the world. He drinks too much. I think he's got a girlfriend in every port." She stopped for a moment as if choosing her words very carefully. "Rosalee is the youngest one. She's adopted. We took her in after her mother left her in the trash bin behind the café." Emma raised her chin. "Her mother was an Indian woman. I saw her do it."

"Really? A Cherokee woman?" Sadie couldn't hide her surprise. "Did you try to stop her? Did you know her? It would be unusual for an Indian woman to abandon her baby. Family is so important to Indian people."

"Maybe she was an alcoholic, or on drugs."

"Maybe so, but even then, a family member would normally step in to take care of a baby."

"Well, I don't know nothing about that. But we treated that child like our very own all the years she was growing up. She doesn't really look Indian, so I think the father must have been white."

Sadie felt a surge of heat rising to her face. Abruptly, she stood.

Emma looked surprised. "What's wrong?"

Sadie walked to a nearby chair and slid into it. "It must have been hard for Rosalee growing up in a white family knowing she was half Indian, not knowing who her real mother and father were."

"Oh, no, honey." Emma's voice took on a sound of alarm. "She doesn't know. We never told her she was adopted. And we would never tell her that her mother was Indian. We wanted her to be just like us."

"Hasn't she ever seen her birth certificate?"

"It doesn't matter. We paid a lawyer to fix it. The original is sealed." Emma pulled a tissue from her purse again and wiped her nose. "She won't ever know. She doesn't look too Indian."

"Did the tribe know about this?"

"Nobody knows about it and nobody ever will. I don't know what possessed me to tell you. I guess I'm just overwhelmed today."

Sadie thought about her own struggle to be successful in a white world, her strained relationship with her white mother, and the good memories she had of her late Cherokee father. She didn't know which was worse, hiding the truth or trying to find it.

"To make it worse, I have no idea where she is," Emma continued. "She took up with a bad crowd, and the last time I heard from her she was in California." She frowned and added, "Just because you got kids, honey, doesn't mean they're going to take care of you when you get old."

Sadie nodded. "I guess not."

"What about you, Sadie, don't you have a family? A woman your age surely has a husband and kids hanging around somewhere?"

Sadie smiled, relieved the conversation was shifting away from Emma's wayward child. "No, nothing like that. I've got an aunt and uncle in Eucha. That's about it." Sadie thought about her failed, short-lived marriage, a rebellious act to get away from her mother. "Unlucky when it comes to finding a husband, I guess. I'd love to have a house full of kids, but you can't do that without a husband."

Emma raised one eyebrow. "Oh yes you can, my dear. I've seen it happen with my very own eyes."

"I know, but . . . "

"Well, when it's meant to be, honey, it'll be." Emma stood, then stopped and turned toward Sadie. "If you'll have me, I'd like to stay on at the café, just for a while until I can decide what to do."

Sadie's eyes lit up. "Are you sure?"

"I'm sure, honey. We'll make our own family."

13

Doc Brown followed Lance Smith through the door that led to the holding cells. The public defender in Tahlequah had asked him to visit Pearl Mobley and conclude, based on his expert opinion, whether or not she was mentally competent. The report would help determine whether Pearl's confession to the murder of Goldie Ray would stand up in court. In the meantime, she would have to stay in Liberty because the Cherokee County Jail remained full.

They approached Pearl's cell and Lance retrieved two folding chairs from against the wall. "Do you want to go in, or do you just want to observe from here?"

Doc Brown set his briefcase on the floor, looked at Pearl, then at the empty surroundings. "This is fine. If you want to stay as a witness, you're more than welcome."

Lance nodded as he set up the chairs. "Okay."

"How're you doing today, Pearl?" asked the doctor.

Pearl stuck out her chin. "If I say okay will you let me out of this stinking pigpen?"

"I just need to ask you a few questions, Pearl. Are you willing to help me?"

"Sure, what do you want to know? I already told the man in charge that I'd be glad to shoot her and I'm glad she's dead. I can go back to that hospital now."

"Okay, Pearl," said the doctor. "What's your full name?"

"My name's Pearl Elizabeth Mobley."

"Do you know what today's date is, Pearl?"

"Oh, I don't know. Around the middle of July, I reckon. You ought to know what day it is if you're a doctor."

"Okay," he said. "How old are you, Pearl?"

"About sixty-six or so, I guess. You're trying to get at my Social Security check, aren't you?"

"No, Pearl, nothing like that. What is your date of birth?"

Pearl looked around the cell as if trying to decide on an answer. "August fourteenth, I think. I'm not rightly sure which year it was."

"Do you know who the president of the United States is, Pearl?"

Pearl spit on the floor. "Duh," she said, and a moment later finished the word with a wide-eyed "bya."

Lance couldn't quite contain his amusement at the answer. The doctor looked at Lance and frowned. "What's so funny?"

"I guess she doesn't like our illustrious president," laughed Lance. "At least she knows her politics."

The doctor turned back to Pearl. "Is that what you mean, Pearl?"

"He's a spoiled brat," she stated. "You remember that old goat that kept saying 'I'm not a crook, I'm not a crook' and holding his hands up in the air?" Pearl held her hands in the air, making the victory sign with her fingers. "They're all crooks."

The two men both broke out in laughter at her antics. The doctor finally shook his head and stood. "Okay, Pearl, you win."

Lance and Doc Brown left the holding-cell area and walked back into the outer office. Lance was still chuckling when he sat down at his desk. "If you want to get to the heart of the matter," he grinned, "all you got to do is bring up politics."

The doctor nodded. "Seriously, Lance, I don't think she's crazy at all. I think she's sly as a fox. She wants us to think she's crazy so she'll get off." He opened his briefcase and stowed the notepad he had been using. "I guess we'll see how it plays out."

As the doctor headed out the door he almost collided with John Mobley. Lance stood and greeted the man.

"You here to see your mom, John?"

"Yes, sir."

"I'll have to search you first," said Lance.

John emptied his pockets onto the nearby desk and held his arms out while Lance patted his sides.

"Thanks, buddy," said Lance. "You're clean. Follow me."

John scooped the items from his pockets and followed Lance to his mother's cell. Lance offered him a folding chair and left so they could talk in private. When he returned to the outer office, he found Sadie waiting with Pearl's supper.

"Hello there," he said. "How's Mrs. Singer doing after the funeral?"

"Remarkably well," said Sadie. "I took her by Goldie's house. She's going to move in for a while."

"Oh, really? I thought she lived in Missouri."

"She does. But she's already let the lease on her apartment go, so she wants to stay on and help with the café. She wasn't very friendly at first but she seems to have warmed up to me now. Sometimes I don't think she actually hears what she says. She's very derogatory toward Indians in general."

Lance nodded his head.

"Do you want me to take this back to Pearl?" asked Sadie, motioning toward the plate.

"She's got a visitor right now, her son. I'll take it to her when he leaves."

"Oh, okay." Sadie stepped forward and placed the plate on the corner of a nearby desk.

"How in the world did you end up buying a café in Liberty, Sadie?"

Sadie smiled and sat on one of the faded chairs. "It's been a dream of mine since I was a kid," she said. "I only went into banking because I thought that's what I was supposed to do after I got my degree in business administration. But after the robbery and all the mess with that . . . well, I did a lot of soul-searching." She drew a circle on top of his desk with her thumbnail. "I did a lot of praying, Lance, and then there it was, an ad in the paper for the Liberty Diner." She looked at Lance and smiled. "It's like it was meant to be."

Lance leaned against the desk with arms folded and ankles crossed and continued to listen.

"I drove down here and met Goldie. She said she needed to sell the café because of her health. Her financials looked good. She wasn't getting rich, but she was making money. So I made her an offer and she took it. And here I am in the middle of another mess . . . with Goldie being killed and all." Silence fell over the office. She stood and lifted the corner of the towel covering the plate she had brought. "Pearl's food is going to be cold."

"I thought the bank asked you to come back to work for them," Lance said.

Sadie returned to her chair. "They did. And I agreed to help whenever they need someone to fill in for vacations and such, but I'm tired of the banking business. I want to do something for me for a change." She squirmed in her seat. "I've been in the branch they opened here in Liberty, and it's pretty nice."

John Mobley suddenly burst through the door from the holding cell. He stomped out the front door without saying a word, pushing past George Stump, who was climbing the steps to the doorway.

"Somebody's house on fire?" George asked in a facetious tone. He walked into the office and closed the door behind him before he noticed Sadie. "Oh, sorry, Lance. I didn't know you were conducting business."

Lance ignored Stump's comments and looked at his watch. "I guess we can take Pearl's supper to her now."

"Oh, yeah," said Stump. "How's the prisoner doing?" His nasal tone had returned.

Lance's dislike for George was growing harder to hide with every passing day. He was beginning to think this job wasn't going to last very long. "Here, why don't you take her this food," Lance motioned toward the plate, "then you can find out for yourself."

Stump raised his nose in the air, daring Lance to call him Deputy Dawg in front of Sadie. "Sure," he said. He went to his desk and took his time shuffling through a stack of papers. He sat down for a moment and made some notes on the back of an envelope as if waiting to catch part of Lance and Sadie's conversation.

The two sat in silence.

Then with a smirk Stump pulled a huge set of keys from his desk drawer, picked up the plate, and walked through the door that led to the cells. He had been gone for only a moment when he quickly ducked his head back through the doorway with a look of distress and yelled, "Hurry up, Smith. She's swinging!"

Lance was on his feet, halfway across the room and yelling orders before Sadie's brain could comprehend what George had said. "Sadie, stay here. Call the doctor. Tell him it's an emergency." Then he disappeared behind George.

Sadie jumped to her feet and in the flicker of a moment, before the door closed behind the two men, she could see Pearl's limp body hanging from the ceiling. In that instant, she recognized the red-and-white checkered dish towel Pearl had kept from yesterday's supper. The sturdy cloth made up the middle section of a braided rope the prisoner had made from her bedding. Pearl had hanged herself.

After summoning help, Sadie ran outside onto the sidewalk and vomited into the street. Then she sat down on the steps of the police station and held her head in her hands. "What am I doing in this crazy place?"

14

The graveside service for Pearl Elizabeth Mobley lasted less than twenty minutes. The Indian preacher from the Liberty House of God Church read a short passage from his Bible and offered a prayer, half in Cherokee and half in English, before the small group dispersed.

Sadie sat with Emma, watching at a distance from inside her Explorer. Although Emma had suggested they attend, at the last minute she'd decided she was "unwilling to stand near the coffin of her sister's murderer." The wound, she said, was simply too fresh.

"I thought I'd be glad she was dead," said Emma. "You know the Bible says 'an eye-for-an-eye' . . . "

Sadie listened to Emma talk, unconvinced that Emma really understood the true context of that Scripture and doubtful that Emma could actually stomach that philosophy in real life. She had hoped Pearl's suicide would perhaps bring some sort of closure and help lessen her new friend's pain. But so far, it hadn't.

Sadie could see Red and Lance standing near the cemetery gate but she didn't recognize anyone else. She shifted her gaze to the other side of the road. A mixed herd of Charolais and Hereford cattle ambled across a large pasture, with several steers grazing by the fence among a flock of white egrets. Her mind wandered as she watched the long-legged, long-billed, white birds feeding on insects on and near the livestock.

Emma disturbed the silence. "Are those herons?"

"Egrets. Similar to herons, I guess."

"The Old Testament forbade humans to eat herons," said Emma. "They're awfully skinny birds for anyone to consider for dinner." Then she sighed. "I should have come sooner. I waited too long to work things out with Goldie. If only I could turn back time . . . If she'd just found a nice white boy to marry, everything would be different." Emma turned her face away from Sadie, and the silence in the vehicle returned.

Behind the small herd, Sadie noticed an Indian man emerge from a ravine carrying a minnow bucket and a fishing pole. He crossed the pasture toward a dilapidated truck resting on the shoulder of the road. A small boy ran from the same narrow valley to catch up with the man, holding his hands straight out in front of him. As the two got closer, Sadie realized the youngster had a crawdad in his right hand. The gleeful look on his face propelled her mind back to her first crawdad catch.

As a young child she had stood motionless in a cold stream, the water barely below her knees. Her grandmother slowly reached into the water and began lifting flat rocks. The crawdads either zoomed away when the old woman removed their shelter, or lay deathly still, camouflaged against the flint rocks on the bottom of the stream. Aiming carefully at the midsection of the crawdad, steering clear of the pinchers, she had grabbed her first crawdad. The surprise and elation of her first catch still remained with her today as she recognized that same joy reflected in the young boy's face.

"What in the world has that boy got in his hand?" asked Emma.

"*Tsisdvna*," replied Sadie. She grinned and looked at Emma. "Crawdad."

"What's he going to do with it?"

"Probably take it home for his momma to cook, so he can eat it. I hope he has more than one," Sadie laughed.

"That's gross." Emma's voice registered alarm.

"You grew up in Oklahoma and never ate crawdads?" Sadie sounded surprised.

"Good gracious, no."

"Lots of Indian people eat crawdads," explained Sadie. "This is the best time of the year to catch them. You just clean them, take off the pinchers and the shells if you want to, roll them in flour, and fry them just like anything else."

"Some people will eat anything." Emma sounded disgusted. "I think I'll pass."

"It's a traditional Cherokee food, and no different than eating any other crustacean."

Emma wrinkled her nose.

Sadie elaborated. "You know, like lobster or shrimp, except crawdads live in fresh water. Lots of Cajuns eat boiled crawfish. It's the same thing."

"Oh." Emma turned her face away from Sadie again.

Silence returned. As Sadie watched the crowd disperse through the gate, she wondered if Emma had any idea how offensive her comments sounded.

In the distance Sadie noticed a woman standing away from the crowd. She continued to watch as the stranger bent low on one knee and placed flowers on a headstone not far from Goldie's grave. A toot from a car's horn brought Sadie's attention back to the present as the traffic began to flow away from the cemetery.

"What do you think, Emma? It's already two o'clock. You want to call it a day and start fresh tomorrow?"

Emma nodded her head and spoke softly. "That's okay with me, honey."

"I'm going to drive into Tahlequah and pick up some supplies. Do you want to go?"

"No, you go on. I could use the rest."

Sadie turned west at the four-way stop and the two women rode in silence until they pulled into the driveway of Goldie's house.

"Would you mind coming in for a few minutes?" asked Emma.

Sadie said she wouldn't mind, and the two walked from the car to the house. Sadie opened the unlocked door for Emma and they went in. Emma dropped onto the sofa and kicked off her shoes. Sadie stood at the door, not sure what to do.

"Where was the son?" asked Emma.

"Who?"

"Her son. Why wasn't Pearl's son at the service?"

"Oh, I don't know. Lance said he'd been looking for him for two days. He wants to question him about what happened right before he left Pearl the day she—" Sadie stopped in midsentence, joined Emma on the couch, and slid her feet out of her shoes, too. "But I guess it doesn't matter since Lance said she left a note."

"Note?"

"Suicide note, explaining that she didn't want to live anymore after what she had done."

Emma's eye grew wide. "Oh? That's the first I've heard of that." She stared at Sadie for a moment before she stood, picked up her shoes, and walked toward the bedroom. "I guess that's it, then. Case closed. Time to move on."

"Yeah, I guess so." Sadie contemplated Emma's words for a moment, slipped into her own shoes, and walked to the door. "Anything I can bring you?"

The phone rang. "Can you wait just a moment, Sadie?"

Sadie could hear Emma speaking with someone she obviously knew. Not wanting to intrude, she got up and turned her attention to a group of photos nestled within a trio of handwoven, double-walled baskets on top of the piano. Sadie picked up one of the baskets and recognized the signature design of a local award-winning master weaver, a Cherokee woman who lived north of Eucha. Goldie must have had an appreciation of Cherokee artwork, she thought. Something her sister didn't exactly exude.

She replaced the basket and turned her attention to the photos. In one picture, Sadie recognized a radiant teenaged Goldie gazing into the eyes of a young Indian man decked out in a starched army uniform. Two other photos included the same person.

After a few moments Emma emerged from the bedroom dressed in a worn pair of slacks and a soft pullover. She looked tired. "That was my son Jeff on the phone," she said. "The one who lives in New York. I left a message for him earlier today and he just called back. I thought I should at least tell somebody in the family what happened. He knew I was coming here to be with Goldie, but he didn't know . . . " Emma pulled a tissue from her pocket and wiped her forehead.

Sadie coaxed Emma toward the sofa.

"That isn't all." Emma used the same tissue to wipe at her nose. "Jeff said Rosalee called him. She needed money to get out of jail, so he wired her five hundred dollars. He said she was somewhere in Oklahoma. I wish that girl would get her life straightened out. You never know when something might happen, you know, like it did to Goldie."

Sadie patted Emma's shoulder.

The front door opened, startling both women. Sadie stood and Emma froze. A woman about Sadie's age with stringy blond hair hiding half of her face stood in the doorway. Sadie immediately recognized her as the stranger she had seen earlier at the cemetery. The woman dropped her large purse on the floor and closed the door.

"Rosalee?" Emma let out a gasp. "Is that you?"

"I can tell you're thrilled to see me, Mother."

"Good grief," exclaimed Emma. "Where in the world have you been? You look awful."

Rosalee wore a multicolored flowered-print skirt and a jacket, two-toned in purple and turquoise. Her black lace hose and white sandals echoed the contrast of her bleached hair and distinctly darker roots. "If I could remember I'd tell you," she muttered.

Sadie walked toward Rosalee and offered her hand. "Hello. I'm Sadie Walela." When Sadie looked into the woman's face, she could see her eyes were red and swollen as if she had been crying.

"I'm Rosalee Singer, the black sheep of the family. I see you already know my mother."

"This is not a good time for that kind of talk," snapped Emma. "Especially with what's happened to your aunt."

Rosalee approached her mother, bent and kissed at the air near her cheek. "I know," she said.

"When's the last time you had a bath?" asked Emma. "You smell like beer."

Sadie could see the pain on the faces of both women and decided this was a good time to leave. "I was just on my way out."

"That's okay," said Rosalee. "Don't let me interrupt. I can't stay."

"Now where do you think you're going?" asked Emma. "Can't you stay here, at least for a little while? You can clean up. Maybe some of Goldie's clothes will fit you."

"I've got my own clothes here."

"Here?" Emma looked surprised.

"Yes, here, Mother. I've spent a lot of time with Aunt Goldie in the last six months or so. She cared about me, and I cared about her. She really wasn't very well, you know." Rosalee stared at her mother with cold eyes. "She told me I was adopted, Mother. Is that true?"

"Oh, honey, she had no right—"

"She told me when you came to visit we would sit down together and you would tell me the truth. So I guess it's up to you and me to talk about it now."

Emma covered her mouth for a moment as if she might be sick, then lowered her hand. "There's nothing to talk about. We took you in and we raised you like you were our own. We gave you a good home. That's all you need to know."

"Who was my real mother?"

"I don't know, Rosalee." Emma's voice took on a defensive tone. "She abandoned you. I told you, we took you in. I didn't know who she was then, and there's no way to find out who she is now. It's not like we got you through an adoption agency or something. We were good to you. Isn't that good enough?"

"I think you all need to have some time alone." Sadie withdrew toward the door again. "It was nice to meet you, Rosalee." Then she turned her attention to Emma. "Emma, do you want me to pick you up on Monday morning or are you going to drive Goldie's car?"

"That old beat-up thing? No, honey, I'm used to walking. It's not that far and I need the exercise to stay in shape. If it's okay with you, I'll just meet you there."

Sadie got into her car and drove back toward the main intersection of Liberty, then headed south toward Tahlequah. She wanted to find out more about Pearl Mobley and try to decipher some of the babbling about Goldie and "someone having her way with her." It sounded like Pearl might have been raped. But, even so, what would that have to do with Goldie? Maybe she could learn something from old newspaper articles.

Twenty minutes later, she parked in front of the Tahlequah Public Library, entered the building, and approached the information desk. The woman behind a stack of books looked too young and fit to be working inside a library all day. She had vibrant eyes, a sunny smile, and highlighted hair framing her friendly face. Sadie explained what she was looking for, and the woman led her to a room full of filing cabinets.

"We'll have to resort to old-fashioned microfilm." As the two women walked, the librarian continued to talk. "It's too bad the small-town newspapers like you're looking for aren't archived on the Internet yet." She led Sadie to a bank of filing cabinets and directed her to the top row of drawers. "Here are the dates for each newspaper," she said. "You can view the film on one of these viewers." She pointed at two monster machines that looked to be about the same age as the building—old.

Sadie thanked the librarian and began to search through the file drawers. She didn't know exactly what she was looking for, but she felt like

Liberty's past might help explain the present. Pearl's riddle about a missing child had piqued her interest, and now Emma's admission of an under-the-table adoption added to the puzzle. Based on Rosalee's age, something should show up in 1967, she thought. Sadie pulled open the drawer marked for that year and starting pulling out spools of film taken from the Tahlequah paper.

Three hours later, the woman from the front desk arrived to remind her they would be closing in thirty minutes. Sadie looked at the mess she'd made of film and canisters on the table beside the viewer.

She closed her eyes, chose one last spool, and fed the end of the film into the viewer, pulling images of newsprint across the screen once more. She groaned when she realized the microfilm had been misfiled. It was the wrong year: 1966. As she reached to hit the rewind button, something caught her eye. The headline read: "Liberty Rape Remains Unsolved." Sadie quickly scanned the article, positioned it between the marks on the screen, and punched the button to make a copy. The old machine growled and spit out a page of paper. She replaced the spools of film on the counter as requested by the librarian, paid ten cents for her one copy, and retreated to her car.

She sat behind the steering wheel and read the article, then folded it and pushed it deep into her purse. After she finished shopping for supplies, she would have plenty of time to think on the long drive home to Eucha.

15

When Lance Smith left the cemetery after Pearl's service, he drove
north out of Liberty past Wilson's sawmill toward Billy Goat Hill Road.
The undeveloped countryside on both sides of the gravel road displayed an
abundance of oak, sycamore, and pine trees, billowing over dense under-
brush. He maneuvered the police car down the steep winding hill for which
the road was named. When the road flattened out, it continued hugging
the base of the ridge and ran through a strip of bottomland. He stopped at
the mailbox marked "Mobley."

A worn path led from the road through tall grass to a dilapidated
trailer house sitting among a grove of red oaks. This was his third trip to
this point in the road this week. "Hot dog," he said. "Third time's a charm,
Smith." He could see John Mobley's Harley sitting at the end of the mobile
home, covered with a worn tarp.

Lance nosed his car off the road onto the path and made his way to
the trailer. He parked behind the motorcycle, lowered the driver-side window, and sat in his car for a few moments. A recent deer kill hung from the
lowest branch of a mulberry tree at the corner of the house. It was covered
in flies, and stank.

Lance honked the car horn and waited for John Mobley to come to
the door. Sure enough, after several minutes John opened the door and
stood in the entryway. His shaved head looked as if he'd been standing
bare-headed in the Oklahoma sun too long.

With beer can in hand, John raised his chin and spat into the yard. He
wiped his mouth with the back of his hand and teetered for a moment before he took a step and tumbled to the ground.

"And you white boys thought you could conquer us Indians with fire-
water," Lance mumbled as he rolled out of the car and walked over to the

fallen drunk. "Take a lesson, my friend," he said to himself. "Who is standing, and who is eating dirt?"

John pushed himself up with his arms, looked at Lance, and belched.

"You're going to have to get a hold of yourself. Getting drunk like this isn't going to do anybody any good, John. Get up." Lance took hold of John's arm, pulled him to his feet, and helped him back into the mobile home.

John sank onto the couch and reached for a beer bottle sitting on the windowsill. An assortment of bottles and cans lay strewn across the table, countertop, and floor. The sink overflowed with dirty dishes and Lance could smell spoiled food. The place look as if it hadn't been cleaned since the old contraption had been dragged across the pasture and had its wheels removed. From the look of things, that had been a while.

"You got any coffee around here?" asked Lance.

John didn't respond, so Lance ventured a peek into the cabinets and found a jar of instant coffee. He used the cleanest dirty pan he could find to heat some water.

By then John had come out of his stupor enough to realize something wasn't quite right. "Hey man, what are you doing in my house, anyway?" His slurred speech indicated he had a long way to go before he would be able to carry on any kind of a conversation.

Lance poured the boiling water into a mug and stirred in the freeze-dried granules to make a quick cup of brew. Then he set it on the kitchen table. "Come on, John. Let's see if we can sober you up so I can talk to you."

Four hours later, Lance had gone through all of the instant coffee available and then resorted to plain water. John stood at the front door and relieved himself into the front yard so many times that Lance thought surely most of the alcohol had been flushed out. After convincing John it was a good idea, Lance helped him into the small shower, turned on the cold water, and listened to him whine. After a while, John emerged from the back bedroom in a pair of dry jeans and a muscle shirt. A U.S. Marines emblem tattooed on the top of his right shoulder caught Lance's eye.

"Say," said Lance. "You a Jarhead, too?"

John rubbed his hand over the indelible image—Semper Fidelis, the Latin words lettered in script under his skin. "Yeah, so?"

Lance offered his hand. "Semper Fi," he said. "The Nam. 1972." For a moment, Lance thought he had found a way to connect to John, as the slogan from Vietnam surfaced in his mind. *There are only two kinds of people who understand Marines: other Marines and the enemy. Everyone else has a second opinion.*

John ignored Lance's gesture. "What do you want?"

"Okay, then. We'll do it your way, all business." Lance returned his hand to his belt. "You weren't at the cemetery today to pay respects to your mother. Why not?"

"She was just a crazy old woman," John grimaced. "All I need is another beer."

"Hold on. After I leave, you can drink yourself to death for all I care. But before you do that I need to know what happened when you visited your mother the other day."

John frowned again. "You don't have any aspirins on you, do you?"

Lance held his rock-hard stare.

"Nothing," said John. "Nothing happened. She wouldn't even talk to me. She turned her back on me and wouldn't listen to a thing I was saying. I didn't know what she was doing. It looked like she was braiding a rug or something. I got mad and left."

"Did she ever admit to you that she killed Goldie Ray?"

John glanced out the window. "No. My momma would never hurt anybody . . . not on purpose."

"Did you know she was going to hang herself?"

"I guess I should have figured it out, but I'm used to her doing loony stuff. I tell you she was just a crazy old woman."

Lance thought for a moment. He felt relatively sure John was telling the truth. "Whose house is this, John?"

"I bought it for my mom a while back. She was living in an old shack that was about to fall in on her head. I pulled this thing over here from Arkansas and gave it to her."

"So it's in her name?"

"Hers and mine. What difference does it make? She's dead. I ain't got no daddy, no brothers or sisters. So all her stuff is mine anyway." John looked around his surroundings. "And that sure as hell ain't much, is it?"

"You told me the other day that you kept your guns at your mom's house. Did you mean here?"

John sniffed. "Yeah, so?"

"Your mom confessed to killing Goldie."

John looked at Lance with a blank face.

"We've got the gun she was toting around that morning," continued Lance. "Virgil Wilson took it away from her after she pointed it at some people in a restaurant. But I need your permission to see what other guns she might have had access to."

John shrugged his shoulders. "Knock yourself out. They're all in the hall closet."

"Would you get them for me, John?"

John got up, walked to the closet, and retrieved four shotguns—two 20-gauge, one 12-gauge, and a small .410. He handed them one by one to Lance. Lance checked each one to make sure it was unloaded before leaning it against the wall. The chambers were all empty. Then John handed him a 30.06 Remington rifle. Lance checked the magazine. It too was empty. He handed it back to John.

"That's quite a collection you got, John. Is that all of them?"

John nodded as he replaced the rifle in the closet. "I like to hunt."

"I guess you realize deer season's about four months away."

John wiped his face with his hand. "Man's got a right to eat, don't he? We got so many deer now, they're half starved from lack of food. I don't think anyone's going to miss one doe. I shot it on my way home after you stopped me . . . for nothing. Harassment, if you ask me."

"How'd you get a deer home on a motorcycle?"

"Good balance," John sneered. "Everyone around here thinks I'm crazy as my momma, don't they? Including you."

"That deer wouldn't have been killed with a slug from a shotgun, would it, John? I thought you weren't riding with any loads that day."

"I wasn't," John grinned. "But I stopped by the hardware store on the way out of town."

Lance shook his head. "John, you'd better take advantage of my good mood today and not cross me again." Lance picked up the guns and carried them out the door toward his car, then stopped, looked back at John, and nodded toward the smelly carcass hanging in the tree. "That thing's past keeping. You'd better get it down before someone turns you in."

John wiped his face again. "Yeah, thanks."

"I'll get these guns back to you in a couple of days," said Lance. "How long are you going to be in town?"

John stared into the distance. "I don't know. I imagine my job's already gone over at the pie factory."

"Is that where you work? Mrs. Smith's in Stilwell?"

John nodded.

"Well, you might want to give them a call. I'm sure they'd understand with a death in the family and all."

John nodded again. "Yeah, sure."

The locusts had already begun humming their nightly serenade when Lance placed the shotguns in the trunk of his vehicle and headed back toward Liberty. As he guided the cruiser back up Billy Goat Hill, he thought about John Mobley the alcoholic, and about what had happened to John Mobley the Marine. Not every man was good enough to be a Marine. Being a former Marine himself, he knew that. Sadly enough, the shell of a man he had just left sitting in the middle of a junk heap was most likely the direct result of his experiences in the Corps—a classic case of Post Traumatic Stress Disorder. Lance knew firsthand there was no cure for PTSD. He also knew John was going to need a lot of help before he could ever learn to live with it.

As Lance pulled up in front of the police station, he could see Red walking down the sidewalk, a black-and-tan hound following close behind. Lance popped the release on the car's trunk, got out, and began unloading John Mobley's shotguns.

Red and his four-legged companion arrived a few moments later and offered to help. Red took two of the shotguns, one under each arm, and followed Lance up the steps. The dog followed the two men to the door, stopped, and sat on the threshold.

Lance laid the guns across the desk and motioned for Red to do the same. Then he turned to close the door. "Who's your buddy, there, Red?"

Red smiled and nodded. "That's Judy. She's been following me around town all day."

"A friend of yours?"

"Judy is everyone's friend the day after a coon hunt," he chuckled. "She belongs to Jake Youngblood. Don't worry. One of Jake's boys will show up before long to get her."

"Hmmm." Lance raised one eyebrow, contemplating the idiosyncrasies of small-town life. Everybody knew everyone else's business, down to the visiting habits of their coon dogs. "I see."

As if the dog understood her place, she walked back down the steps, circled twice, and slid down against the wall next to the stairs. Lance shook his head and closed the door.

"Say, you're going to be at the gospel singing Thursday night, aren't you?" asked Red.

"Why do you ask? You need a ride?"

"No, I'm going with some of the singers. Creeks don't miss too many meals."

Lance grinned.

Red nodded at the gun collection. "Did you make a big bust somewhere?"

"Not exactly."

Red patiently waited.

Finally Lance decided to elaborate to see what Red's reaction would be. "John Mobley's," he said.

"What'd he do?"

"I don't know that he's done anything. I'm still trying to piece together what happened to Goldie Ray."

"Seems to me that was fairly apparent."

Lance didn't respond as he pulled the notebook out of his pocket and tore out a few pages. He scribbled on each one before attaching it to a gun.

"Thought Pearl confessed and you already had the murder weapon . . . and the shell casing." Red thought for a moment. "I guess that means they didn't match up."

Lance remained silent.

"Why did you need to bring in all of these guns? The shell casing is from a 20-gauge. It can only be tested against these." Red pointed at the two middle-sized shotguns on the desk.

"You are very astute, old timer."

"I'm not as old as I look."

About that time, George Stump walked through the door, pulled off his hat, and hung it in its usual place on the nail by the door. "I wish Youngblood would teach his coon dogs to go home instead of lounging around in downtown Liberty." Then the shotguns caught his attention. "Hell of a cache, Smith. Somebody must be sorry they ran into you." He picked up the .410, raised it to eye level, and pointed it out the window. "This is a dandy little piece. Did you confiscate it? We get to keep it?"

"Not exactly," said Lance as he searched the chief's face, assessing the seriousness of his comment. "I'm getting ready to put these in the property locker."

Stump frowned as Lance proceeded to move the guns into the back room and into the gun safe.

A few minutes later, the sound of Judy's barking mixed with the grumbling sound of an old truck with squeaky brakes could be heard outside. Red jumped up and hurried toward the door. "Got to go. Sounds like my ride."

Lance closed the gun safe and followed him outside and onto the sidewalk. He watched as Red got in the front seat of Elmer Youngblood's old blue truck and sat next to Judy, the hunting dog.

"See you Thursday." Red waved as Elmer backed out and drove off.

16

When the alarm on his clock radio kicked on the fuzzy sounds of a country music station at 5:00 a.m., Lance was already awake. Questions had churned all night about Goldie Ray's murder and he'd visited every possible scenario of her death—some while he lay awake, others in his dreams.

Technically, according to George Stump, the case was closed. In her suicide note, Pearl had said she didn't want to go on living after everything she had done. Stump took that as an affirmation of the murder confession he had overheard at the church. Lance thought it could have meant anything.

Lance rubbed his face with both hands, shook off his thoughts, and got out of bed. He had been looking forward to this day for a long time and he refused to let his job creep in and ruin it. This was the first day he had managed to take off since taking the job at the Liberty police department three weeks earlier. A well-deserved mental health day, he called it.

After he dressed, he nibbled on a piece of fried Spam left over from the night before while he waited for a strong pot of coffee to brew. When it finished, he filled a thermos, grabbed his hat and walked into the predawn darkness. He threw his fishing gear in the bottom of the boat trailered in his driveway, connected the battery cables, and checked the fuel tank. With everything in order, he got into his truck, backed it up to the trailer, and connected the two.

Charlie McCord, his friend and former colleague from Sycamore Springs, had agreed to meet him at daybreak at Lake Eucha. They would rendezvous at the Old Eucha campground, the site where Eucha had stood before the City of Tulsa built the lake, forcing the small town to relocate to its present site several miles away, now known as New Eucha. In less than an hour, the two lawmen would be drifting on the smooth waters of their favorite fishing lake. Lance was ready for a day of relaxation and could care less if they bagged a single fish.

Lance drove the leisurely back roads north from Tahlequah through Liberty to Kenwood and around the south end of the lake to the meeting place. When he pulled into the otherwise empty campground he could see Charlie waiting.

After a few words of greeting between the two men, Charlie added his fishing rods and a tackle box to Lance's gear, and Lance backed the boat down the ramp. Charlie shoved the boat off the trailer into the water and at the last possible moment he jumped in and guided the boat to a nearby dock and waited for Lance to park the truck and trailer.

Lance joined his friend in the boat, turned on the ignition, and cranked the starter no less than a dozen times before the outboard motor began to purr. He guided the boat east toward Rattlesnake Cove, his favorite fishing spot.

The lake, fed by countless underground springs, had been built in the early fifties and served as the main water supply for Tulsa, ninety miles away. Lance remembered the stories told of a man who supposedly rode his motorcycle through the finished pipeline from one end to the other before they released the initial gush of water. Seemed like a silly thing to do, but Lance never doubted the tale. Now, with no swimming or speed boats allowed on the lake, most fun-seekers and campers migrated either north to Grand Lake or south to Lake Tenkiller. The wide open lake was now an angler's delight and had supplied the best fishing environment in northeastern Oklahoma for decades.

Lately, however, high levels of nitrogen had caused algae to grow out of control in the lake, leaving the people of Tulsa with a foul taste in their drinking water. Litigation was underway to stop the chicken farmers in northwestern Arkansas from polluting the streams that fed the lake, but the conflict had turned into a state versus state battle with no end in sight. For now, the fishing remained good, and sportsmen came from miles around to dip their hooks in the water of Lake Eucha.

Fog rose like steam from the water, and as the boat gained speed they passed through alternating pockets of warm and cool air over water hovering at a warm eighty-five degrees. Lance guided the boat slowly eastward through the misty patches as pink-fringed clouds appeared, announcing the arrival of the new day. Charlie pointed at a dozen mallards, disrupted by the boat's early morning appearance, taking flight in their customary formation. Lance acknowledged with a nod and a smile. Minutes later the fiery sun burst into view, evaporating the fog. By then, Lance had completely forgotten Goldie and Pearl. Everything in life, he thought, could probably be solved from the fisherman's end of a rod and reel.

When he found the cove he was looking for, Lance eased the boat near the shore and killed the motor. The two men began to plot their strategy.

"What do you think, Charlie? Worm or lure?"

"Well, what are you fishing for?"

"Everything and anything."

"Then it doesn't matter." Charlie laughed.

They both chose squiggly plastic lures that resembled small fish, in the hope that the bigger fish in the deep water below would buy into the ruse and bite into the hidden hook. Then they fell into the quiet rhythm of cast, reel, and cast again.

Water lapped against broken layers of the ancient bluffs that created this part of the shoreline of the manmade lake. The sound soothed the two men into a comfortable silence as the boat bobbed slightly in the water. It was good, Lance thought, to be with a friend who knew when conversation wasn't necessary.

Finally, Charlie broke the silence. "Heard you had a prisoner go south on you, Smith. What happened?"

Lance groaned. "Yeah, you would have thought she could have at least waited until she got to county jail."

"Maybe she was just saving the taxpayers some money. Murder, wasn't it?"

"So she said. I'm not so convinced."

"Oh?"

"The consensus seems to be that she was nuts. And I'll agree she was a little strange. But why she would want to confess to a murder doesn't make any sense to me, except there seems to have been some bad blood in the past between her and the victim. Maybe she was so glad the old woman was dead, she was willing to take credit for it. I don't know."

"Murder weapon?"

"Yes and no."

Charlie looked blankly at Lance, placed his rod on the deck of the boat, and picked up a different one dangling a plastic worm. He cast again, waiting for Lance to explain.

"The buckshot the coroner took out of the victim was from a Field and Dove load. Probably came from a 12-gauge, or a 20-gauge at full choke. I've got a shell casing that was found at the murder scene that came from a 20-gauge, I've got a sawed-off 20-gauge that was taken off the crazy woman about an hour after the murder, and I've got a whole bevy of long guns gathered from the crazy woman's house. Now you'd think something would pretty well wrap it up, wouldn't you?"

Charlie shrugged. "Sounds like it."

"Well, it doesn't."

"Ah." Charlie nodded as if he already knew what Lance was about to say. "What about fingerprints?"

"The lab says they couldn't pull any identifiable prints off the shell casing, and the marking on the shell doesn't match the firing pin on any of the confiscated shotguns," Lance said. "So who do you believe? The crazy woman or forensic science?"

"Oh, I'd pick the crazy woman every time," quipped Charlie, "if I was basing anything on the accuracy of the OSBI. They're not exactly batting a thousand these days."

Lance rolled his eyes. "Thanks, Charlie."

"No other suspects?"

"Red, the guy who turned in the shell casing seems a little suspect, but Sadie's made friends with him." Lance glanced at Charlie. "Does that sound familiar?"

"Oh, boy." Charlie whistled through his teeth, remembering another questionable man from Sadie's past.

"Right now I don't have anything to else to go on. If it wasn't the crazy woman, then we both know if the perpetrator is still hanging around, he'll screw up." Lance adjusted his hat. "I can wait."

They continued to fish in silence until they lost the cool comfort of the early morning hours. The sun, moving high into the sky, sent the August temperature climbing toward triple digits. Perspiration soaked through Charlie's shirt and pooled under the brim of his fishing cap.

"You know, Smith, these fish are smarter than we are. Let's find some shade."

Lance agreed.

The men secured their rods and Lance revved the engine. The boat sped across the water. Before reaching the boat ramp, they had to pass an area on the north shore known as Powderhorn, a popular recreational area that had delighted visitors for decades. The terraced landscape, natural stone stairs, and pools of sparkling springwater had once sheltered over a thousand kinds of plants and cacti. Unfortunately, the enchanting site now rested at the bottom of the lake, all except for a flat limestone shelf that created a landing several feet above the water's edge. Now, it served as a favorite fishing spot for many locals.

Lance slowed the boat. "Let's try just a little while here. Lots of places for fish to hide."

Charlie nodded and the two resumed fishing. The water slapped against the boat and Lance lowered the trolling motor into the water to give him the control he needed to maintain a safe distance from the rocky shoreline.

"Say," Charlie said. "How's Sadie doing?"

Lance grinned and shook his head. "Poor thing. She bought a restaurant, of all things, and right off the bat she had a run-in with Pearl. The woman who committed suicide," he explained. He pulled in his lure and recast. "Pearl about scared her to death with a shotgun, then the old woman came back a little while later and smashed out the front window of the café with a rock. Then, of course, the former owner being murdered didn't exactly make her day."

"Well, at least she's out of the banking business."

"It's too bad I'm not ten or twelve years younger." Silence fell between the men again and Lance lost himself in thought. Sadie's slender build and long coal-black hair reminded him of someone else. Someone from another time and place—the tail end of his tour in Vietnam.

He had been in country for over a year, thankful for each and every day he remained alive. Only two wake-ups to go and he would be on a long and welcome plane ride home. It was to be the happiest day of his life. He had prearranged everything through the Marine Corps to return as a civilian with the love of his life, a Vietnamese woman named Mai. Her name meant "yellow flower," she had told him, the yellow flower that brought good luck and bloomed every year on the first day of Tet, the lunar New Year.

He had held her in his arms and kissed her before she pushed him away. She wanted to spend her last night at home with her family. He protested. She insisted. He could hide her, he told her, and she would be safe. Instead, she kissed him again and hurried away. Before she faded from sight she looked back at him, smiled, and waved.

He awoke a few hours later to the sound of incoming mortar rounds and instinctively ran to his post to return fire. The fire fight lasted for several hours, and with every passing moment the dread in the pit of his stomach grew. As soon as morning arrived and he could safely escape the Marine stronghold, he ran the entire two miles to her village. What he found when he got there was seared into his memory forever.

Wisps of smoke rose from the burning remains of what had been the small structures the villagers called home. He searched in desperation but it was too late. The entire village, along with his lovely Mai, had been wiped from the earth. The thought that it could have been his own artillery that took those lives—her life—tore a hole in his heart more painful than he could bear.

When he returned home to Oklahoma a few days later, he struggled to forget that horrific scene. But the sights and smells had never left him and he knew they never would. And on those nights when she came to him in his dreams, he would sit straight up in bed, shaken and drenched in sweat. Heat crawled up his spine for only an instant before he regained control of his thoughts.

"You okay, Smith?" asked Charlie. "You look like you just seen a ghost."

Lance shook off the memory. "Yeah, I'm okay."

"What are you? About fifteen years older than Sadie?"

Lance nodded.

"You know, these days, folks don't pay much attention to age. Especially when it's someone you care about, and it seems like you care for Sadie."

Lance stared at the water while he thought about Mai, how much he had loved her and the ache that clung to the inside of his heart about how she had died. The pain was buried so deep, he couldn't even share it with his friend Charlie.

"'Course Sadie had quite a roller coaster ride with that guy she was so crazy about in Sycamore Springs." Charlie shook his head. "Man, he turned out to be a bad deal all the way around."

"Yeah, I think she was really crazy about that guy too."

"You ought to pursue her, Smith." Charlie grinned. "However," he added, "my track record with women is pretty dismal, so take it for what it's worth."

Lance laughed and agreed.

Charlie cast his lure and it fell close to the rocks, where it dropped into a crevice and became entangled. "Damn it," he said. "That was my favorite lure."

Lance steered the boat closer with an oar, but when Charlie pulled on the line it snapped.

"Oh, forget it," said Charlie. "The water's too deep here. With my luck I'd fall in. I'll get another one."

Lance peered into the water, trying to guess an approximate depth.

"Don't even think about it." Charlie shook his head. "It's not worth it."

Lance gave up, pushed away from shore, and they headed back toward the boat ramp.

Two teenagers climbed out onto the shelf at Powderhorn. They settled on the edge of the rock formation, dangled their legs over the water, and gazed into each other's eyes. The girl opened a leather pouch and pulled out a small plastic bag half filled with marijuana. She dug into the small bag again and came up with a package of cigarette papers. The boy watched while she meticulously rolled three marijuana cigarettes.

"I hope this doesn't bring me too far down before we can score some more meth," he said.

The girl shrugged her shoulders as she lit the first cigarette and inhaled. The two teens puffed themselves into a smoky stupor as the afternoon clouds floated high above.

Eventually, the boy returned to their vehicle and retrieved a six-pack of beer, a bag of potato chips, and a handful of candy bars. The girl lit another marijuana cigarette and staggered toward the edge of the shelf, eyeing the water below.

"Don't jump," he warned. "The current will suck you under."

The girl released a stream of smoke from her lungs and stuck out her lower lip. "I'm a good swimmer."

"Not that good."

He dumped the food and beer on the ground and ran to grab her arm just before she fell. He pulled her toward him and they tumbled to the ground, their legs and arms entwined. They smoked pot, drank beer, and munched on chips and candy until they eventually swirled into another drug-induced daze.

When the girl awoke, the sun had already begun to sink in the western sky. She looked for her friend and found him climbing on the rocks below. She watched as he carefully lowered himself all the way to the water's edge.

"Hey, let's go," she yelled. "I'm hungry and I need to pick up my kid."

"Hold on, I think I found something."

"Well, bring it with you. We need to go."

A few minutes later, the boy emerged carrying a shotgun in one hand and a shiny, squiggly lure in the other.

17

As Sadie drove north toward Eucha, she scrunched her shoulders in an attempt to relieve the ache in her neck and back. She thought about Emma and the unexpected arrival of her daughter Rosalee. They obviously had unresolved issues, and Sadie didn't particularly want to know about them. Their tense reunion only dragged up memories of her unhappy relationship with her own mother.

She turned off the highway and drove the lane up to her house, parking the car in its usual place next to her old truck, between the back porch and the gate that led to the barn. Sonny bounced over to greet her with the exuberance only a dog can have for its master. He barked wildly, scolding her for being gone too long, and then playfully circled her as she carried several bulging plastic Wal-Mart sacks toward the house.

After putting away her groceries she returned to the porch and sat down on the top step to talk to him. She scratched his ears and told him all of her problems while he licked her face and nuzzled her arms. When she stopped, he seemed content that all was well. He followed her to the barn and watched while she dumped out a can of oats for Joe, then retreated to his favorite shady spot under a large walnut tree.

When Sadie returned to the yard, she took a minute to admire the dark red blooms of the Indian Blanket wildflowers that graced the northeast corner of the yard. Her Cherokee grandmother had transplanted some many years ago from a patch that grew in the upper pasture and they had returned every year since. The flowers triggered a tender memory of her grandmother's sweet spirit and love of nature, and how she had made Sadie promise she would never sell what she called her Indian Land—her folks' original allotment from Indian Territory before statehood. Sadie stopped, picked five of the daisy-like flowers that were almost as large as the palm of her hand, and carried them into the house.

After centering her bouquet on the table in an old water pitcher that doubled as a vase, she dropped onto the couch, kicked off her shoes, and punched on the television with the remote. After watching a short version of *CNN Headline News*, she dug in her purse and pulled out the old newspaper article she had found at the library. She read it again and then closed her eyes in thought.

Maybe Pearl's rape had caused her to have a mental breakdown, especially if it had resulted in a pregnancy. Pearl had said Goldie had taken her little girl, but that didn't make sense. Pearl had had a son, not a daughter. Could a thirty-something-year-old rape have anything to do with Goldie's murder? A nagging voice inside Sadie's head kept telling her it did. If she could just think about it long enough, she could figure it out. Before long she began to float between sleepy layers of consciousness.

The phone rang and she almost rolled off the couch onto the living room floor. Her heart raced as she grabbed the phone. To her surprise, it was Lance Smith.

"Lance, is something wrong again?"

"Not really. I was just wondering if you still have that paint horse."

"Joe? Of course. Why?"

"I need to borrow a horse to ride into the hills over by Kenwood and I thought I might talk you into loaning me one. In fact, I'd really like for you to ride with me."

"Kenwood. Why?"

"It's for a friend of mine. He thinks some kids are trespassing on the back of his property, but he can't catch them. I want to ride in and see what they might be up to. Nothing official."

Sadie frowned. "What do you think they're doing?"

"Oh, I don't know. I'm going to guess there's a little marijuana cultivation going on, but it's easier to sneak up on someone if you don't look like the law."

Sadie laughed. "But, Lance, you *are* the law."

"Yes, but it's not official. Certainly not in my jurisdiction anymore since I left the Cherokee marshals. Besides, you look harmless. Maybe if we go together we won't make them too nervous."

"Thanks a lot, Lance."

He lowered his voice and chuckled. "We'll go incognito."

"This isn't something you made up just to ask me out on a date, is it?" The line went quiet before Lance spoke again. "Never. Want to go?"

What was she thinking? She wouldn't miss this for anything. "Of course, I'd love to. I can borrow one of my uncle's horses for you and I'll ride Joe. When is this undercover operation supposed to take place?"

"Daybreak."

"In the morning?" Sadie grimaced. "Lance, I've got a café to run."

"Tomorrow's Sunday," he reminded her. "You're not open on Sunday."

"Oh, so it is." Sadie sat up straight, realizing her mind was still in a daze. "I usually have Sunday dinner with Aunt Mary and Uncle Eli, but that's okay. I'll call them as soon as we hang up and make arrangements with Uncle Eli for a horse and trailer. Why do you want to do this on Sunday?"

"They have a habit of showing up there on the weekends. They won't be expecting the law on Sunday morning. It'll look like we're just out for a ride."

"Okay. You remember where I live?"

"I'll be at your place around five."

"That early?" Sadie groaned. "Oh, all right. I'll be ready."

She hung up and smiled.

I have a date with Lance Smith in less than ten hours.

The thought excited and scared her all at the same time. She liked Lance even though she thought he was a walking contradiction. He had a lot of traditional Cherokee values, but she had never heard him utter one word in the Cherokee language. He exuded strength, yet he had an air of gentle compassion that she could feel when she watched him with other people. Being a police officer gave him a position of power, yet he came across as a humble being. He seemed to be old fashioned, almost a male chauvinist. That characteristic in anyone else would have been an insult to her as an independent woman. Instead, his mere presence made her feel safe, something she craved.

Her first husband had physically abused her and then ended up doing time for running drugs. She had been scared of him when he was released from prison and shamefully relieved when he died a violent death.

The next man she fell in love with had turned out to be a master of deception, and her involvement with him had almost cost her her life. She shuddered to think what would have happened if Charlie McCord hadn't been there to save her.

Now she guarded her heart and inner soul, reluctant to allow any man to get very close. She had been unlucky in love her entire life, but she held out hope that someday when the time was right, it would be a man like Lance Smith who would change all of that.

She began to plan for the next morning. What in the world would she wear?

By the time Lance pulled across the cattle guard and up the lane toward Sadie's farmhouse, Sadie had already been next door where she had retrieved a buckskin gelding named Tornado and a horse trailer. She left Tornado waiting in the trailer while she saddled Joe. She draped his reins over the top of the fence to remind him to stay put until she told him otherwise. Sonny stood at the side of the truck, his ears at attention and his nose twitching at the early-morning scents.

Lance parked and got out. "Good morning," he said.

Sonny barked.

"*Unelagi*," said Sadie and the wolf-dog relaxed. "Good morning, Lance," she added.

"I really hate that."

"What?" Sadie raised her eyebrows.

"A dog that knows more Cherokee than I do."

"Then you'd better bone up on the language if you want to talk to my dog. But I wouldn't feel too bad if I were you. He doesn't speak it very well either." Sadie smiled, patted Sonny's head, and walked to Joe. "Are you ready, big guy?"

Lance opened the back of the trailer. "Nice buckskin."

"That's Tornado. You'll like him. He's nothing like his name." She lifted Joe's reins and guided him to the rear of the horse trailer, walking him in beside the other horse.

"I miss having a horse," Lance said. "Unfortunately, I have neither the time nor the money."

"I know what you mean." Sadie pitched a key to Lance. "You want to drive?"

After making sure Joe and Tornado were secure in the trailer, Lance opened the passenger-side door for Sadie. He walked around the front of the truck, then stopped and looked at Sonny sitting patiently nearby. Sadie whistled and the wolf-dog jumped into the bed of the truck. Lance climbed into the driver's seat and they were off.

The fresh morning air ripped through the open windows of the truck as Lance pulled the trailer first west from Eucha, then south below the Lake Eucha Dam through the Spavinaw Hills State Game Refuge toward Kenwood. When they reached Kenwood Road, he turned back east for a short distance before pulling off onto a dirt road to the right. He came to a stop, got out and opened a gate, then pulled the truck and trailer through and parked in a clearing. Sonny jumped out and trotted into the field to scout out the new territory. He sniffed several places before marking a bush. Sadie joined Lance to help unload the two horses.

Lance made sure Sadie was on Joe before he climbed on Tornado. "Let's ride toward that tree line over there." He motioned with his head. "Then we can move south and west along the creek."

Sadie nodded. "I'll follow you."

Lance centered himself in the saddle, clicked his tongue, and urged the buckskin gelding across the field. Sadie trailed on Joe, and Sonny ran ahead. The early morning mist embraced the small valley, bringing a crisp coolness, one they both knew wouldn't last long once the sun started creeping skyward.

Before they reached the stream, they could hear the sound of water rushing over the flint rocks that made up every creek bed in Cherokee country. Lance eased Tornado over a fallen tree limb. Joe placidly followed.

Mourning doves cooed and a woodpecker tapped on a distant tree in staccato bursts. As a quick and agile squirrel made his way from the limb of one tree to another, a resonating sound caught both riders by surprise. Whoo-whoo-whoo, who-whoo, to-whoo-ah.

Lance pulled up on his reins so hard the gelding stopped and started backing up.

"Whoa," Sadie instinctively commanded as she stopped beside Lance. "*Uguku?*" she asked. "An owl?"

"Yeah." Lance frowned and eyed the nearby tree line. "Sounded like a blasted hoot owl to me, too."

Sadie winced. Her grandmother had reminded her on countless occasions of the Cherokee belief that owls are messengers of bad omens. Somebody's going to die, she would say.

Suddenly they could hear Sonny barking as if he had cornered something on the other side of the creek.

"So much for a surprise appearance," groaned Lance.

Sadie turned Joe to the left, searching for a safe place to cross the stream. Lance followed.

In a few short minutes Sadie found a crossing. She sat back in her saddle and nudged Joe with her thighs, impelling the strong horse to plunge into the clear, icy water and climb the embankment on the other side. She directed Joe toward the sound of Sonny's barking. The agitated wolf-dog turned in half-circles and tried to stand on his hind legs, his attention riveted to the upper part of a tree.

She rode up beside Sonny, holding onto the brim of her hat with one hand to help shade the bright morning sun. Instantly, the same sound boomed above her head. It sounded like a recording of a hoot owl, stuck on continuous replay. Then Sadie saw the source of all of their concern and laughed out loud.

"What's so funny?" asked Lance as he reined his horse to a stop beside her.

Sadie pointed at the lowest limb of the tree. "There's your carrier of bad news, my friend."

Lance saw what she was pointing at—a plastic replica of a hoot owl perched precariously in the crook of a tree limb. Every time Sonny jumped, the plastic bird's head spun around, its eyes lit up, and it produced a hooting sound.

Failing to appreciate the humor of the situation, Lance dismounted, picked up a long stick, and prodded the noisy contraption loose. It crashed to the ground and broke into three pieces, killing the sound. Sonny growled and ran to investigate. He sniffed, nosed it over on its side, then picked up a piece, carried it to a cluster of ragweed, and put it down.

Sadie jumped off Joe. "Sonny, give it to me." She picked up Sonny's prize and walked back to Lance, who stood bent over inspecting the other pieces.

"Who in the world would put up a mechanical owl out here in the middle of the woods?" she asked.

Lance dropped the plastic owl head back on the ground. "I don't know. It looks like this one has a sensor, so when it detected Sonny's movement on the ground, it started hooting. I'm sure that's the same thing we heard on the other side of the creek." Lance swung around and searched the landscape. "Or maybe it's a signal. Come on." He stuck the tip of his boot into Tornado's stirrup, mounted the horse and rode south toward a green meadow before Sadie could turn around. Sonny barked with excitement.

"Go catch him, Sonny," she said. "We're right behind you."

The wolf-dog darted away as she repositioned her hat to allow cool air to strike her perspiring scalp. "Good boy." She stroked Joe's neck and climbed into the saddle.

As she reined Joe to trail Sonny, a shot rang out in the distance. Her heart drummed in her chest and she rose up high in the saddle. She could hear Sonny barking, but Lance was nowhere in sight.

"Lance! Sonny!"

The sound of another mechanical owl echoed in the distance as Sonny's bark climbed to an even higher pitch. Joe snorted in anticipation of her next command and raised his head as if sensing the electricity tracing through her veins. She squeezed the stallion with her knees, dug her heels into his flanks, and they raced across the field in the direction Lance had ridden. As she topped a knoll, she could see Tornado standing by himself with his reins hanging loose on the ground. A surge of adrenalin shot through her.

When Sonny started barking again, Joe pranced and shook his head. Sadie turned Joe toward Sonny's barking and called out again.

"Lance! Sonny!"

Suddenly she could hear Lance yelling words that sounded like Cherokee. His voice came from a small stand of trees under a rocky cliff. She pointed Joe toward the trees but stopped short when a teenaged Indian girl stepped into the open. Lance followed her, limping. Sonny circled the pair, still barking.

"Would you tell your dog to shut up please?" Lance sounded irritated.

"*Eluwei!*" yelled Sadie, and the excited dog ran to her side. Sadie dismounted when she realized the young girl was wearing handcuffs. "What happened? Who is she? What happened to your leg?"

Ignoring Sadie's questions, he glanced around for his horse and whistled. Tornado raised his head and looked at Lance, all four hooves planted firmly in place.

"Oh, come on, Tornado. Give me a break." He clicked his tongue against the roof of his mouth.

Sadie mounted Joe, rode over to Tornado, and retrieved his reins. The buckskin snorted and bobbed his head before allowing Sadie to lead him back to his rider. Lance took Tornado's reins, grabbed the saddle horn, and climbed on.

"What about her?" Sadie asked. "Are you going to make her walk?"

"Yep."

Sadie wrinkled her forehead in disapproval. The girl looked so young and scared.

Lance caught her look and grimaced. "Maybe she'll decide to talk by the time we make it back to the truck."

Sadie glanced at her friend and gasped. "Lance, the side of your face is bleeding."

Lance grunted and wiped his temple with the back of his hand. He looked at the blood and then wiped it on his pants.

For the first time, Sadie noticed the handle of a handgun sticking out of Lance's back waistline. "Lance, what happened?"

Lance ignored Sadie again and spoke to his prisoner. "This nice lady is going to ride her horse toward the creek over there," he said, nodding at Sadie. "When we get there, we're going to cross the creek and walk through the clearing on the other side to a truck. If, before we get there, you decide to tell me who your buddy was that ran from me and what you were doing trespassing on private property, well, then I might entertain the idea of relieving you of those handcuffs. If we make it all the way to the truck, then the handcuffs are yours to keep and you get a free ride to the county jail. It's your call. Let's go, Sadie."

Sadie decided this was not the time to ask any more questions. She reined Joe back in the direction they had come and nudged his flanks. She pushed her sleeves higher and repositioned her hat as the trio moved slowly across the steamy field.

When they reached the banks of the creek the young girl stopped. She looked at Lance and started crying. "I'm sorry. Please don't make me tell. He'll beat me."

Reining in, Lance dismounted. "What's your name?"

"Gertie."

"Gertie what?"

"Just Gertie."

"Okay, just Gertie, how old are you?"

"Eighteen."

Sonny approached the girl and sniffed at her leg. As she tried to avoid the dog, she slipped on some loose gravel and fell on her behind. She began to sob.

Sadie jumped off her horse and rushed to comfort the teenager. "That's enough, Lance."

Lance dug in his pocket and fished out a handcuff key. He helped the girl stand up and set her hands free. "Keep talking or these go back on."

The girl launched into a tearful explanation. Her boyfriend was growing pot on the other side of the meadow. They had spent the night sleeping in a cave under the cliff where Lance had found her. When they heard the mechanical owls signaling someone approaching, they had hidden in the trees and waited. When Lance arrived, her boyfriend ran.

"What'd you say his name was?"

"Lennie." She wiped her nose on the back of her forearm. "Lennie Campbell. He lives on the Old School Road, about a mile that way." She pointed east.

"Where do you live, Gertie?"

The girl raised her nose in the air. "Anywhere I want to," she said. "I'm old enough."

Lance stared at her. "So in other words, you live with Lennie."

Gertie nodded.

"Where are your folks?"

She turned her face away. "I don't have any real folks. My mom and dad are dead, and the court said I had to live with white people, chicken farmers." Her eyes fired at Lance. "I'm not going to be a chicken farmer. Got that?"

"What do you mean you have to live with white people?" he asked.

"My parents were in the Guard. Got killed in Iraq. My momma's truck hit a roadside bomb." She stopped for a moment, dropped her head, and then continued. "My daddy died trying to get to her." Her eyes riveted through Lance with an iciness that almost melted Sadie's heart.

"Who are these white people you live with?" asked Sadie.

The girl looked at Sadie as if she'd forgotten she was there. "Lester and Fannie Mae Anderson. They're my grandparents on my momma's side." She began to cry. "She was white too, but she wasn't anything like them. She never would've made me work in a chicken house."

"What about your other relatives?" Sadie asked. "Your father's side of the family. Where are they?"

"They live in Anadarko," she said and then looked at Sadie with sad eyes. "I'm half Kiowa," she explained. "They came for me, but the judge said I had to live with my white grandparents. They said there was nothing they could do, so they left me here and went back home. As soon as I get a job and make some money I'm going to get my own place. Then I won't have to answer to nobody."

"Okay, Gertie," Lance said. "You lived up to your part of the deal. So will I. You're free to go. But if I were you I would run, not walk, as far away as you can possibly get from your friend Lennie, because he's nothing but trouble for you. You're going to end up in jail, or hurt, or killed. Understand?"

Gertie nodded.

Lance got back on Tornado and held his hand toward her. "Climb on. We'll give you a ride to your grandparent's place. I think I know where it is."

Gertie backed away, shaking her head. "Please," she begged. "They don't know about the baby. They'll make me give it up. I promise I won't get in trouble again. I promise I'll get away from Lennie. I promise. I can walk back to his house from here, and then I'll find someplace to go."

Lance stared at the girl and then looked at Sadie. "Okay, let's go."

"Lance, we can't just leave her here." Sadie's voice strained.

"Why not? It's her choice. She said she was eighteen."

"Because it's not right." Sadie shook her head as Gertie disappeared into the nearby trees. "She said she had a baby."

"Then she shouldn't be spending the night in a cave with a drug dealer." Lance urged Tornado across the creek and Sadie followed in silence as Sonny barked and gave chase to a rabbit through the tall weeds. When they reached the truck and dismounted, Sadie led both horses into the trailer. After securing them for the ride home, she climbed into the front seat without saying a word while Lance secured the back of the trailer.

Sonny arrived soon after, panting wildly. "Come on, Sonny," she said. "Get in." The wolf-dog jumped into the bed of the truck and plopped down as Lance slid into the driver's seat.

"Lance, I cannot believe you left that girl out there by herself."

"She'll be all right."

"Surely you didn't buy that line about finding someplace else to live."

"Probably not."

"And she can't be a day over sixteen."

"Probably right again. I'll contact someone at the Department of Human Services and she can be their problem. You forget I'm not on the clock today."

Sadie glanced at Lance to see if she could read his face.

"When I get a chance," he continued, "I'll go by and have a chat with a white chicken farmer about his half-Kiowa granddaughter."

"If she's not dead by then."

Lance backed the trailer out onto the road and drove toward Eucha.

"By the way," said Sadie. "What exactly happened back there? How did you hurt your leg?"

Lance thought for a moment and then launched into an explanation. "Little Gertie, there, and her boyfriend ambushed me."

"Ambushed you?"

"Gertie hit me in the head with a rock."

Sadie's eyebrows shot up.

"And I fell off my horse."

Sadie tried to stifle a laugh.

"Your dog cornered Gertie," he said, "and when I got there a copperhead was mad as hell about the whole ruckus. It wanted to fight instead of run, so I obliged and shot its head off."

"Oh, no." Sadie began to laugh.

"That's the last thing I need today, a blasted snakebite."

"Lance, that was a plastic owl," she teased. "I don't think that counts as an omen of death. Besides, copperheads usually travel in twos, so if they'd really wanted to get you they would have."

"Maybe the other one was a smart snake. At any rate, I'd say he's going to have to find a new buddy." Lance looked at Sadie and grinned. "Your dog didn't understand my lame attempt at Cherokee, and I couldn't get him to shut up until you got there."

She smiled, dug in her pocket and pulled out a handkerchief, then slid closer and dabbed at the side of his face. "You're bleeding again."

Lance winced. "Stupid kids."

"Ambushed, you say?" Sadie wanted to stay mad at him but couldn't. His wall of machismo began to fade when she started giggling. He gave her a dirty look as she held her sides and tried to quell her giggles, to no avail. He eventually gave in and their laughter spilled from the windows of the truck out into the passing countryside.

18

By the time Monday morning arrived, Sadie couldn't figure out where the weekend had gone. As she drove the winding road between Eucha and Liberty, she thought about Lance. She'd truly enjoyed spending the day with him. He was a bit older than she had earlier thought, and a gentleman, unlike most of the men her own age. He kept a proper distance and that was a relief. Deep down, she hoped they would see more of each other.

Her mind shifted to the café and all the events surrounding Goldie's murder. Emma appeared to be coping well with the loss of her sister, but her strained relationship with her daughter Rosalee seemed to be taking a toll on her. Based on the stories Emma had recounted of Rosalee's past, Sadie assumed it wouldn't be long before Rosalee moved on.

Sadie parked in front of the café at 5:45 a.m. Some of the regulars waved as they left the café and walked by. She shook her head, got out, and went inside. Red occupied his normal spot, and she could see Emma's movements through the swinging doors that led into the kitchen.

"*Osiyo*," said Red.

"*'Siyo*." Sadie smiled. "It sounds like you're Cherokee today instead of Creek."

"Oh, no. Just trying to be neighborly. *'Stonko?*" he said, then winked at her. "We don't really say hello in Creek," he explained. "We say, Is all well with you? *'Stonko?*" he repeated.

Sadie nodded. "Yes, all is well with me. Thanks." Sadie stored her purse in one of the drawers behind the counter, then walked into the kitchen and found Emma with her hands buried in a gooey flour substance. The aroma of fresh-baked bread filled the air. "My goodness, Emma, you're at it early. It smells heavenly in here."

"I hope you don't mind, honey." Emma transferred floury debris from her fingers to her white apron. "I know this is your place and I don't want you to think I'm trying to take over, but I didn't sleep very well last night and it felt good to get in the kitchen and do something. I found some of Goldie's plum jelly. It will melt in your mouth."

"How could I complain about homemade biscuits, Emma?" Sadie found a warm biscuit and slathered it in butter. "Let's sit down and talk about how we want to proceed. I know Goldie ran this place by herself, but frankly, I think it may be a while before I can do that."

"Oh, sure, honey. Goldie wasn't that special. Anyone could have done what she did. I know I could have."

"I bet you could, too, Emma, and I would love to have your input. I can pay you by the hour or a flat salary."

Emma opened the refrigerator and handed her a jar of jelly. In a few short minutes both women were seated at a corner table near the kitchen devouring bacon, eggs, and biscuits, washing it down with hot coffee and scheming about how to run the café. Emma agreed to handle the kitchen while Sadie did everything else, and the deal was struck.

"You know . . . " Sadie poured cream and spooned sugar into her coffee. "I can't eat like this every morning or I'll start gaining weight."

"You can't work all day on an empty stomach," said Emma. "Besides that, you could use a little extra meat on your bones."

"Oh, yeah? And, what about my cholesterol?"

Sadie had risen to retrieve the coffeepot when the front door opened and Rosalee walked in. She looked like a different person. She wore whitewashed jeans, a varsity tee shirt, and tennis shoes. Her dark roots had disappeared, and her golden hair framed her freshly scrubbed face, complimenting her hazel eyes and freckled cheeks. Her sadness had disappeared, replaced with a beautiful smile.

"Good morning," said Sadie. "Come join us for breakfast."

"I'll get her something." Emma took the last bite of a jelly-covered biscuit. "But I'll take some more coffee if you're coming this way with it."

Sadie nodded as she picked up another mug and delivered the coffee to their table.

"Thanks." Rosalee pulled out an empty chair, dropped her purse on the floor next to it, and sat down. She poured sugar into the hot coffee, stirred, and sipped.

Sadie returned the empty coffeepot to its burner. When she had filled the strainer and pushed the red button to start another pot brewing, she turned to check on Red. A peculiar look covered his face as he stared at Rosalee.

"I'll have some more coffee for you in just a minute, Red."

"Who is that young woman?" he asked.

Sadie looked at Rosalee, then back at Red. "She's too young for you, old man. That's Emma's daughter, Rosalee."

"Hmmm." Red nodded. "She looks familiar."

"Do you know her?"

"Probably not." Red pulled out a five-dollar bill and laid it on the counter. "I've got to go." He glanced toward Rosalee and Emma once more before leaving.

Sadie cleaned the counter of dirty dishes and waited on two more groups of customers. When the activity died down, she returned to the table where Rosalee had just dug into a heap of scrambled eggs. Emma sat across from her daughter sipping coffee.

"It's nice to see you again, Rosalee," said Sadie. "You're up awfully early this morning."

Rosalee took a bite of bacon, then wiped her mouth with her napkin before she spoke. "I'm on my way to Tahlequah to a meeting."

"I'd better check on the pies." Emma abruptly retreated into the kitchen, coffee cup in hand.

Rosalee continued to eat while her eyes followed her mother. "My AA meeting is at nine o'clock and I want to have plenty of time to find the new place." She looked at her watch. "I'll be going to Tahlequah on Tuesdays and Fridays. It embarrasses Mother when I talk about Alcoholics Anonymous, but I don't care. Logan proved to me that it's better than the alternative." She finished off her biscuit. "Let's just say I fell off the wagon for a while. I really need to get back on my program."

"Is Logan a friend of yours?"

"He was. He's dead." Rosalee hesitated and then continued. "Got killed in a bar fight not too long ago." Her voice quavered. "I really miss him."

"Oh, I'm sorry to hear about your friend, but I'm glad he got you started with AA. I understand it's helped a lot of people. So you've been living in this area for a while? I don't think your mother knew that."

"Yeah, I've been hanging around for a while. I used to visit my aunt a lot. You know, she never judged me. She just loved me the way I am. I can't believe she's dead, too. Seems like everyone's running out on me." A tear spilled off her cheek as she took another drink of coffee. "I'm sorry I arrived unannounced like I did."

"No problem," said Sadie. "Your mother seems glad to have you here."

"Not really. I'm sure she's putting on a good front for you, though. Say, I really need a job. Do you need any help here?"

Sadie raised her eyebrows. "So you're going to be staying in Liberty?"

"Just 'til I can get back on my feet."

Sadie thought for a moment and then tried to explain. "I'm just barely getting started here. And, to be honest, I hadn't planned on hiring a waitress just yet."

The front door opened again and Tom Duncan walked in. Sadie excused herself from her conversation with Rosalee and went to greet him. This was the first time she's seen him since the day she closed the deal on the café.

"Hi, Sadie." Tom took a seat on one of the stools at the long counter. "This place must be good for you. You look great."

Sadie placed a glass of ice water in front of him and smiled. "Sounds to me like you're trying to butter me up for something. What is it, Tom?"

"Got any cinnamon rolls?"

"No, but we have biscuits this morning, and I can give you some honey-butter."

"Sold. And I'll take a glass of milk."

Sadie quickly retrieved three floury biscuits surrounding a scoop of honey-butter. She placed the small green plate in front of him and leaned on the counter waiting to hear the latest gossip from the bank.

Tom ate and talked with his mouth full. "I know you must be having fun here, Sadie, but you said if I ever needed any help to let you know."

Sadie cocked her head to one side, waiting to hear the rest.

"My fraternity brother, known him since kindergarten, well, he's getting married this weekend and he's asked me to be his best man. I just have to go, Sadie, but there is no one to cover for me. And if there was, I doubt they would want to drive all the way to Liberty to do so. You already know the system. Everything is the same as it was in Sycamore Springs. You won't have to do anything but show up and be there to make any minor managerial decisions. I promise it will be a piece of cake." He stopped talking long enough to down his glass of milk.

Sadie stared at him. "Tom, I hate the banking business. I can't believe you are asking me to do this."

"I've already talked to Thelma in the personnel office. She said it would be okay for you to fill in. She has you listed as retired from Mercury Savings, so you are eligible to return to work if you want. It's only Thursday and Friday."

"Retired?" Sadie rolled her eyes and looked away. "That's a stretch." Three men came in and took a seat at the other end of the counter. "I'll think about it," she said. "Call me later."

Tom nodded, dropped several bills next to his plate, and left.

Sadie poured fresh coffee for the men at the counter, took their orders and delivered them to Emma in the kitchen. Then she returned and sat at the table where Rosalee had just finished eating. "Rosalee, I think we might be able to work something out after all."

Rosalee's face glowed. "Really?"

"Yes, I just realized there's going to be times when I need to be away. You could fill in for me. When are your meetings in Tahlequah?"

"Tuesday mornings and Friday nights," she said with a concerned look.

"Then I will hire you on one condition."

"Name it."

"No drinking. If you miss one AA meeting while working here, that'll be the end."

Rosalee smiled. "Thank you," she whispered.

"Now the important question. Do you have any restaurant experience?"

"Some. But I'll be honest. Most of it was in a bar." The two women looked at each other in silence before Rosalee spoke again. "I give you my word. I'll work hard if you'll give me a chance."

Sadie placed her elbow on the table and rested her fingers against the side of her chin as she looked at Rosalee's face. "Okay, I can't pay you much. Minimum wage plus tips and two meals a day—breakfast and lunch."

"Sounds good to me." Rosalee's eyes lit up.

"You'll have to go into Tahlequah to the County Health Department and get a food handler's permit. You have to watch a video and pay two dollars. Do you have two bucks?"

Rosalee nodded.

"If you have a problem, be up front with me, and I'll give you the same courtesy." Sadie walked behind the counter, opened a drawer, and pulled out some forms she had seen earlier. She sat back down, pushed the breakfast plates to one side, and placed a blank application in front of Rosalee. "I'll need you to fill this out for my records and sign this W-4 for Uncle Sam. When can you start?"

Rosalee looked at her watch. "As soon as I get back from my meeting. I'll go by and get the permit while I'm in Tahlequah."

"Good."

Emma emerged from the kitchen, delivered plates to the men at the counter, and refilled her coffee cup. She walked back to the table where Sadie and Rosalee were talking and sat down. She noticed the papers in front of Rosalee and frowned. "What's this?"

Sadie spoke before Rosalee had a chance. "I asked Rosalee if she could work for me. Since you've agreed to handle the kitchen, she can help me in the front. That way if I need to be gone, you won't be here by yourself."

"Oh, really?" Emma looked surprised. "Why, Sadie, you can't depend on her. Besides, I didn't realize you were going to be staying that long, Rosalee."

"Don't worry, Mother. It won't be for very long . . . unless you don't want me to stay at all."

"No, that's fine. But if you're going to live under my roof, you'll have to keep your nose clean. No more running around with wild hooligans. Just because you think you're grown doesn't mean you won't have to follow the rules in my house. If you think you can handle that, then you can stay with me."

"Hooligans! If you're talking about—"

"It's settled then." Sadie spoke quickly in an effort to defuse a volatile twist in the conversation. "Rosalee, when you've finished filling out those forms, you can put them in that top drawer over there." She turned her attention to Emma. "I'll get another W-4 for you, Emma. In the meantime, how's everything coming back there for lunch?"

Emma's voice returned to its usual docile tone. "I'll have everything under control, honey, as long as the meat man shows up some time this morning."

As if on cue, they heard the sound of a delivery truck at the back door. "I'll get it," said Sadie. "You all watch the front."

Sadie disappeared through the back door to accept the food delivery, and Emma retreated to her sanctuary in the kitchen.

Rosalee gritted her teeth and watched her mother walk away. She would continue with her plan regardless of her mother's sour response. She checked her watch again and hurriedly filled out the forms. She opened the drawer and placed them inside as Sadie had instructed, but before she closed the drawer something caught her eye. A copy of an old newspaper article had spilled from Sadie's open purse. She looked around before carefully sliding it into better view. She began to read to herself under her breath:

> "An unidentified woman was found Friday morning behind The Liberty Diner in Liberty, Oklahoma. Preliminary reports say the woman had been raped and beaten. Goldie Ray, a nineteen-year-old café worker found the woman in the alley near the back door of the restaurant when she arrived to open the café around six a.m. Authorities stated that the woman displayed signs of confusion and became violent when emergency workers arrived. The name of the victim has not been released, but an anonymous source at the scene identified her as Pearl Elizabeth Mobley, of Liberty."

Rosalee looked around, pushed the paper back toward the open purse, and headed out the door.

19

"Why would you trust me to work for you?" Red leaned over Sadie's shoulder as she counted change into a small cash drawer.

"Why would you volunteer?" Sadie unzipped a bank bag and showed it to him. "There are extra coins in here, but I don't think you'll need them. Besides, you're not really working, you're just taking money from customers if Rosalee gets too busy. And, as far as the matter of trust, if you're willing to put your life on the line to save me from being shot by Pearl Mobley and you have possession of the key to the front door, then I think you're trustworthy enough to handle a couple of bucks." She placed the bank bag under the counter and slid the drawer shut. "If you need anything, call me at the bank." She pulled out a paper napkin, scribbled a phone number on it, and handed it to him. "Thanks, Red. I'll be back in the morning about six o'clock."

She walked toward the door, then stopped and turned. "Oh, yeah, Hector will be here today to paint the window. Didn't break his arm after all. Just a sprain. Call me." The door rattled as it closed behind her.

Sadie jumped into her vehicle and drove the short distance to the bank, got out, and stared at the First Liberty Bank building, an archaic structure resting on the northeast corner of Third Street and Washington Avenue. An empty laundromat shouldered it on Third, and the adjacent building on Washington looked as if it had been vacant for at least a decade. She cupped her hand above her eyes to protect them from the sun. It was going to be another scorcher.

Tom had told her the story of how First Liberty, a family-owned bank, had struggled during the oil bust of the eighties. It pulled ahead during the nineties but couldn't compete with the large conglomerates of the twenty-first century. The family had finally given in and decided to sell.

That's when Merc State Bank, the former Mercury Savings Bank, stepped in. They bought First Liberty for pennies on the dollar and turned it into a branch office. Sadie had seen it happen repeatedly and hated to see the small banks with their homespun atmosphere fall victim to the giant companies. But the same thing had happened to the mom-and-pop grocery stores and hardware stores that were forced to close when Wal-Mart and Lowe's marched into communities across Oklahoma. Opening side-by-side, the big-box stores monopolized business and pierced the small towns with a two-edged sword: low prices and low wages.

As she assessed the situation on this warm August morning, she wished she hadn't agreed to take the job. She walked up to the front door, turned her key in the deadbolt, entered, and relocked the door. Memories of a past bank robbery crawled up the back of her spinal column like an army of ants and she involuntarily shivered. She couldn't believe she was entering another bank alone after what she had gone through two years earlier. This time, at least, motion detectors protected the building.

Harsh, staccato sounds sliced the air, and she hurried to the alarm key-pad to punch in the code Tom had given her. The sharp beeping stopped. She walked to each corner of the lobby, making sure she was alone before she walked to the front window and opened the blinds, signaling the other employee now waiting in the parking lot that it was safe to enter.

The mingled smells of new paint and carpet glue still hung in the air. The furniture, while new, was flimsy and cheap, giving Sadie the impression that this was a low-budget branch. They had made the lobby smaller by putting up a freestanding partition that divided the old tellers' cages from the newly built counter.

The vault stood in full sight in a corner behind the single teller station. It looked out of place, too big for its small surroundings.

The clock on the wall chimed and Sadie jumped. All of a sudden she hated herself for taking on this task. She walked to the front door and unlocked it for the teller. After relocking it, she introduced herself to the woman. "Hi, I'm Sadie Walela. You must be Polly Gibson."

The middle-aged woman wore a lime-green cotton-knit outfit that hugged her pudgy body in all the wrong places. She scrunched her forehead and looked at Sadie. "I thought you worked in that old café downtown."

"I do," said Sadie. "But I'll be filling in for Tom for a couple of days."

Polly balanced two donuts on top of her flat purse and licked the sticky icing from her fingers. "You know, Tom doesn't make me wait in the car like a kid. He lets me come in the same time he does. I've been working for this bank for more than three months, and I know the code to turn off the motion detectors."

Sadie sized up the woman's round face before she spoke. "You don't have to worry, Polly, I don't want your job. I'm just trying to help out a friend."

Polly blinked several times as if her eyes burned as she walked behind the teller counter. She stacked the donuts next to the calculator, wiped her purse on her thigh and stowed it in the cabinet below before speaking again. "I hope you know how to open this vault."

"I make no guarantees," said Sadie, "but we'll give it a shot. Do you have the key?"

Polly nodded and handed Sadie a ring with several small keys attached.

Sadie retrieved the small piece of paper with the combination on it from her purse, picked the key with the name Mosler inscribed on it, and inserted it in the middle of the dial. She reeled the circular device back and forth, careful to match the marks on the dial with the correct numbers on her note, counting the number of spins each time. After the last turn, she held her breath and stopped on zero. The internal mechanism clanked as she turned the handle. She tugged at the door and pulled it open.

"Okay." Sadie let out a sigh of relief. "We're in." She flipped the light switch on the outside wall to illuminate the inside of the vault and waited for Polly to get her cash.

Polly entered the vault, unlocked her cash drawer, carried it to her teller station, and carefully slipped it into the empty drawer.

Sadie followed. "Tom asked me to conduct a surprise audit," she said. "Can you get me the audit form?"

"Oh." Polly's pink face turned pale. "Tom usually does the audit on the first Monday of the month."

"Well, it wouldn't be a surprise audit if it was on a schedule, would it?" Sadie's attempt at humor fell flat. "Come on," she continued in a friendly voice, "it will only take a minute. You can count and I'll watch."

Polly retrieved the audit form and handed Sadie the calculator tape out of the cash drawer that reflected the previous day's ending cash. Sadie watched Polly count and marked off each denomination as Polly counted the loose bills out loud. The drawer included a strapped bundle each of ones, fives, tens, and twenties. Polly held each bundle in the air, called off the amount, and returned them to the drawer.

"We'll need to break the straps for the audit, Polly."

"Why? They're dated and stamped," Polly contested. "Tom says never to break a strap unless you have to."

"Strapped money can be wrong, too, Polly. Tom asked me to do this, and I have to sign off on it."

"I can't count money fast like the others can," she whined.

Realizing that Polly was beginning to feel uncomfortable, Sadie offered, "Do you want me to count it while you watch?"

Polly nodded.

Sadie slipped the paper strap off the ones and quickly shuffled the money from one hand to the other. Then repeated the procedure again.

"Polly, I count this bundle to be one bill short. Go ahead and count it slowly onto the counter and I'll watch."

Polly counted one bill at a time from hand to counter. It was indeed one bill short. Sadie made a note on her form and looked at her watch. This was taking longer than she had anticipated. She moved onto the other bundles in the drawer. Once again, each bundle was one bill short.

"Polly, I show the drawer to be short thirty-six dollars, do you agree?"

"I guess so, but Tom's the one that straps money, not me."

"No problem. Just sign the audit form and I'll leave it for Tom to sort out."

Polly frowned and reluctantly signed the bottom of the paper. She dropped the pen on the counter, stuck her nose in the air, and went for the coffeepot that sat on a stand next to a large water dispenser. "I'm going to make some coffee. My donuts are probably cold by now."

The clock chimed again and Sadie unlocked the front door. As she retreated to Tom's desk in the corner of the small branch, she longed for the easy-going conversation in the café. Tom was going to owe her big-time for this favor.

She tried the temporary password Tom had given her to log onto his computer. Amazed that it actually worked, she stared at the menu on the screen trying to remember the reports he had asked her to review. After a few minutes, she became absorbed in the world of banking.

The phone rang twice and she realized Polly was busy talking on another line, so Sadie grabbed her phone and answered. It was Thelma from the main office in Sycamore Springs making sure everything was moving along smoothly.

"Sadie, it's good to hear your voice," said Thelma. "How in the world have you been? I was so glad to hear that Tom talked you into working for him."

Sadie gulped. "As long as you realize it is only for two days, Thelma. I have a café to run now."

"That's what Tom said. I thought maybe he was exaggerating. After working at Mercury for all those years, well, I would think it would be hard to get banking out of your blood."

"No, he's not exaggerating." Sadie laughed. "In fact, I hate to tell you this, Thelma, but I would rather be at the café than here."

"Oh, I almost forgot what I called for. Be sure and download the first three reports for Tom so he can work on them as soon as he gets back. He's got some transactions he needs to look at."

"No problem, Thelma."

"I've got to get to a meeting. You keep in touch, you hear?"

Sadie smiled. "I will."

As she hung up the phone she heard the front door open. It was George Stump. He ignored Sadie and walked straight to where Polly stood nibbling on her pastries behind the teller counter. Polly walked over to the coffeepot, poured coffee into a Styrofoam cup, and handed it to the police chief. They spoke in whispers for a moment before George turned on his heels and approached Sadie's desk.

"Is there a problem here this morning?" he asked.

Sadie sat straight in her chair. "Excuse me, Chief?"

"Mrs. Gibson said you were accusing her of stealing some of the bank's money."

Sadie looked past George's shoulder at Polly who was now busy placing paper in the copy machine. "No, sir." She returned her eyes to the police chief. "We do not have a problem here that cannot be handled internally. But I'll be glad to tell the manager to give you a call when he returns if he thinks it's necessary." It was hard for Sadie to hide her amusement. From the look on George's face, one would have thought she had accused Polly of robbing the bank at gunpoint.

The phone rang again and Polly hurried to answer it. George nodded, turned and looked at Polly, then left.

"It's Tom," said Polly as she climbed back on her stool behind the teller window and sipped coffee.

Sadie turned her back to Polly and picked up the phone.

"I just landed in Seattle," said Tom, "and wanted to thank you again for filling in for me. Is everything going okay?"

"Everything's under control. Only next time, . . . No, let me rephrase that, because there's not going to be a next time."

"Oh, Sadie, don't talk like that."

"No, I mean it. Next time you can do your own teller audit."

"She was short, wasn't she?"

"Tom, I'm going to kill you."

"Forgive me Sadie, but I needed another witness. It was in her bundles, wasn't it?"

"You already knew? You scum. So tell me," she continued, "what's the deal with the police chief?"

"Oh, I bet she called George, didn't she?" It was a remark more than a question. "I think they've got a fling going. I've seen him bring her to work every now and then."

"Ohh." Everything began to make sense to Sadie.

"Don't worry. I'll take care of everything on Monday. Sure you wouldn't want to come back to work for the bank? I think I'm going to need a new teller."

"Good-bye."

"Wait, did Thelma call yet about a report?"

"Yes, she asked me to download something for you."

"Look in my top drawer," he said. "I've been working on the dormant accounts. If you're bored, give it a whirl. I'm sure you remember how it works."

"My memory is failing more with every passing moment, Tom. But I think you said something like, Sit around and make managerial decisions. No wait, you said minor managerial decisions."

"Okay, you win. See you next week."

"Good-bye, Tom." She didn't wait for an answer before she hung up. She walked across the lobby and poured herself a cup of coffee. Polly, totally absorbed in a crossword puzzle, didn't notice as Sadie stirred both sugar and cream into the cup and returned to her desk.

Sadie downloaded and printed the reports Thelma had requested. Before she placed them in Tom's tray, she thumbed through the pages looking for familiar names. She recognized several, then Goldie Ray's name jumped at her from the page that listed the recently closed accounts. Sadie instinctively went to Tom's computer and pulled up the account. There were very few transactions. Mostly cashier's checks. Sadie clicked on each one to view images of the cleared items. Every check had been issued to the Northeastern Oklahoma Heart Center. Even the final check that closed Goldie's account the day before she was murdered had been made to the same medical facility. Sadie thought about it for a moment. Goldie's health problems must have had to do with her heart. That's why she wanted to get out of the restaurant business. And, Sadie surmised, since she closed her account in Liberty, she must not have planned on returning. Sadie looked at the transactions again, then dismissed them from her mind.

The morning moved at a snail's pace before Polly volunteered to pick up lunch. As a peace offering, Sadie offered to treat and sent Polly to the café to pick up a couple of cheeseburgers. When she returned, they had a quiet lunch. After eating, Polly picked up her puzzle again, and Sadie went back to her corner desk.

Sadie pulled out the dormant account report Tom had told her about and skimmed the list. Nothing looked out of order, but she looked up account transactions on the computer for a while to help pass the time. The clock chimed announcing it was only three o'clock. Two people had graced their door since they'd opened at nine, not counting George Stump. Only two hours left today and eight tomorrow, she thought, then she would never have to look at the world from the back side of a banker's desk again.

After spending the rest of the afternoon browsing account information, Sadie was relieved to hear the clock deliver five chimes. She noticed Polly had already balanced her drawer and as soon as Sadie locked the front door, the teller carried her cash drawer into the vault.

A few seconds later she emerged from the vault and picked up her purse. "I'm ready to go. Do you want me to wait for you? I have my own key, you know."

Sadie looked at the unhappy teller. "No, go ahead and go. I'm going to put these reports in the vault for Tom and then I'll be leaving too."

"I just thought since you were all paranoid about security and all . . . "

Sadie frowned. "I'm fine. I can set the alarm on the vault. See you tomorrow."

Polly headed for the door and let herself out with her key. Sadie turned off the computer and walked behind the teller counter to make sure everything was put away. She carried the stack of reports into the vault and placed them on a small counter next to a metal file box containing signature cards.

She returned to the huge vault door and opened the back compartment to set the overnight timers. After thinking for a moment, she decided on twelve hours. That way, the timers would expire before 6:00 a.m. They wouldn't need to open the doors until eight o'clock, but she liked to allow a little leeway. She turned all three timers, careful not to exceed the determined hour, then hit the light switch on the wall outside the vault extinguishing the lights inside.

A cold chill swept over her just before a gloved hand reached from behind her and covered her mouth. Adrenalin surged through her body as she struggled with her assailant, trying to scream. But she was no match for the arms of steel that turned her toward the vault and flung her inside. As she fell forward, she tripped over the step stool used to reach the top safe deposit boxes and fell hard to her knees. Before she could turn and see her assailant, the heavy vault door closed with a thud behind her and the locking mechanism clicked shut as the wheel spun, sealing her inside.

Darkness enveloped her. In a claustrophobic panic, she thought for a moment that her heart might explode from the sheer volume of blood pumping through it. Fire shot through her right knee where she had fallen on it. She rolled over onto her rear and rubbed her leg.

After a few moments the pain subsided slightly. She blinked her eyes three times as if that might help her see. It didn't. She stuck out her right arm and tried to feel the wall of safe deposit boxes. Nothing. She listened to see if she could hear what was going on outside the vault. Nothing.

Her mind raced. This didn't make any sense. If it was a robber, they weren't very smart because all the money was already locked up. Then it hit her. It wasn't a robbery. It was a personal attack on her.

She drew in three deep breaths and tried to regain her composure. Who in the world would blindside her like that? And why? Polly couldn't possibly be that strong. Where did her attacker come from? There was no one in the bank when Polly left.

She tried to relax. At least she was safe for the time being. The vault was sealed up tight for at least twelve hours. Then panic struck again. This was a very old vault and she didn't know if it even had an air vent. For a split second she wondered how long it would take her to die and how painful it would be when she ran out of oxygen.

She searched her memory for the layout of the vault. Was there a phone? Was there a light switch somewhere? She couldn't remember.

She began to inch backward, crawling on the floor. After several feet she reached her goal: the back wall of the vault. She pushed herself into a standing position, causing her kneecap to ache again. Ignoring the pain, she followed the wall, moving to her right until she came to the work station where she had left Tom's reports.

She bumped her injured knee against the counter and cursed loudly. She bent over to hold her knee and, when she did, she struck her head against the wall and the stack of reports slid off the counter. The fear and frustration of her situation suddenly engulfed her. She yelled at herself, the bank, and the world in general before sinking down onto the floor.

After a few minutes, determined to regroup, she stood up and began feeling the walls around the work area in a methodical manner. She moved her hands up the wall, then back down again. She repeated the procedure again, but to her dismay she found neither light switch nor phone. Unwilling to give up, she tried again, stretching as far as she could on her tiptoes, seeking with her fingertips. Finally she felt something. It was a wire.

She held onto the wire with everything she had, following it down the wall and around a corner near the back of the work station. She came to the end of the wire and felt a small, rectangular box mounted on the wall. She couldn't figure out what it was, so she retraced her steps, following the wire as far as she could in the opposite direction.

She could feel the reports on the floor beneath her feet. She kicked them out of the way and continued to follow the wire. When she found the light switch at the other end, she let out a cry of relief. She flipped the switch and a bright light glowed over the counter, nearly blinding her. "*Wado, Unelanvhi,*" she whispered. Thank you, God.

She looked around. There was no phone but at least she had light. She scooped up the reports, piled them back on the counter, and searched for an air vent. Above the door she could see a cylinder that she believed was the device that would pump in fresh air. She looked around and found the step stool she had tripped over earlier, rolled it to the door, climbed on it, and flipped the old switch. Nothing happened. Then, to her relief, she felt a cool current of air rush in. She let out a sigh of thanks, "*Wado, wado.*" She climbed down, pushed the step stool into the corner, and examined the rest of the fixtures. Surprisingly enough, most of the inside of the vault had been redone. The only thing missing was a phone.

That's okay, she thought to herself. She only had to wait until someone missed her, and hopefully that would be Lance Smith when she didn't show up for their prearranged meeting at a benefit gospel singing later that evening. If not, maybe her uncle and aunt would notice when she didn't come home. But that was unlikely. She had been keeping long and erratic hours since opening the café.

Suddenly, she thought she could hear someone yelling. It sounded like a woman. Maybe Polly had come back and the assailant had assaulted her, too. "Polly!" she screamed. "The vault! I'm in the vault!"

Nothing.

"Polly!" she yelled again. "Go get help!"

Nothing.

It must have been her imagination. There was no one at all to help her. She looked at the reports and groaned.

20

Lance Smith drove the highway east of Tahlequah and turned onto a dirt road that would take him to a small church that the local people referred to simply as the Old Indian Church. He hadn't been to a Cherokee gospel singing in a long time and looked forward to an enjoyable evening. Good singing, good food. What else could anyone ask for? The ladies of the church always sold Indian Tacos to raise money, and just thinking about the homemade pies made his mouth water.

Since he was off duty and far from the city limits of Liberty, he hoped this gathering would give him a chance to disappear into the crowd and relax. Nevertheless, he parked on a shoulder of the road away from the other cars, an unconscious habit he had of always allowing for a quick and easy getaway if the need arose.

He stepped out of his truck and heard what sounded like the clank of clashing billiard balls. Following the sounds, he discovered a group of men standing on a dirt field aiming pool balls at holes etched neatly into the ground.

The sight brought back memories of how his uncles had tried to teach him to play this traditional game of Cherokee marbles when he was a boy. He had tried to gain control over the golf ball–sized rocks they used, but he never did get the hang of it. Not to mention that the ground was so rocky and uneven where he grew up that they had to reinforce their holes with PVC pipe. He had to admit he hadn't seen that unique type of hole at any tournament play. Most resembled the perfectly round holes this group had made by pressing pool balls into the soft soil.

The marble field contained five holes, about forty feet apart, spread out in the shape of a large L. One of the players stood near the first hole, shaking out his throwing arm in preparation for the game. The player pitched some practice balls as he explained the game to a group of young boys standing nearby.

"The game of marbles is about twelve hundred years old," the player explained. "They used to use marbles shaped from limestone, but we use pool balls now because they're easier to come by. Everyone is responsible for bringing your own ball. You can buy them at Wal-Mart if you don't have any at home." The player pointed to a mound of balls near a group of women sitting in lawn chairs. "There are a few extras over there if someone needs one. Now, the object of the game is to prevent the other team members from making it into the holes while your team moves through each hole. The team that reaches the fifth hole and then returns to the first one, wins. The best team at this tournament gets to advance to one of the finals at the Cherokee National Holiday coming up on Labor Day. But be prepared, because that's where the experts play. Everybody ready?"

The small crowd of youngsters clapped as the man started the game by throwing his cue ball underhanded at the first hole. "We have to put our marbles in the hole," he continued to explain, "then we can take two turns knocking the opponents' marbles away from the other holes."

The teams lined up and began to play and Lance decided to move on. A crowd had already assembled near the small building that housed the kitchen. Three picnic tables sat under a large maple tree, each covered with homemade pies, cakes, and cookies clustered between gallon jugs of Kool-Aid and tea, and a pot of coffee. He stopped to see if by chance someone had brought his favorite dessert: raisin pie. Someone had.

A large metal tub held bottles of water and cans of generic soda pop soaking in ice water. Two older Indian women stood behind the third table; one took money while the other served corn soup, fry bread, and Indian Tacos.

This is going to be good.

He walked past the food tables to the grassy area where people had already gathered to eat and visit, some sitting in lawn chairs, others clustered on blankets spread on the ground. Kids of every size and shape squealed and chased each other, running in and out of the crowd.

The grassy area gave way to a steep incline where steps made from large smooth rocks created amphitheater seating. At the bottom of the hill rested a large wooden platform that served as a stage, complete with microphones and lights. Several men were busy setting up a drum set at the back of the stage and positioning speakers on each side. A group of women in traditional Cherokee tear dresses stood away from the stage, fanning their faces with handheld paper fans, waiting their turn to sing.

Lance surveyed the crowd and then returned to the food line to fill up before they ran out of raisin pie. After paying for his food, he carried it to the corner of the top step, sat, and proceeded to eat. If Sadie showed up as she had promised, he would at least be through eating and wouldn't have to worry about his manners. He thought she ate like a bird anyway.

Lance took his time and enjoyed the food. He loved fry bread and could never get enough of it. He decided he was going to ask Sadie why she didn't offer it at the café. After cleaning the last morsels of food off his paper plates, he carried them to a nearby trash barrel and dropped them in.

As the singing began, Lance cruised the perimeter of the crowd searching for Sadie. When he couldn't find her, he selected a tree to lean against while he listened to Cherokee songs performed by some of the best singers around.

He instinctively analyzed the crowd. It was predominately Cherokee, lots of family groups. Words and phrases of the Cherokee language drifted softly around him. Lance felt comfortable and secure among his people and imagined that this scene could easily have taken place a century ago, except for the soda pop and the Kool-Aid. And the marble players would have been throwing rocks instead of pool balls.

The melodies of Cherokee hymns rang in the air. The language was still alive in this place and, although his ability to speak Cherokee was limited, hearing it rejuvenated his spirit and reminded him of his mother.

She had sung Cherokee songs to Lance when he was a child, and he still held those melodies in his heart. But after his father injured himself in an industrial accident at the chicken plant in Jay, both parents had turned to drinking. His father never regained the use of his left hand and became so miserable and full of hatred that he had become impossible to live with. Not long after Lance left for the service, both his parents died in a horrific automobile accident. When Lance received the news in Vietnam, he vowed never to abuse alcohol like they had.

Lance spotted Red down near the wooden stage. He watched as Red mingled in and out of the crowd, stopping to visit with each and every group of people. Red seemed to know most everyone, yet he always seemed to be alone. As Lance contemplated the mysterious Creek Indian, Red stopped and looked straight up at Lance as if he could sense the lawman's intrusion into his being.

Red nodded, excused himself from the group, and headed toward Lance. "Say, it is good to see you without a badge pinned to your chest. Did you try some of the pineapple upside-down cake?"

"You never miss a thing, do you, old man?" Lance said.

"Not when it comes to food. I like to eat." Then he added, "I'm not as old as I look."

Lance grinned and returned his attention to the singers. The Indian Methodist Church Choir had just taken the stage, and Lance was impressed with their performance. One male singer stood in the back row, singing into his own microphone, a karaoke-type boombox that allowed him to project his bass voice into the crowd, adding a full-bodied harmony below the women's voices. When they got to the chorus, Lance recognized the old favorite called the "Sunday School Song." He began to hum along as the singers sang: *Di ka no wa dv sdi, Do dv ni te lv ni, A na la sga si sv, A ni lv gwo di ha.*

"Do you sing?" asked Red.

Lance grinned. "Not in public."

An old woman, walking with a cane, limped toward the two men. When she stopped she used the end of the cane to point straight at Lance. "You the new man in Liberty?"

Lance looked around and then back at the old woman. "Yes, ma'am." He stepped forward and offered his hand. "Lance Smith."

"You can call me Annie." She leaned on her cane and accepted his hand. "I went to get my bottle, and there's something wrong at the bank."

Lance frowned. She didn't smell like she was intoxicated. He was off duty and had no desire to deal with this kind of problem tonight. He looked at his watch. "What bank's that, ma'am? Most banks close around five o'clock, I guess, and it's after eight now. Did you need some money?" Lance dug in his pocket for his money clip.

"Nah," she said, obviously perturbed that he didn't understand her dilemma. "I don't need money. I'm trying to tell you. I keep my good stuff, a bottle of eighteen-year-old scotch whiskey, in the safe deposit box in that bank in Liberty. You know, the new one. I only get it out for special occasions, that way no one can sneak in and drink it up. My niece brought it to me all the way from Kansas City. It's better than the liquor I can get around here."

"Okay." Lance thought perhaps if he agreed with her, she would go away.

Red spoke up. "Sadie is working at that bank in Liberty today. Remember?"

"What?" Lance suddenly became interested in what he was hearing.

"I told you she was at the bank when you were in the café today," Red reminded him.

"I thought you meant she'd gone to make a deposit. I didn't know you meant she was actually staying there all day." Lance returned his attention to the old woman. "Annie, what did you mean when you said there's something wrong at the bank?"

"It was right at closing time," she said. "I was afraid I was too late. The door was still open, but the place was empty. Didn't seem right."

"Did you go in?"

"Yes." The old woman nodded her head to emphasize her affirmative answer.

"Maybe she was in the restroom or something," offered Red.

"No, I called out and no one answered. I thought it was kind of strange. There was a car parked out front, but there was no one inside, and they went off and left the place unlocked like that. I just wanted one drink, that was all."

"What did the car look like?"

"It was red."

Lance didn't even stop to thank Annie. He ran straight toward his truck, unaware that Red was right behind him. When Lance hit the keyless remote and jumped in, Red yelled, "Let me in!"

"I don't have time for you now."

"Just open the door." Red already had his hand on the door handle waiting for Lance to unlock it. "I won't get in the way."

Lance hit the remote again and Red jumped into the passenger's seat.

"Then put on your seat belt," barked Lance as he turned the key in the ignition and slammed the shifter into low gear. Together they tore into the night, back toward Liberty.

21

A male ruby-throated hummingbird perched on the railing to rest near a teardrop-shaped feeder. He stretched his fiery red throat, poked his bill in the air, and swiveled his iridescent green head first one way and then the other as if he had only one good eye. He puffed his feathers, causing his tiny body to appear larger, and expanded his silver-grey chest to its maximum, daring any other hummingbirds to dip into the red sugar-water. Sadie thought he looked like a miniature penguin.

A female hummer flew into his airspace. She hovered near the feeder, slowly edging her bill toward the yellow flower-shaped plastic portal of artificial nectar. In an instant the male took flight, his body transformed into a small missile aimed directly at his adversary. He sideswiped her. They twirled in midair in a dance of grace and precision and then zoomed off. Sadie shook her head, grinned, and watched. A few seconds later, the male bird returned to his duty station.

"You are so tough for such a tiny bird," teased Sadie.

Another dazzling hummingbird ventured near. Showing its aerial agility, the bird held its flight pattern high near the roof of the porch. The guarding hummer flew toward the intruder and found himself caught in an abandoned spider web. He fluttered and reversed flight, pulling strands of the sticky web across his wings and body. Sadie gasped and ran to help, determined to rescue the little creature. Just as she reached for him, he maneuvered, pulled free, and escaped. But she had reached too far. Her foot slid off the edge of the porch and suddenly she was falling. She fell hard on her knees and rolled onto the ground. When she tried to get up, her legs would not move.

"Sadie, what are you doing on the ground?"

The soft voice caught her unaware.

"Grandma?" Sadie's voice echoed as if it were in a tunnel. "Is that you? I'm hurt. Alisdelvdi," she said. "Help me."

"You must help yourself, Sadie. You are strong. You are a Walela. Get up."

Sadie moved her legs, trying to increase blood flow to her tingling toes, and opened her eyes. She had been dreaming. Certainly no hummingbirds flew inside this cold steel vault. But the spirit of her grandmother, she was sure, had been there while she slept.

Her knee still hurt from the spill she had taken and it was swelling. She looked at her watch. It was only a little past nine o'clock and she wished she had access to a restroom. It was going to be a long night.

She took the reports she had scraped off the floor earlier and decided to put them back in order. She studied the different headings, some of which made absolutely no sense to her. Guided by the report numbers at the top of each page, she began to sort through the mess of paper.

"Dormant accounts," she muttered to herself. "Who cares about dormant accounts?"

She scanned the report, thinking she might recognize a name or two. Nothing. Then suddenly a dollar amount jumped out of the column on the right-hand side of the report. It was an odd amount. She had seen it earlier in the day. She concentrated, trying to remember where. Probably the same page, she thought. "I'm looking at pages I've already looked at," she reminded herself. She continued to scan through more reports. Again, the same dollar amount leapt off the page at her. "What report is this?" She looked for page one. Unable to find what she was looking for, she laid out the pages on the floor, grouping the different report numbers together. Before long she saw a pattern of questionable transactions, the same odd amounts going in and out of different accounts. "Why doesn't this stupid report have names on it?" she said aloud. She would have to remember to bring them to Tom's attention.

"Why am I doing this?" She spoke out loud again. "I don't care about strange transactions. This is ridiculous."

She bunched the papers together, stacked them on top of the counter, and sat on the floor. Her knee throbbed. Maybe if she could go back to sleep, she thought, morning would arrive sooner.

But her mind wouldn't rest. She searched her memory, trying to figure out who would lock her in the vault, and why. This was all so hard to believe. Friend or not, she promised herself she would never consider working in another bank as long as she lived.

Eventually her mind drifted. She thought about her aunt and uncle, the farm and the café, Sonny and Joe. She remembered her life as a banker and silently lamented the toll it had taken on her. She replayed the events in her life since buying the café—Goldie's death, the broken window, Pearl's suicide, Emma and Rosalee's arrival, and their sour relationship. Next she thought about Lance Smith and how he had reappeared in her life. For a fleeting moment she wondered if there was a place in his nice, orderly world for an unorganized ex-banker who, so far, was willing to place her trust only in a horse and a dog. Her fluid thoughts moved on to Sonny and Joe. She knew they would be all right but she didn't like to be away from them. She drifted into dreams of riding Joe at the edge of the creek with Sonny scouting the path ahead of her.

Lance knew the signal on his cell phone would be too weak to reach Maggie Whitekiller until he reached the hill north of Tahlequah on Highway 82. So he held the phone in his left hand, poised to dial, and as soon as he could he punched the send button. Maggie answered on the second ring.

"Maggie, where's the chief? Have you had any alarms or calls coming in from the new bank?"

"Everything is pretty quiet around here, Lance. The chief is, uh, out-of-pocket. I have orders to call him only if there is an emergency. What's wrong? I thought you were off tonight."

"What does out-of-pocket mean, Maggie?"

"It means he is busy, uh, in a personal sort of way."

"That's great." Lance didn't try to hide the disgust in his voice. "Do you have an emergency contact for the bank?"

"Hold on."

When Lance placed the phone on his lap, waiting for Maggie's voice to return to the tiny speaker, Red began to talk.

"Your dog-man is out-of-pocket, you say?"

Lance ignored the question.

"He's probably at Polly Gibson's house," Red offered. "She got divorced last month after her husband got suspicious of all the overtime she was working at the bank."

Lance continued to drive north at breakneck speed until he had to slow down to make the turn off the highway onto Moody Road. "Maggie? Where did you go?" He looked at his phone, realized he had lost his connection, and threw the phone on the seat. It bounced onto the floor of the truck and Red retrieved it.

"Gibson?" asked Lance. "She works at the bank?"

"Yes, she is the teller."

Lance absorbed the information without expression and floored the accelerator.

Sadie woke to the sounds of muffled voices. It took a moment before she remembered where she was. She jumped up. A bolt of pain shot through her knee and her bladder at the same time. Ignoring both, she called out. "Help! I'm in the vault!" She waited a moment, then repeated her cry for help.

Her mind raced. According to a small digital clock on the work station, it was almost ten-thirty. Maybe whoever shoved her in had come back to finish her off. She recoiled against the back wall and looked for something with which to defend herself. Her mind ran wild. How would they get to her unless they had access to the combination, and even if they did, she was sure the alarm would go off when they pulled the door open. An ink pen was the closest thing to a weapon she could find; she grasped it in her hand, poised to plunge it into her assailant's eye at the appropriate moment. Her knee hurt, so she slid back onto the floor and waited in silence.

After a few minutes, she closed her eyes and let out a heavy breath. "Please let it be someone I know," she prayed.

22

Lance recognized Sadie's vehicle before he parked in front of the Liberty branch of First Merc State Bank. He could see the lights on inside the building and thought for a moment he may have jumped to conclusions. Sadie was a dedicated worker and was probably just working late. Then reality set in, and he realized it was after ten o'clock. Not even Sadie was that dedicated.

"Where's your gun?" asked Red.

"Stay here," ordered Lance as he opened his truck door. He reached behind his seat, pulled out a .357 revolver, slid it inside the waistband of his jeans at the small of his back, and clipped his badge to his belt. He entered the bank through the unlocked door and searched the entire building. He felt like a rock dropped in the pit of his stomach when he found Sadie's purse sitting under a desk and her keys sprawled on top of it in full sight. Where was she?

"Hello?" Lance yelled. "Anybody here?"

Nothing.

"Sadie? Are you here?"

Suddenly he thought he could hear something. He stood completely still and listened. Then he heard it again. Someone was in the vault. He leaned against the vault door, cupped his hands around his mouth, and shouted. "Sadie, are you in there?"

The reply was muffled, but he knew in his heart it was her. He returned to his vehicle and called Maggie again. In less than an hour he had rousted both the chief of police and Polly Gibson out of bed and contacted the head of security at the main office of First Merc State Bank in Oklahoma City. They would send someone named Walker out from Sycamore Springs to open the vault. No alarms had been tripped, and

Polly Gibson swore Sadie was closing up when she left the branch a little after five o'clock.

Lance forbade anyone from entering the bank until he could determine if he needed to take fingerprints. He thought the cash would be gone and expected soon to be working a robbery. While he continued to wait for Walker to arrive, a thought occurred to him. He walked back to where Polly Gibson was sitting inside her car and leaned down to her open window.

"Polly, are you sure you don't know how to open that vault?"

"No, sir. They keep the combination a secret because I have the vault key. You know, dual control. I didn't do anything wrong by leaving before she did. She told me to. And Chief Stump says I don't have to say anything. I'm just here as an employee of the bank."

Stump heard his name and walked over to Polly's car. His hair was wet and he smelled like Ivory soap. "What's the problem, Smith?"

"I just thought perhaps Mrs. Gibson might be able to open the vault and we wouldn't have to wait for the banker from Sycamore to arrive. I'd kind of like to make sure the other employee is all right."

"Well, if you ask me, when a woman is dumb enough to get herself locked in the vault, she ought to have to wait until morning to get out," sneered Stump.

Lance turned on his heel and reentered the bank. He cupped his hands against the vault door and yelled again. "Sadie, can you hear me?"

He could hear her answer, but her words were inaudible. It sounded like she said she was "cursed" and it was "funny."

He laughed to himself and tried again. "You are not cursed, Sadie. Where's the combination to the vault?"

It sounded like the same muffled words were trying to escape the heavy door.

"Hang on," he said. "Someone's on their way to get you out."

Poor girl. When it came to bank robberies he was beginning to think she *was* cursed. He scanned the small office, trying to figure out this strange scenario. "Okay, Smith," he mumbled to himself. "This can't be that hard." He sat at the manager's desk, looked at every item on it, and thought. He took the pen out of his pocket and carefully pulled out each desk drawer, searching.

If I was filling in for a bank manager, he contemplated, *I would need to write down the combination somewhere. Where would I put it?* His first answer was in his spiral notebook in his shirt pocket. *Okay, if I was a woman where would I put it?* He looked at the floor and suddenly laughed out loud. "Damn, Smith, if it had been a copperhead you'd be dead by now."

He picked up Sadie's purse and hesitated. Then he dumped the contents out on the desk. "Why do women carry all this crap around?" he continued to himself. He pilfered through gum wrappers, ink pens, a checkbook, a hairbrush, and a couple of unopened pieces of mail. When he unzipped a small beaded coin purse, he remembered teasing Sadie about her bad habit of wadding up her money and shoving it all together with her coins. Just before he rezipped the bag, a small piece of white paper caught his attention. He dug it out and unfolded it to discover a string of numbers.

He jumped up from his chair and ran to the door. "Chief," he yelled. "Can you bring Mrs. Gibson and her vault key in here? I think I've found the combination."

It took Lance four tries before frustration set in. The air conditioner had been off for a while and cool air had escaped each time the front door was held open. Sweat dripped from his forehead and onto his hands. "I don't think this is right," he complained. "It doesn't work."

Polly shrugged her shoulders. "Don't look at me. I've never been allowed to open the vault. I don't know how."

Stump interrupted. "If you don't need Mrs. Gibson for anything else, Lance, I'm going to take her home. This doesn't seem to be too serious. The man from Sycamore should be here any time."

"What about my key?" Polly protested.

"We'll take responsibility for it, Polly," said Stump. "Let's go."

Lance followed the two to the front door. He was beginning to wish he'd never taken this job. He watched the chief escort Polly to her car, open the car door for her, slide into the driver's seat, and drive off.

Red appeared out of the darkness. "I can probably open it."

Lance raised his eyebrow. "Oh, yeah? What makes you think so?"

Red held up his outstretched hands and smiled. "I have very sensitive fingers."

"Be my guest. They're going to have to change this combination anyway."

The two men returned to the vault door. Lance inserted the key in the middle of the dial while Red studied the numbers. Then Red stepped up and started spinning the dial to the left over and over. "This kind of clears it out," he said. Then he held up the small piece of paper and stopped the dial on the first number, reversing the spin in each direction twice more before coming to rest on the final digit. He grabbed the lever and yanked it to the left. Nothing.

Lance's shoulders slumped. "Obviously your fingers aren't sensitive enough."

"Shhh. I'm working here. Are you sure these numbers are right?" Red spun the dial once more several times to the left and repeated the turns according to the numbers on the paper. "Bingo."

Red stepped back and Lance jerked the handle. Clunk.

"Way to go, Red." Lance pulled the heavy door open.

Sadie sat on the floor at the back of the vault holding her knee. "I never thought I'd be so glad to see two Indians. Can somebody help me up?"

"Are you all right?" The two men exclaimed together.

"Was it a robbery?" continued Lance.

"How could it be a robbery? The money's all in here. Hurry up. I've really got to go."

Lance and Red both helped her stand and watched while she limped with determination toward the ladies room. As the door to the restroom closed, the sound of a ringing phone pierced the night. Lance instinctively plucked a tissue off a nearby table and used it to pick up the receiver. It was Maggie.

"Lance? I thought you might still be there. The bank alarm just went off."

"That's okay, Maggie. We just got the vault open. I'm sure that set it off."

"Is Sadie okay?"

"Seems to be. Go ahead and tell the security company that Liberty Police is out in force."

"Will do."

As Lance hung up the phone, Sadie came out of the restroom wiping her face with a paper towel. "Wow. Thanks, Lance. I don't think I could have made it much longer."

"Don't forget to thank Red, too," said Lance. "I couldn't have done it without him."

"Really?" Sadie turned to Red. "Thanks, Red."

Red grinned and waved her away.

"So what took you so long?" she asked.

"It took me a while to figure out where you hid the combination."

"Why?" Sadie seemed puzzled. "I kept telling you it was in my purse, in my money."

"Purse? Money?" Lance laughed. "I thought you said you were cursed and it was funny."

Sadie gave him a serious look. "This is not funny."

"How did you get locked in the vault anyway? What happed to your leg?"

"I was shoved in by a very strong, pushy person. I fell over the step stool in the vault. Sprained my knee, I guess."

Lance frowned. "Do you know who it was? Man? Woman?"

"If I knew that, I'd be on my way right now to strangle them. But I can tell you this. They meant for me to fall pretty hard."

"Do you think you could look around and see if anything is missing?"

Sadie limped to Tom's desk and looked around, then moved behind the teller counter. "I don't know, Lance. I don't see anything. Can't we just lock it up and go home? Somebody else can figure it out tomorrow."

A car door slammed and Lance tensed. A middle-aged man in jeans and a tee shirt trotted up to the front door and entered. He zeroed in on Lance's badge, walked over, and offered his hand. "I'm Timothy Walker. I got here as fast as I could. I'm vice-president over the branches in this area for First Merc State Bank." He handed Lance a business card. "I understand we had a break-in or something?"

Lance studied the man's card while Sadie stepped forward and introduced herself. Walker nodded and shook her hand. "Yes, I remember meeting you at the main office one time. I understand you were filling in for Tom Duncan today. He speaks very highly of you."

"Thank you," she said. "I really think everything is okay here. The money was already put away so I know it is safe. I think it was just a prank. Polly had already gone and someone must have been hiding in the unused part of the old lobby or . . . someplace. I don't really know. They just snuck up on me, pushed me in, and slammed the door."

Walker looked at Lance. "Did the alarm go off? If it did, we didn't get a signal."

Lance shook his head. "I don't think the alarm was ever triggered."

"Then how did you know she was in the vault?"

Lance smiled. "It's a small town. We try to take care of one another." He guided Sadie toward the door. "We'll wait for you outside while you secure the building."

"I'd appreciate that," he said.

Red and Lance followed Sadie to her car. "Are you sure you're all right?" asked Lance.

"Yes, I'm fine," she said as her Explorer purred to life and she cranked the air conditioner on full blast. "I just need to get some ice on this knee. Say, you wouldn't mind checking on me tomorrow, would you? I'm obligated for one more day of banking."

"I'm going to need to get your statement, but I think it'll be all right to wait until morning. I'll meet you here when you open up."

"Thanks." She pulled the shifter into reverse and started to back out, then stopped and lowered her window. "Red, you need a ride?"

"Yeah, if you don't mind. I'll ride to Billy Goat Hill."

"Get in. It's on my way."

Red slid into the passenger's seat and lowered the window. "She's quite a woman, Smith. You ought to take better care of her."

Lance leaned on the car door with his hands. "By the way, Red, how did you get so good at opening vaults?"

"It's a long story. You learn a lot of strange things in the military. Someday I'll tell you all about it."

Sadie spoke up. "What made you decide to come looking for me, anyway?"

"A nice little lady named Annie," said Lance, "just wanted a good drink of scotch whiskey tonight."

Sadie wrinkled her forehead. "Who?"

"I'll explain," said Red.

Lance nodded and watched as they rode off into the night.

23

The next morning as Sadie turned right onto Third Street she could see Lance sitting in his police car in front of the bank. She parked beside him and got out, favoring her injured knee.

"You still here?" she teased.

"Hey, I've not only changed clothes since I saw you last night, I've had a shower."

Sadie playfully sniffed the air. "I'm glad," she said as they walked toward the bank. Before they had time to enter, a blue generic-looking sedan drove up and parked on the other side of Sadie's Explorer. It was Timothy Walker.

Walker jumped out of his car and greeted the duo at the front door carrying his sport coat in one hand while he rolled down his long sleeves with the other. "Good morning," he said. "The home office thought I'd better help out here today."

Sadie thought the young vice-president looked entirely too corporate in his button-down shirt and polished leather loafers. "That sounds great to me. Does that mean I can go home now?"

"No, I'd appreciate it if you could stay at least through today. I will need to get back to Sycamore as soon as I've written up a report for the security department on last night's, uh, situation."

Sadie turned her key in the deadbolt and entered the bank with Lance and Walker close behind. Lance immediately began to search the building. Walker headed for the restroom.

About halfway across the lobby Sadie realized the air was void of the shrill beeping of the motion detector. She continued on to the keypad and studied it. The steady green light meant the alarm had not been turned on.

"Uh, Mr. Walker, did you set the alarm on the motion sensors last night?"

When no one answered, she turned around and realized she was alone. Her heart jumped as she limped to the front window, opened the blinds, and looked for Polly. The teller was nowhere in sight. Walker came out of the restroom, adjusting his belt.

"Mr. Walker, did you activate the motion detectors last night?"

Lance rounded the freestanding partition. "The building is clear, Sadie."

"Thanks, Lance," she said. "The alarm wasn't turned on."

Walker spoke up. "I guess that's my fault. I thought I had it set last night before I left, but I guess it was operator failure. I'm glad you had a police officer here to check the place out this morning."

"Yeah, me too," said Sadie.

"No problem," said Lance. "Once you get situated, Sadie, just call the office and I'll come back and take your statement. If I'm not in, Maggie can get me on the radio. I'll check on you about closing time."

Sadie nodded as Lance left. By then, Polly was making her way up the steps. She brushed through the front door and walked past Sadie.

"Good morning," said Sadie.

"Yeah, whatever," replied Polly. "I can't believe you got locked in the vault. I didn't get any sleep last night with all the commotion going on." As she moved toward her teller station, she saw Walker and stopped short.

"This is Mr. Walker from the Sycamore Springs branch," said Sadie as she relocked the front door. "I guess you had already gone by the time he got here last night."

Walker acknowledged Polly with a nod.

Polly's pale face flushed to a warm pink. "Oh, I guess so." She put her purse down and went straight to work.

The morning flew by. Walker worked on his laptop computer at an empty desk, and Polly made herself look busy doing nothing. Sadie downloaded and printed Tom's reports, then gathered yesterday's reports from the vault and proceeded to put everything in order for the absent manager.

When Walker finished typing his five-page report, he asked Sadie to read it. She did and made a few suggestions, which he readily accepted. A few customers stopped in. Some transacted business, others came for a cup of coffee, curious about all the activity that had taken place overnight.

Shortly before noon, Chief George Stump stopped by and struck up a conversation with Walker. They made small talk for a while, then Sadie heard Stump asking about the night before and whether anything was missing. She sat up straight in her chair and stared at the two men when she heard him apologize to Walker for any harm that might have been done to the vault or alarm system by Lance's enthusiastic efforts to save his "girlfriend." Walker assured him everything was fine and that no harm had been done. Sadie decided it wasn't worth wasting thoughts or words on either man.

Before he left, Stump walked to the teller counter, made a transaction, and spoke in quiet tones to Polly, who was obviously still in an unhappy mood. She began to talk back to him, and as she did, her voice carried across the small lobby. "Stop it. It won't work."

Aware that their conversation had drifted in the wrong direction, Stump turned his back to the teller and changed the subject. "Boy, if it gets any hotter, my cornfield is going to be burnt up."

Walker looked up from his work. "Do you raise corn in this area?"

"Nah, not much," replied Stump. "I plant just enough to feed me and my neighbors." He poked something into his shirt pocket and made his way to the door. He stopped, looked at Sadie, and said, "Now, don't you go getting yourself locked up in the vault again, young lady."

Sadie bit her lip and went back to work. The door closed behind the chief and Walker walked over to Sadie. "Here is a copy of my report. It should suffice as your statement for the local police. I will be staying until lunch breaks are over. I'd prefer no one be left alone in the branch again."

Sadie nodded in agreement and sent Polly to lunch. "If you'll stop by the café and pick up a sandwich for me, Polly, I'll buy your lunch." That seemed to be the first thing that had brightened Polly's face all day. "What about you, Mr. Walker, would you like some lunch?" Sadie asked.

"No, nothing for me. I'll get something on the way out of town."

Polly took her purse and disappeared out the door and down the street.

"Do you work out of Polly's cash drawer when she is gone?" asked Walker.

"Yes," answered Sadie. "Since this branch has only two employees, I have no choice." An experienced vice-president would already know this, but Sadie elaborated anyway. "I leave all of the transactions out for her to verify before she puts them away, and I note any cash that was taken in or given out."

"I guess it would be pretty hard to pin any outages to a single person then, wouldn't it?"

Sadie took a deep breath. She was sure this wasn't the only branch of this bank that operated with less than adequate personnel. "I'm just filling in," she said. "You'll have to ask the manager about his experience with cash discrepancies at this branch when he gets back."

Walker nodded and returned to his computer.

Sadie sat on Polly's tall chair and sorted through her tickets—first the debits, then the credits, then the checks. Nothing seemed to be out of order. She eased off the chair and began to straighten items on the top of the counter. Anything to keep her busy so the day would go by faster. Suddenly she stopped, returned to Polly's tickets, and thumbed through them again. There was nothing with Stump's name on it. She made a mental note and put the tickets back.

Polly returned and the two women had an uneventful lunch. After they finished, Walker stowed his laptop into its bag, picked up the sports jacket he had never bothered to put on, and approached Sadie. "I need to go. I think you will be all right. I understand your police officer friend will be back at closing."

Sadie nodded.

"If you have any problems," he said, handing Sadie his card, "call me on my cell phone. It's listed on the bottom of the card."

Sadie smiled. "You found a phone that works in this area?"

"Most of the time," he said as he walked out the door.

After Walker left, the afternoon moved right along. Several people, mostly Indian and Hispanic, came in to cash payroll checks from a nearby greenhouse. Polly denied the majority of their requests because they either didn't have an account with the bank or she didn't like their form of identification.

When the flow of traffic began to slow, Sadie approached Polly. "Why couldn't you cash those men's checks?"

"'Cause their checks aren't drawn on this bank."

"Yes, but they're corporate checks drawn on First National. The greenhouse has been in business for thirty years. Those men are going to have to drive all the way to Tahlequah just to cash their paychecks."

"I don't care. I'm just following the rules."

"I guess so. By the way, did you cash a check for George Stump this morning?"

Polly looked at her and blinked. "I don't know, why?"

"I was just curious. I don't think he has an account here either, but I saw him put something in his pocket."

"I'm tired of your accusations," snorted Polly. "I quit." She picked up her purse, stuck her nose in the air, and walked out the door.

"Well, fine," muttered Sadie. "I hate this business."

Sadie dialed the cell phone number on Walker's card. A recording came on the line, so she hung up, called Thelma and apprised her of the situation, assuring her that no one needed to come from another office. She would have Lance come by while she finished out the day and closed the branch. Thelma agreed no one could get there before closing time anyway and thanked Sadie for taking control of the situation.

Sadie hung up, called the police station, and breathed a sigh of relief when Maggie answered instead of Stump.

"Maggie, could you locate Lance Smith and ask him to call me at the bank?"

"Do you have an emergency, Sadie?"

"No, no. Nothing like that. I just want to visit with him."

"I'll radio him."

Sadie had barely hung up when Lance's police car parked in front of the door. He got out, looked around, and entered the bank.

"What's up?" he asked. "Where is everybody?"

"Well, Timothy Walker has already gone back to Sycamore Springs and Polly quit. I didn't want to close up by myself for fear the guy who came by at closing yesterday might come back again today. Besides that, I need to give you this report Walker wrote up about last night."

"It's great to be needed." He looked at his watch. "You close at five?"

Sadie nodded.

"What happened to Polly?" he asked.

"I don't know. I guess I just have a way with people. She didn't like me questioning anything she did. I think she might have been tripping around the edge of doing something illegal . . . like taking money. I think she's come up short in her cash drawer a few times. I don't really know, and I don't really care. I think Tom wanted to get rid of her anyway. This just makes it easier."

"How does the saying go?" Lance pulled out a chair and sat down facing the front door. "You just can't get good help anymore."

As soon as the money was safely locked away in the vault, Sadie set the motion detector and the two left together. Sadie locked the front door and turned to Lance.

"I would like to thank you for coming to my rescue last night. Can I fix dinner for you?"

"I can't." Lance looked into the distance. "I'm busy tonight."

"Oh, I'm sorry. I didn't know you were seeing anyone."

Lance laughed out loud. "I'm not," he said. "Unless you want to count Charlie McCord as a date."

Sadie rolled her eyes. "I didn't mean—"

"Charlie asked me to ride along with him on a meth lab raid tonight up in Delaware County. I imagine it will take up most of the night. How about a rain check?"

Sadie smiled. "You got it."

24

Lance drove east from Liberty on a seldom-used back road and hit Highway 10 a few miles south of the Arrowhead Resort and Canoe Rental. He traveled the highway that curved alongside the Illinois River, past Peavine Hollow and the Hanging Rock campgrounds. Darkness had enveloped the countryside hours earlier, bringing the nocturnal animals to the road like bugs to a country porch light. He dodged two armadillos, one chubby raccoon, and an unseen but very smelly polecat as he followed the highway north.

When he reached the small community of Kansas, Oklahoma, Lance pulled into the parking lot of a convenience store and parked in an inconspicuous spot to wait for Charlie. In less than ten minutes, Charlie arrived in a dark-blue sedan—an obvious undercover vehicle—and parked next to Lance's truck.

Lance lowered his window and spoke in a gruff voice. "They'll never see us coming on that horse, Keem-o-sabi." He shook his head and laughed.

"Hey," Charlie retorted, "my truck is in the shop and this was the only available vehicle that's not black-and-white. Besides, since this is the sheriff's party and we are just going along as spectators, I thought we could take your ride."

"Mine? What are you talking about? I'll have you know I like my truck and will not tolerate some druggy shooting holes in it."

Charlie was already loading his gear in the floor of Lance's truck. "You've been watching too much television, Smith. This is not one of those new reality shows."

"Okay." Lance chuckled. "We'll go as Indians. Maybe no one will notice you're white. Get in."

Charlie obliged and nodded toward the highway.

Lance followed Charlie's directions and drove east, then turned north onto a county road before they got to the Arkansas state line. They drove past two mobile homes and an abandoned hay barn. After rounding a curve, Lance could see a shack on the left with a car sitting on blocks in the front yard and an old van parked next to it.

"That's it," said Charlie. "Go on down and turn around and we'll stake out the northeast corner. The sheriff said they would come in from the south. We'll already be in place when they get here."

Lance continued on the dirt road for about a mile, then turned off his lights and made a u-turn. They worked their way back slowly in the dark. Lance parked off the road near a clump of trees and killed the motor.

Charlie pulled out a pair of night-vision binoculars and surveyed the area. "Good job, Smith. I can see the front door and the vehicles." He pulled a portable radio out of his gear, squeezed the transmitter, and spoke into it. "This is McCord. Anyone out there?"

After a few seconds he got a response. "Affirmative. We're in a wait-and-see mode."

"Roger. Out."

"They hide in the bushes pretty well," remarked Lance. "I didn't even see them."

"That's pitiful for an Indian, isn't it?"

Lance nodded. "Out of practice, I guess."

Lance and Charlie looked at each other and smiled. Lance missed his friend's politically incorrect humor.

A huge golden moon, in the shape of a deflated football, began its ascent in the clear sky surrounded by a smattering of bright stars. Charlie continued his vigil with the binoculars, while Lance watched lightning bugs wink at each other in the adjacent pasture.

"You'll never believe this." Charlie kept his voice low and handed the lenses to Lance.

Lance peered through the glasses and blinked twice to clear his sight. A white-tailed fawn wearing a bright red collar stood in the front yard next to the van. A golden retriever, almost as large as the deer, joined it and relieved himself on a nearby tree. "What the—?" Lance continued to watch the animals as they meandered farther into the yard. "There ought to be a law against that."

"There is." Charlie picked up his transmitter. "This is McCord. Come in."

"Yeah, Charlie. We see it, too."

"Well why don't you send one of your boys after a warrant then? It's illegal to possess wildlife without a permit."

"He's already on his way. Out."

Charlie dropped his radio on the seat and stretched his legs and arms. "We should be in business in about an hour with a warrant."

"Good. I'm getting bored."

About forty-five minutes later, Charlie's radio gurgled to life. "We're going in with the warrant, McCord. Watch for any runners that get away from us."

"Roger."

Charlie and Lance got out of the truck and moved toward the house in the darkness. Lance instinctively removed the leather thong off the hammer of his .357. They watched two deputies and the sheriff line up at the front door, while two others circled behind the house. A woman answered the door, then disappeared as the three lawmen rushed in.

Charlie's radio sputtered. "We got a runner going out a window on the back side. We're on him."

A few minutes later, it was all over. Two men emerged from the house in handcuffs, one in nothing but his underwear, the other in jeans, shirtless with no shoes.

"That was exciting," offered Lance in a sarcastic tone.

The sheriff emerged from the house pushing a blond-haired woman wearing shorts and a tank top toward his vehicle.

Lance and Charlie moved in closer to lend a hand. "Is the house clear?" asked Charlie.

The sheriff shook his head. "No."

"Find what you were looking for, Sheriff?" asked Lance.

"Meth," he said. "This place is a mess."

"Whoa." Lance froze. "Have they been cooking meth in here? Because if they have, I'm not going to go in and breathe that crap without some kind of protective gear."

"No, these are just users, all small potatoes," assured the sheriff. "But don't worry, we'll get their source, too."

Lance pulled his weapon and followed Charlie through the front door. He hated what he felt. The stench of methamphetamine chemicals hung in the air. Knowing the sheriff was wrong, he pulled out his handkerchief and covered his mouth and nose. Meth had taken such a toll on the small communities of northeast Oklahoma, he longed for the days when he and Charlie had made similar raids near Sycamore Springs and found only marijuana.

As he stepped over a pile of filthy clothes, he noticed a child's sippy cup and a stuffed toy peeking out from under the edge of the couch. Those were the real victims, he thought, the children who would end up ingesting drugs through the ignorance of their drug-addicted parents.

Charlie quickly headed toward the hallway and Lance took the kitchen. Lance observed encrusted dishes piled in the sink, trash on the counter and on a small table, but he found no one hiding. He checked a small pantry and broom closet. They too were full of junk but no suspects. He opened the back door to allow fresh air to enter and discovered the bench where they had been cooking meth. "Damn it," he said and closed the door. Through the window, he could see the bobbing of a flashlight beam in the trees a few hundred yards away. He assumed the two deputies, who had given chase to the runner, had been unsuccessful in their pursuit.

He met Charlie in the hallway, coming out of a bedroom. "Kitchen's clear," said Lance.

Charlie nodded. "Yeah, this bedroom is too. But look at this." He held up a fishing lure. "This is my lure. I know it is."

"I doubt you're the only fisherman in Delaware County who ever owned a lure like that, Charlie, but get the damned thing and let's get out of here. Did you check this other bedroom?"

"Headed there right now."

Lance flipped the light switch on and the two men entered the empty room. Charlie quickly checked under the bed and shook his head. Suddenly, the closet door burst open and a young black-haired child ran screaming toward the men, attaching himself to Lance's leg like a mad dog. In a split second, Lance saw an Indian girl with a familiar face emerge through the hanging clothes. It was Gertie, the young girl who had hit him in the head with a rock near the field of marijuana a few weeks ago. She had a shotgun.

"I won't let you take my baby deer!" she screamed. "You can't have her! She's mine!"

"Drop it!" commanded Charlie.

"Stop!" yelled Lance. He could see Charlie's .357 aimed directly at Gertie, his own gun down as he tried to push the child out of danger. The blast of two guns firing simultaneously rendering Lance deaf, but he could feel the stinging in his shoulder as he tried desperately to protect the child by shielding him with his own body.

The room began to swirl in slow motion around Lance's head. The child shrieked, the shotgun hit the floor, and the girl fell backward into the closet with a bullet wound in her chest. The last thing Lance saw before he lost consciousness was blood everywhere and a shiny, squiggly lure vibrating on the floor beside him.

25

It was Saturday morning and, knowing the café was in good hands, Sadie had allowed herself the unusual luxury of sleeping late. It was already past 8:00 a.m. when she walked off the back porch and sat down on the bottom step to have a heart-to-heart conversation with Sonny before she drove toward Liberty. She positioned her injured leg on a nearby rock, allowing Sonny to sit next to her other foot while she scratched his head. The longer she scratched, the closer he inched, leaning hard against her good leg.

She dug in her purse and pulled out her new cell phone. She turned it on and watched as the reception indicator tried to climb, then fell again. The woman at the booth inside the Wal-Mart store had promised her the reception in northeast Oklahoma had improved so much that she would refund Sadie's money if she wasn't satisfied within the first thirty days. She was beginning to think a refund would be in order, but she would wait for now. She wanted to appease her Aunt Mary, who thought she needed one for safety's sake after the episode in the vault. It seemed more reasonable than her uncle's suggestion, which was to start carrying a handgun. She flipped the top down on the phone and dropped it into her purse.

The last few days had been unseasonably cool, void of the usual triple-digit temperatures and stifling humidity. Several yellow leaves, caught in a brief gust of air, drifted from a nearby walnut tree and came to rest near the porch. With only four days left in August, the sight of those falling leaves gave Sadie a peculiar feeling, as if something wasn't right.

She began to think about the Cherokee National Holiday scheduled for the upcoming Labor Day weekend. There would be thousands of tourists descending on Tahlequah for the festivities and powwow. Sadie liked to watch the parade, hear the chief deliver his "State of the Nation" address, then drive out to the Heritage Center and cruise the arts and crafts tents.

Maybe Rosalee would like to go with her this year. Emma had a bad habit of making derogatory comments about Indians in general, so asking her was out of the question. Better yet, maybe Lance would be going.

She nudged the huge wolf-dog. "That's my toe you're sitting on," she said and then laughed when he leaned his head back on top of her knee and looked at her with his pitiful icy-blue eyes. "What's the matter, Sonny? Haven't been getting enough attention lately, have you?" As if he could understand her sympathetic confession, he thumped his tail against the porch and leaned a little harder. Right on cue, Joe whinnied.

"That's it," she said as she stood. "If you guys are going to gang up on me, I'm out of here."

Sonny jumped up and barked.

"Sorry, boy. You have to stay here." He sat back down when he heard the word "stay." She threw him a kiss over her shoulder as she got into the car. "I promise to make it up to you."

As she drove toward Liberty, she thought about how glad she was to be going to the café instead of the bank. Emma told her the night before that everything had gone without a hitch for the two days she had filled in for Tom Duncan. Rosalee had done a good job, Emma reluctantly conceded, and Red agreed when Emma suggested Sadie stay off her injured knee for a few days. Sadie argued, then promised to call the doctor's office and stop by on her way into town to make sure it wasn't anything serious.

Doc Brown's office, located two blocks west of the café, was the only choice for medical care on Saturday morning unless she wanted to drive to Tahlequah and spend the rest of the day sitting in the waiting room at Hastings Indian Hospital. The other option, which she seriously considered, was simply to prop her foot in the air, grab the television remote, and lean back on a couple of feather pillows and chill out. But that thought was short-lived; her personal commitment to her new calling as an entrepreneur won out.

The young girl who had answered the doctor's phone when Sadie called the day before had told her they had a nine o'clock cancellation. Sadie quickly grabbed the time slot.

Sadie pulled into the last empty parking space in front of Doc Brown's office, a two-story white house set back from the street with a manicured lawn and a hedge of mature azaleas. The only thing that designated the house as a doctor's office was a small hand-painted sign hanging on the wall next to the front door. Sadie got out of the car, climbed the steps, and limped through the front door with five minutes to spare.

She signed in at the desk in the corner and sat on a worn couch in what she envisioned must have been a living room or parlor in ages past. A few minutes later, Doc Brown emerged from another room, ran his finger down the list of names, then turned and noticed Sadie. "Come on back, Sadie. We're almost full-up this morning, but you can take my office at the end of the hall. I'll be there in just a moment, and we'll check out that knee of yours."

Sadie let herself into a small room that looked like it doubled as an examining room and office, with a small desk in one corner and a row of metal filing cabinets against one wall. She scooted onto the end of the examining table and waited.

A few moments later the doctor stuck his head in the door. "I'm sorry, Sadie, my nurse is not here today and I've got to do everything. I'll be here just as soon as I stitch up a cut on Willard Fox's hand. It will only take a minute."

"No problem," she offered. The doctor had already closed the door and disappeared before she finished her words.

She slid off the table and began to read a certificate that hung in the middle of the wall. It declared the doctor's graduation from the University of Oklahoma Medical School in 1966. That made him old enough to be her father, she thought. Two photographs flanked the certificate, one of an old barn and the other of a green-headed mallard swimming in the middle of a farm pond. The signature "Brown" in the bottom right-hand corner of each identified the doctor as a skilled amateur photographer.

She searched for a magazine or something to occupy her mind while she waited for the doctor to return. She spotted a newspaper on top of one of the filing cabinets and decided to see if it was current enough to warrant her interest. It was only one section of an Oklahoma City paper, and a week old. Someone had circled an article about a soldier killed in Cambodia more than thirty years before. Plans were underway to return his remains to Oklahoma. She quickly glanced at the rest of the page, decided it was old news, and put it back.

Her knee hurt and she leaned against the wall for a moment. The filing cabinet to her left bore a worn label that read: "Medical Records

1966–1967." She couldn't believe her luck, or even that medical files that old would still be intact and in public view. Was it possible that Rosalee's 1967 birth records could be right here beside her?

She argued with herself. She was new in Liberty. If she got caught illegally rummaging through medical records, it would ruin her reputation. She looked over her shoulder and strained to hear activity in the hallway. Silence.

I'll be quick. No one will ever know.

She stole a quick peek. Only a few files remained in the old cabinet, but the name "Pearl Mobley" jumped out at her. She looked around again to make sure no one was watching and pulled the folder open. She found several six-by-eight typed cards inside. She read quickly, scanning the old records. "Twins?" she gasped.

When she heard the doctor's voice in the hallway, she quickly replaced the folder, closed the file cabinet, and hobbled back to the examination table. Just as she did, Doc Brown burst through the door.

"Okay, young lady, let's take a look at that leg of yours." He sat on a short stool, rolled over to Sadie and took her knee in his hands. Gently pressing his fingers around her kneecap, he then worked his way up and down her leg. "Where does it hurt?" He held her thigh with one hand and carefully tried to bend her knee with the other.

"Everywhere."

"Any sharp pains?"

"Everywhere," she repeated.

He opened a nearby drawer and retrieved a stretchy bandage. "I can send you to Tahlequah to get an X-ray, but my guess is that it's just badly bruised. Best thing you can do is stay off of it for a few days." He began to wrap her knee.

"Say, Doc, did you know Pearl Mobley for very long?"

"Pearl? Why, I guess everybody around here knew Pearl." He continued to work on Sadie's knee. "As a matter of fact, Pearl was one of my first patients when I came here right out of medical school."

"Really?" Sadie tried to sound surprised.

"Yes, her folks brought her in because she was sick. It turned out to be morning sickness."

"Pregnant with John, I guess."

"Yes."

Sadie remembered the article she had found at the Tahlequah library about Pearl being raped. "Was she married?"

The doctor gave Sadie a curious glance as he finished tying her bandage. "Why are you so interested in Pearl?"

"Just curious."

The doctor opened a nearby cabinet and produced several prescription sample packets. "This will help with the pain and swelling. You can take two a day."

Sadie nodded. "Someone said they thought Pearl had twins," she lied.

"I know Pearl's dead, but I still have to respect her privacy."

Sadie nodded again. "Thanks, Doc. I think I'll take your advice and go put this foot up." She slid off her perch and turned around, but the doctor had already disappeared through the door. She grabbed her purse, limped down the hall, and checked out with the girl at the front desk.

After leaving the doctor's office, she got back into her car and drove down the street in front of the café. Before turning into the alley behind the café she slowed to admire the freshly painted windows. The name change was now official. "The American Café," she whispered. The words brought a smile to her face. As she parked, she thought about her great-aunt and how hard it must have been to run a café back in the forties. She hoped she could be as strong and successful.

When Sadie walked through the back door and into the kitchen of the restaurant, she could hear the clatter of dishes and the soft mumble of customers. "Doesn't the front window look great," beamed Sadie.

Emma pulled two loaf pans out of the oven and the aroma of freshly baked bread filled the air. "I guess so. I don't know what was wrong with the Liberty Diner. But I guess with Goldie gone, it doesn't matter."

Rosalee carried a platter of dirty dishes into the kitchen and dumped them in a rubber dishpan. She noticed Sadie and smiled. "Hi, Sadie. You're supposed to call some guy named Charlie." Then she disappeared through the swinging doors back into the café.

"What did the doctor say, honey?" asked Emma.

"The same thing you did," reported Sadie, "to stay off of it and take a couple of aspirin."

"Well, you ought to mind him. The morning rush is over and we're going to offer beans and cornbread and chicken-salad sandwiches for lunch. I've got apple and peach pie, too. It'll be easy to clean up and we'll be out of here by three. You go get some rest."

"Sounds tempting," said Sadie. "How about a sample?"

Emma sliced a loaf of bread that had been cooling on a wire rack, piled it high with chicken salad, then topped it with a tomato slice, a lettuce leaf, and another piece of bread. Sadie filled a small cup with brown beans, spooned in a dab of sugar, and headed for her favorite table in the back of the café near the kitchen door.

Emma followed, filled a tall glass with sweet tea, and sat down across from Sadie. The café had emptied and the two women were alone at the table.

Sadie took a bite and raved. "Mmmm. That's good chicken salad, Emma. Never had anything quite like it. What'd you put in it?"

"It's just boiled chicken, except that I only use the white meat. Then, let's see, there's celery, grapes, almonds, some Miracle Whip, and a little salt and pepper."

Sadie abruptly changed the subject. "You know, Emma, I think Pearl Mobley may have had twins when John was born."

"Oh, good grief," remarked Emma. "Not you too."

Sadie wrinkled her forehead and stirred her beans. "What do you mean, me too?"

"Rosalee said she read an old newspaper article about Pearl being raped behind this café. She's got it stuck in her head that Pearl was her mother."

"Oh, really?" Sadie frowned, wondering about Rosalee's source of information. "It could be a possibility, though. Did Goldie ever talk about finding Pearl that night?"

"No, and besides that she probably wasn't even raped. In the sixties, everybody was having free sex, married or not."

Sadie held her sandwich, poised to take another bite. "Do you remember the incident?"

"Not really. I had my hands full with the kids. I don't really remember much about it."

"I thought you said Rosalee's mother was Indian."

"She was. Like I said, I saw her myself." Emma took a gulp of tea. "And I've explained all that to Rosalee. Why, Pearl was as white as a spoonful of Crisco. Anyone can tell by looking at Rosalee the poor thing has got some Indian blood in her. She hides it fairly well with bleaching her hair, though. Don't you think?"

Sadie finished off her sandwich and wiped her mouth with a paper napkin as Rosalee approached their table.

"How are you feeling, Sadie?"

"Not bad, now that I've got a full stomach. How about you?"

"Okay, I guess. Don't forget to call that Charlie guy. He sounded kind of upset."

"Charlie McCord?" Sadie had never known the man to get riled about anything, but she couldn't think of another Charlie that would be calling her.

"I heard you two talking about Pearl," said Rosalee. "I'm going to prove Pearl was my mother."

"How in the world do you think you're going to do that?" asked Emma, visibly shaken. "I don't know why you want to insist that Pearl Mobley was your mother. Besides, if that article really is about Pearl and she was raped, then John is probably the result."

"I heard Sadie say she thought Pearl had twins," said Rosalee, and turned toward Sadie. "Why do you think that?"

Sadie looked away. "I'd rather not say."

"Well, it would all make sense," continued Rosalee. "Didn't you say back when you were talking to Pearl she said she had a little girl and Aunt Goldie took her?"

"Something like that," answered Sadie. "But you have to remember, Rosalee, Pearl was saying a lot of crazy things back then."

"Honey, Pearl wasn't right," said Emma. "She had to be out of her mind to murder someone in cold blood. Bless her poor soul."

Rosalee would not relent. "What if she really did have a girl and they took her away from Pearl and put her up for adoption. That could be me."

"Rosalee, I wish you would give it up." Emma's face began to turn red and her voice cracked with anger. "You don't look a bit like Pearl. And if John Mobley was your twin brother, you'd think you two would bear some sort of resemblance. I just don't know why you keep at it except you want to hurt me. I told you, your mother was some Indian woman who brought you here and dumped you. I have told you over and over that I took you in out of the goodness of my heart. I don't know what else you want to hear."

Rosalee held up her arm. "Do these freckles look like they belong on a Cherokee, Mother?"

Emma looked as if she wanted to spit, shrugged her shoulders, and looked away.

"And I always thought I got them from you," added Rosalee.

Sadie tried to defuse the conversation. "Well, for starters, you can't always tell by looking at someone whether they are Cherokee or not. Maybe you got those freckles from your daddy."

"That would be hard to tell, wouldn't it?" Rosalee snapped. "Especially since I don't know who my daddy was, either. I'm going to ask John Mobley. Surely he knows whether he had a sister or not."

"You better be careful, Rosalee," warned Emma. "You never know what you might get into with that hoodlum."

Sadie ignored Emma and fished in her purse for her new phone. She turned it on, listened for a dial tone, then dialed Charlie's number from memory, not completely sure whether it was correct. A computer-generated recording came on announcing "the person she was trying to reach was unavailable." She closed the phone and dropped it back into her purse. "Oh, by the way, Emma, here is my new cell phone number in case you need it." Sadie wrote on a napkin, handed it to Emma, and turned her attention to Rosalee. "Do you want me to go with you to see John Mobley? He's probably not as bad as everyone makes him out to be."

"What difference would it make anyway?" snapped Emma. "Pearl's dead." She snatched the napkin and stormed into the kitchen.

Sadie and Rosalee watched Emma's retreat. "You have to realize, Rosalee," said Sadie, "this is hard for your mother."

"Whatever, I don't really care." Rosalee shrugged and then looked straight at Sadie. "You know, people like you never see the real Emmalee Singer. You only see what she wants you to see."

Sadie ignored Rosalee's last remark. "If you'd like," continued Sadie, "I'll call Lance Smith and have him go with us."

"Oh." Rosalee frowned. "I heard he got hurt or something."

"Lance?"

"The police officer, right?"

"Oh, no," gasped Sadie, suddenly realizing why Charlie had called. "Did Charlie leave a number?"

"He said you'd have it."

Sadie hurried to the wall phone and quickly called the police station. Maggie answered on the second ring.

"Maggie, can you ask Lance to call me?"

The line went quiet before Maggie replied. "Sadie, Lance got shot during a drug raid last night out by the state line."

Sadie's knees almost buckled and her voice froze.

"He's out of danger," Maggie rushed to clarify. "They took him to Fayetteville by Life Flight. He's in Intensive Care."

"Fayetteville, Arkansas?"

"It was the closest hospital. I guess he lost a lot of blood."

"Oh." Sadie's head reeled. "Thanks, Maggie." Sadie dropped the phone and ran toward her Explorer as fast as her injured leg would go.

26

Sadie decided the quickest way to get to Fayetteville was to cut over to Highway 10 and go north. When she hit the Cherokee Turnpike, she raced east toward Siloam Springs, a small town that straddled the state line between Oklahoma and Arkansas. As she passed the Cherokee Casino, her steady pace slowed to a crawl as every stoplight turned red at her approach. Then an alarming smoky steam began to seep from under the front of her car. She quickly pulled into the first parking lot she could find. It belonged to Mama's Chicken House.

She eased into the last empty space and killed the engine. As she pulled the hood-release lever and got out to inspect the problem, a middle-aged man and two young boys came out of the restaurant. The man hurried to help her, waving his arms. "Stand back," he cautioned. "You'll get burned."

Sadie heeded the man's warning and helplessly watched as a puddle of green liquid began to form on the asphalt at her feet. After a few moments, the hissing slowed and the man and the oldest boy together pushed up the hood, releasing a huge hot cloud. "I'll bet it's your water hose," said the oldest boy. His younger brother inched closer to get a better view.

"Oh, I don't have time for this." Sadie limped in a small circle. "Besides, this is a new car. It can't have a bad water hose."

The man pulled a handkerchief from his back pocket, wiped his hands, and cautiously craned his neck for a better view. "Wait here," he commanded, and jogged to a nearby truck where he dug under the seat, then returned with a fistful of tools, a roll of silver duct tape, and a red oil rag. His head disappeared under the hood and Sadie could hear him talking to his sons.

"Wow, look at that," remarked one of the boys.

All Sadie could see were elbows and bottoms as the trio worked on her car. She realized her cell phone was ringing. She rushed to her purse, dug it out, and answered. It was Charlie McCord.

"Charlie, I've been trying to call you. What happened? How's Lance?"

"Well, we got into a little shoot-em-up. But it looks like he's going to be all right. He's asleep right now and I'm on my way out to get a bite to eat. Thought I'd try to call you again since they won't let me use my cell phone in the hospital. It interferes with the heart monitors or something. Anyway, some lady at your café gave me your number. She said you'd already found out about Lance and took off. Where are you?"

"Right now I'm standing in the parking lot of Mama's Chicken House in Siloam Springs, Arkansas, with a broken water hose."

About that time, the man backed away from Sadie's vehicle. "It looks like your hose might have been cut."

"Who's that?" asked Charlie.

"A man and his two boys stopped to help me. He thinks my radiator hose was cut. I've got to go, Charlie. I've got to get this car somewhere to be worked on."

"Where'd you say you were?" asked Charlie.

"Mama's Chicken House in Siloam Springs," she repeated.

"Stay put. I'm only thirty miles away. I'll be right there."

The younger boy had lost interest in Sadie's ailing vehicle, but the older boy and his father finished wrapping tape around the leaking hose and added a liter of water one of the boys had retrieved from their truck. Sadie snapped the phone shut, shoved it into her pants pocket, and tried to see what the two were doing.

"Are you sure it was cut?"

"Pretty sure." The man wiped his hands on the oil rag and nodded to his son to close the hood. "I guess it could have been a defective hose, but it would definitely have caused a lot more trouble if you hadn't pulled over when you did. I noticed your Cherokee Nation license plate. You live around here?"

"No. I'm from Liberty, just a few miles north of Tahlequah, going to Fayetteville."

"Well, we wrapped it up best we could, but I wouldn't drive it that far." He pointed with his head. "You might get some help at the Ford dealership down the street. But I doubt the service department is open on Saturday afternoon. Then there's Wal-Mart about a block down. They can probably put on a new hose for you." The man reached into his back pocket, extracted his billfold, and pulled out a business card. "If you want to rent a car 'til it's fixed, we can certainly help you out with that, too." He pointed across the street, then handed Sadie his card. "That's us over there."

Sadie inspected the card. Littledave's Used Cars and Rentals. "Thanks," she said. "It was awfully nice of you and your boys to stop and help me. I'm Sadie Walela."

"Matthew Littledave." He nodded at the boys. "This is Matt Jr., and this is Mark." Each young boy shyly followed their father's example and shook Sadie's hand. Sadie noticed the permanent stain of motor oil under the fingernails of all three.

"Can I pay you for your trouble?" she asked.

"No, ma'am. We kind of like tinkering on cars. Don't we, boys?" He smiled, ruffled the younger boy's straight black hair, then stooped to pick up the roll of tape.

"Well, if you're ever in Liberty," she said, "stop by the American Café and I'll buy you lunch."

"That's two restaurants we're going to have try out." A curious look came over the man's face. "A woman rented a car from me a little while back. She invited us to her place, too. Her name was—" He stopped and rubbed his forehead with his free hand. "Mrs. Ray, I think. Said she owned the Liberty Diner."

"Oh, Goldie." Sadie's voice dropped. "Goldie Ray used to own the café, she . . . uh, it's the same place, just a new name."

"Well, we'll try to drop by next time we're down that way. Are you sure you don't want us to stay until your friend gets here?"

"No need. I'll be fine. Thanks."

"You take care then," he said. Sadie nodded and the three piled into their truck and drove into the traffic.

Sadie climbed into her vehicle to wait for Charlie and stared into space, thinking about her water hose. First the vault incident and now this. Why would someone want to do her harm? She mentally moved down the list of people she had met in Liberty. The only person she could think of who might hold a grudge against her was Polly Gibson. But sabotaging a vehicle didn't seem to fit her personality. Polly might give someone a tongue-lashing behind their back, but Sadie didn't think the former bank teller had the fortitude to cause physical harm to anyone.

She squirmed in her seat and shifted her attention to Matthew Littledave's car lot. A row of vehicles sat lined up in front of a small shack, their windows painted with various messages—the most frequently used phrase seemed to be "$35 weekly." A banner above the office door read "Our cars might look bad, but they run good." Sadie smiled. Only in small-town America.

In less than thirty-five minutes, Charlie McCord arrived and followed Sadie to the Wal-Mart Super Center where she made arrangements with a middle-aged man in the automotive department to repair her car.

"Can you keep the old hose for us?" requested Charlie.

The man nodded.

"We'll be across the street at Lupe's Mexican Restaurant," said Sadie as she penciled her cell phone number on the form.

The man nodded again. "Give us about an hour," he said, then took her keys and disappeared into the noisy work area.

Sadie and Charlie got into his truck and the two rode across the highway to the restaurant and settled into a corner booth. Sadie pulled up a chair and propped up her foot to give her sore knee a rest.

"Lance told me what happened to you at the bank. Have you figured out who pushed you in the vault yet?"

"No," she said, dropping her menu back onto the table. "But they're going to be sorry when I do."

Charlie ordered the combination plate and Sadie opted for one taco, not because she was hungry but so Charlie wouldn't have to eat alone.

She munched on tortilla chips and listened in amazement as Charlie recounted the prior evening's events—how he and Lance had served as backup for the sheriff when they made the raid on the meth house, including every detail, even the presence of the white-tailed deer sporting a red collar.

"Lance said he'd had a run-in with the girl before. She and her boyfriend were growing marijuana somewhere. I couldn't understand all of what he was trying to say. Something about an ambush."

"Oh, my gosh, Charlie. You mean the girl we ran into in Kenwood was the same one who shot Lance?"

"You know about it?"

"I was there. She threw a rock and hit Lance in the head. I think her name was Gertie."

"A rock?"

"I thought it was funny at the time. But it doesn't seem so funny now."

"Was there someone with her?"

"Yeah, but he got away. Lance warned her to stay away from him."

"I bet he's the one that got away last night. What was his name?"

"Gosh, Charlie. I don't remember. Campbell, I think. Gertie said he lived on the Old School Road, east of Kenwood."

"Kenwood? That's in Delaware County. What was Lance doing up there?"

"Doing a favor for a friend, I think. The kids were on his land, so we rode out on horses one Sunday morning to have a look."

"Hmmm. If it's the same Campbell I know, he's been in trouble before."

Their food arrived and the conversation ceased. Sadie watched Charlie eat as if he hadn't eaten in a week.

"So, you've been with Lance all night?" she asked as she nibbled at the edge of her taco.

Charlie nodded. "I rode with him in the helicopter and stayed until they took him into surgery. One of the deputies helped me shuffle vehicles, then I drove Lance's truck home and changed clothes. I was covered in blood."

Sadie replaced the taco on her plate, wiped the edge of her mouth with her napkin, and slowly pushed the plate to the side.

"Then I went back this morning," continued Charlie, "so someone would be there when he came to. Lance never talks about his relatives, so I don't know if he has any around here or not. Do you know?"

Sadie shook her head. "What happened to Gertie and her kid?"

Charlie shoved a heaping fork of cheese enchilada into his mouth. "The girl didn't make it. Died at the scene. One of the deputies took the kid and turned him over to someone who handles that sort of thing."

"Oh, no." Sadie let out a long breath.

"I contacted the Liberty P.D. last night and George Stump showed up at the hospital right before I left to go home." Charlie grinned. "He's a different sort of fellow, isn't he?" He continued before Sadie had time to comment. "Anyway, I tried to call you this morning—" Charlie realized Sadie had stopped eating. "I'm sorry, I didn't mean to ruin your lunch."

"That's okay. I wasn't really hungry."

"Don't you worry about Lance, now. He'll be all right." Charlie continued to eat, stirring his refried beans and Spanish rice together on one end of his plate with his fork before taking a bite. "How is the café business, anyway?"

"It's an adventure. Harder than I thought it would be. The former owner's sister and niece have been a lot of help."

"That's interesting. Whatever happened on that case? Lance was telling me the accused committed suicide in jail. Is that right?"

"Yes. Her name was Pearl Mobley."

"I guess the jury's still out on whether or not she was the real killer." Charlie spread butter across a flour tortilla, rolled it up, dipped it in salsa, and took a bite.

"Oh, really?" Sadie didn't sound surprised.

"Yeah, I understand the lab said the shotgun shell at the scene didn't match the gun of the accused." Charlie took one last bite, stopped eating as if he had suddenly reached the saturation point, and pushed his plate into the middle of the table. "Speaking of shotgun shells . . . " He reached into his shirt pocket, pulled out an empty red cartridge, and placed it on the edge of the table. "I saved this for Lance in case he wanted a souvenir."

"This is the shell from last night?"

"Yep, that's the one she almost got him with."

Sadie picked it up and turned it over in her hand. "I didn't know you could match a shotgun shell back to a specific gun. How can you tell?"

Charlie picked up the shell and pointed to the indentation on the end of the cartridge. "This is where the firing pin struck it."

"You mean you can tell from this little bitty spot?"

"The lab can match it to a firing pin if they've got the gun."

"Do you think this one might match the gun that killed Goldie?"

"Highly unlikely."

"Why?"

"Just is."

"Could you test it to make sure?"

"Have to send it to the OSBI lab in Oklahoma City."

"But you could do that, right?" Sadie placed the cartridge back on the table and Charlie put it back in his pocket. About that time her phone rang. Her car was ready. Charlie took care of the ticket, and the two climbed back into his truck and returned to Wal-Mart.

Sadie paid the man in the automotive department and carried the severed water hose back to Charlie's vehicle. "What do you think?" she said. "Does it look like it was cut?"

Charlie peeled back the well-secured duct tape. "It's really hard to tell with all this tape on here, Sadie, but when a water hose bursts, it leaves a jagged break. This one looks pretty clean. Mind if I keep it?"

"Be my guest," she said. "Let's go check on Lance."

Sadie got into her newly repaired vehicle and followed Charlie to the Fayetteville hospital. When they arrived, he led her to a waiting room on the third floor set aside for families of surgery patients. Sadie waited while Charlie approached the nurse's station, pulled his badge out of his pocket, and inquired about Lance. He was doing fine, the nurse assured Charlie, but he could have visitors for only a few minutes at a time until he was moved to a private room.

Charlie thanked the nurse, and he and Sadie migrated into the empty waiting room. They both chose vinyl chairs facing a small television mounted on the opposite wall. They stared at the silent screen, reading the captions that appeared below the attractive woman newscaster.

Charlie sat on the edge of his seat, resting his elbows on his knees. "If I'd been a little quicker," he said, "Lance wouldn't be in this predicament. Maybe I've lost my edge."

"You can't blame yourself, Charlie. Lance wouldn't like it."

"Yeah, I know." Charlie excused himself and walked to the men's room.

Sadie realized that Charlie was hurting. His friend had almost died in front of him, and now he was blaming himself. She wanted to help him, tell him it was going to be okay, but she knew any words she had to offer were inadequate. There was nothing she could say to make him feel better.

Charlie returned and they both flipped through first one magazine and then another, to pass the time until one of them could visit Lance. Sadie began to feel uncomfortable. Her very presence at the hospital made her feel uneasy. She had not hesitated to run to Lance's aid, but now that she knew he was going to be okay, she wondered if maybe she should leave. She knew she would be embarrassed if he showed up uninvited at her hospital bedside.

She rummaged through the stack of magazines, found an abandoned newspaper, and tried to distract herself with any article she thought might provide a hint of interest. As she passed over the obituary page, a photo of a soldier caught her eye. The young Indian man in the picture looked familiar.

She caught Charlie's attention. "There's an article here about a soldier's remains being returned from Vietnam. Well, Cambodia it says. Do you know him?" She handed Charlie the paper. "They are going to bury him at the national cemetery at Fort Gibson," she added.

Charlie looked at the paper, shook his head, and handed it back to Sadie. "No, I don't think so."

"I didn't think Cambodia was part of that war," she said.

"Well, that just goes to prove your government doesn't always tell you the truth, doesn't it?"

Sadie looked at Charlie. "What do you mean?"

"They said we weren't in Laos, either. But that was a lie. When you get a chance, ask Lance about it. He was over there."

Sadie dropped her nose back into the paper. "Well, if we had a soldier missing in action and his remains were found in Cambodia, then I'd say someone was in Cambodia."

"That's what I mean." Charlie rose and walked toward a Coke machine. "Want something to drink?"

Sadie shook her head. "No, thanks."

Charlie detoured by the nurse's station, returned to his seat, and placed his soda can on a nearby table. "I'm going to go back and check on Lance. You want to go?"

"No, I'll wait here. You can tell him I said hello and that I hope he feels better soon."

Charlie disappeared down the hallway and Sadie continued to stare at the dead soldier's photo. Something gnawed at her gut. Why did he look so familiar? Finally she dismissed the obituary page and had moved on to the comics just as Charlie reappeared.

"What happened?" asked Sadie.

"He's still pretty out of it from the morphine they're giving him for pain."

Sadie thought for a moment. "I changed my mind. I think I will go back and see him . . . for just a second."

"Go ahead. It's the second room on the right. If anyone says anything, just tell them you're his next of kin. I don't think they really care. I'll wait here."

Sadie nodded, made her way down the hallway from the small waiting area, and slipped into the room Charlie had indicated. Lance lay sleeping in the bed closest to the wall, his head turned as if he were trying to look out a nearby window. Several wires and tubes connected his body to various machines and hanging bags of liquid. An oxygen hose ran from the wall to his pillow, circled his ears, and disappeared into his nose. His left shoulder and upper arm were encased in white bandages.

Sadie quietly approached the bed and watched his chest swell in measured movements. Her eyes traveled to the machines where the rhythm of his heart etched a continuous graph across a small screen.

She moved to the other side of the bed, bent and softly kissed his forehead. He opened his eyes, smiled, and closed them again. Overcome with emotion that ripped at her insides, she backed quietly away and left the room. She took a few moments to regain her composure, then rejoined Charlie in the waiting room.

"Is he awake yet?" he asked.

She shook her head. "No."

"The nurse says he's out of danger and needs his sleep, so I think I might as well go." Charlie rose and lumbered toward the door. "There's not a lot I can do here and I've got a mountain of paperwork to do."

"I think you're right. It's getting late and I need to get back to Eucha before my aunt and uncle send out a search party." Sadie stood and then stopped. "Wait." She returned to the newspaper, found the article about the soldier, tore it out, then limped as fast as she could to catch up with Charlie who had already disappeared down the hall.

27

Rosalee carefully maneuvered her red Jeep down the steep dirt road, trying to dodge the large rocks. When she reached the bottom she stopped and pulled out the piece of paper on which Junior Wilson had scrawled the directions to the Mobley place.

When she got to the mailbox that read "Mobley" and looked across the pasture at her destination, she almost changed her mind. But something deep inside steeled her resolve, and she gave the accelerator a nudge. She followed the path across the field, pulled up outside the trailer, and sat with the engine running while she surveyed the run-down dwelling. She honked her car horn twice.

She could see movement behind a window curtain before the door opened. What she saw next caused her to think she had made a terrible mistake. At that moment, she would have given anything for a stiff drink.

A military man stood in the doorway. His pink bald head glistened with perspiration in the morning sunlight. In his dark-blue uniform he looked like he had stepped right off a movie set.

She lowered her window. "I'm looking for John Mobley."

"What do you want?" The man's voice reeked with hateful intimidation.

"I just want to talk to him."

"Who are you?"

"My name is Rosalee Singer. It will just take a moment."

The man looked at his watch, then stared at her before he spoke. "Hold on."

The man disappeared, and Rosalee decided to turn off her engine. She didn't need an overheated radiator in the middle of nowhere. A few moments later, the man emerged from the mobile home. He had put on a white hat and gloves and carried a rifle.

Oh God, could this be John Mobley?

She'd never seen the man up close, but this individual looked nothing like the one she had seen from a distance riding around town on a Harley motorcycle with a bandana tied around his head.

Suddenly the seriousness of her situation struck her like a blow. John Mobley was probably crazy. Just like they all said he was, just like his mother. And isn't that what crazy military men do? Get all dressed up to commit suicide? Or, worse yet, here she was and would herself probably fall victim to his craziness. What a fitting conclusion to her own miserable existence now that she had managed to catch a glimpse of sobriety.

She grabbed for the keys in her ignition but it was too late. He stood at her open window, leaned down, and looked inside.

"What do you want?" he asked.

"Uh, I'm sorry," she stammered. "I think I've got the wrong house."

"If you're looking for John Mobley, then here I am. But you'd better hurry up and state your case because my ride ought to be here any minute. In fact, I thought that's who you were when you drove in. Did Jack send you out here?"

"Jack?" Rosalee's fear began to grow.

"Don't play innocent with me. I saw you sitting in the front row at the AA meeting last week. My sponsor sent you out here to check on me, didn't he?"

"AA? You're a member of Alcoholics Anonymous?" Rosalee felt a tiny bit of relief. At least they had something in common. "No, nothing like that. I don't remember seeing you there. I came here to ask you some questions, about your mother, your family."

"There is nothing to talk about." John dropped his head and looked at the ground. "She committed suicide. What else do you people want? Are you some kind of lawyer or something?"

"No, no. I just want to know if you ever had a sister, a sister who was maybe put up for adoption."

John frowned. "What the hell are you talking about, lady?" He moved slowly away from the vehicle.

Rosalee froze, remembering the rifle he had had earlier, afraid she might have triggered the mechanism that would bring on her own demise. "I'm sorry. I think I may have made a mistake in coming here."

He stood up tall, his feet shoulder-width apart, and began to speak. "The only real family I ever knew was the one that issued me this uniform. Do you know that the Marine dress blues are the only uniforms made up of all the same colors as Old Glory?" He held up his elbow. "Blue stands for bravery." Lowering his elbow, he pointed at the stripe on his trousers. "Red is for blood and sacrifice." Then he adjusted his hat and stuck out his chin. "White is for honor." He lowered his eyes to meet hers. "I wear this uniform because I'm a Marine. People stop and stare at me in this uniform. They respect me because I have on this uniform." Then he lowered his voice. "No one respects a man because he's Pearl Mobley's son."

Rosalee's heart jumped into her throat. He really was crazy. But maybe she could talk herself out of danger. She didn't have a lot to lose.

"Why is it exactly that you have on that spiffy uniform today?" she asked.

John turned and raised his eyes toward the road. Rosalee quickly checked her rearview mirror. Relief flooded through her veins when she saw a car turn off the road and drive toward them.

"Time's up," snapped John. "I've got to go."

The car rolled to a stop not far from Rosalee's Jeep. She could see the driver wearing the same uniform with the same blue jacket and stand-up collar. Without another word, John got into the passenger's side and slammed the door. The vehicle backed up and roared toward the road.

Rosalee let out a sigh of relief, but her hands were trembling when she turned the key in the ignition. She backed up, turned the Jeep toward the road, and swore she would never ever approach John Mobley alone again. At that moment she decided she couldn't possibly be his sister, after all.

Red looked in the mirror and tried unsuccessfully for the third time to tie a square knot in his tie. He pulled the tie from around his neck and let it drop to the floor. He unbuttoned his white shirt, pulled it off, and let it fall on top of the tie.

He sat on the edge of his bed, his left ankle resting on his right knee, and thought about the impending ceremony. After a few moments, he stood, went to his closet and, reaching to a high shelf, retrieved a worn shoe box. He carried the box into the adjoining room where he placed it on a wooden table and sat down to examine the contents. He gingerly removed the lid, set it aside, and shuffled through a dozen old and yellowed envelopes. Choosing one, he leaned back in his chair and pulled out the short letter and several black-and-white photographs it contained.

As he read the letter, a feeling of sadness and helplessness came over him like a stifling fog. He laid the letter on the table and arranged the pictures beside it so he could see them all at one time. Slowly, he studied the young Indian man in each photo—shirtless and dirty, in baggy green pants and heavy-duty boots, with a cigarette dangling from the side of his smiling mouth and an M16 rifle in his hand.

In one of the photos, the man stood at attention, no cigarette, fully dressed in clean, starched fatigues, sporting polished boots and an eagle feather attached to the epaulet on his shoulder. This photograph captured the man's unique expression, as if he were about to say something amusing.

Red dropped the picture and picked up the final one. There were no people in the photo, just a heap of ashes, with pieces of a helicopter's destroyed rotor blades the only distinguishable items. He scooped all of the photos together, shoved them back into the shoe box, and returned to his earlier dilemma.

He walked to the closet, pulled his favorite shirt off a nearby hanger—colorful and long-sleeved—and put it on. Next, he stepped into a pair of neatly hand-pressed blue jeans, fed a tooled leather belt through the loops around his trim waist and attached a beaded buckle. He picked up a shoe brush, carefully shined the best pair of boots he owned, and sunk his heels into them.

Standing back, he looked in the mirror. His silver hair made him look old, he thought, even though, at the age of fifty-five, his body remained relatively fit. Today, the wrinkles in his tired face reflected the painful memories of every battle and fire fight he'd fought all those long years ago in Vietnam. He shook his head. It had taken too long for this day to arrive.

He picked up his hat, carefully removed the hawk feather, and placed it gently on top of the dresser. From the bottom drawer, he retrieved a rectangular cedar box, opened it, and pulled out an eagle feather identical to the one on the man in the photo. Carefully, he secured it to his beaded hatband. Then he placed the hat on his head and stood tall. Thirty-six years after the last date on the letters in the shoe box, on a Sunday afternoon with gentle breezes blowing from the south, under the clear and cloudless Oklahoma skies, Red was finally ready to welcome his brother home.

28

The Monday morning crowd at the café had come and gone like a spring thunderstorm. Sadie leaned against the counter wiping her face with a paper napkin. Rosalee perched on a nearby stool and thumbed through the only morning newspaper Liberty had to offer, the one that came seventy-five miles from Tulsa. She had been carrying on all morning about her experience at John Mobley's place, continuing to insert bits and pieces of the story between each and every breakfast order she delivered. Now she began to recite the experience again.

"Why did you go by yourself?" asked Sadie. "I told you I'd go with you. You should have waited." Sadie filled a glass with ice water for herself and placed it on the counter. "Besides, why don't you just get a copy of your birth certificate and see what it says?"

Rosalee sipped cold Dr Pepper through a plastic straw. "I tried that." Then she took the straw out of her glass and chewed on one end of it. "You wouldn't believe how hard it is to get an original birth certificate unsealed in Oklahoma if you've been adopted."

"Really? I would think if it's your birth certificate, you would have the right to look at it."

"You'd think so, wouldn't you?"

Sadie picked up a wet cloth and absentmindedly wiped at the edge of the counter. "You'll probably find that lawmakers in Oklahoma rarely use logic when they pass legislation if it isn't going to benefit them personally."

Rosalee turned the straw around and began chewing on the other end. "How's your friend Lance doing?"

"Remarkably well, I hear." Sadie dropped the cloth next to the coffee pot. "I haven't actually talked to him, but my friend Charlie McCord told me this morning he's making a fast recovery because he was in such good physical condition. He may get to go home tomorrow."

"That's good." Rosalee laid the straw on the counter and took a gulp of her drink. "I can't believe he belongs to the same AA group I do."

"Who?"

"John Mobley. He thought someone from AA had sent me."

"Maybe you should offer him a ride to your meeting sometime. You could get to know him better and ask him about Pearl and if he had a twin."

Rosalee smirked. "I don't think so."

"What about the tribe? Don't they have to keep track of all tribal citizens' adoptions?"

"Actually, I went to the Cherokee Nation when I was in Tahlequah the other day. My name is nowhere in their database, and they told me I would have to access my original birth certificate and prove I was a descendant of someone listed on the Dawes Rolls before they could help me. They said that was the original list of Indians living in Indian Territory when Oklahoma became a state, or something like that."

Sadie nodded. "It was for the land allotments."

"Besides, I don't think Pearl was Indian."

"You're confusing me, Rosalee. I thought Emma said your real mother was an Indian woman."

"Well, yeah," Rosalee smirked. "But, I think she's lying. You can't believe anything she says."

Sadie didn't answer. She knew all too well how it felt to have a mother who possessed absolutely no skills in communication.

Then with a troubled look on her face Rosalee asked, "Sadie, do you think I'm Indian?"

The door opened and Red entered, giving Sadie a welcome diversion from her conversation with Rosalee. He took his usual place at the end of the counter against the wall.

"Coffee?" asked Sadie as she reached for the coffeepot.

Red nodded, placing his hat on the stool beside him and smoothing the top of his hair.

"Where have you been?" Sadie plopped down a cup and saucer in front of him and poured. "I haven't seen you in a while."

"I had some personal business to attend to," he said and began his ritual of spilling coffee into the saucer.

Sadie replaced the coffeepot. "Want something to eat?"

Red thought for a moment. "Yes, I'll take my usual."

Sadie headed for the kitchen. "Emma, give me two eggs over medium riding high on a short stack, and a side of bacon."

Emma acknowledged the order and went to work. Sadie picked up an armful of clean coffee mugs, carried them to the counter, and began stacking them near the coffeepot. A moment later, the front door opened again and Tom Duncan headed straight for Sadie.

"Get away from me," warned Sadie. "I'm not talking to you."

"Come on, Sadie." Tom looked distraught. "I need to talk to you."

"Oh, all right. But don't even think about asking me to work for you ever again. Got it?" Sadie turned and dipped a glass in the ice machine, then began filling it with water. "Want something to eat?" she asked as she deposited the glass in front of him.

"No. I need to talk to you," he repeated, then gave her a wide-eyed look and emphasized his words. "In private, Sadie."

Sadie looked around and noticed both Red and Rosalee staring at them. "Come on. There's a place we can talk upstairs, above the kitchen."

Tom followed Sadie through the kitchen and climbed the short flight of stairs to a small spare room. She turned and faced him. "Okay, this should be private enough for you. What is it?"

"Sadie, I just heard what happened to you. Tim Walker filled me in on everything. It all kind of freaks me out. I think I'm going to ask for some extra security."

"Okay, but what's so private about all that?"

"I've just spent a couple of hours looking at the reports that you printed out for me. Do you remember those amounts you circled?"

Sadie nodded.

"It looks like Polly was making bogus deposits into a dormant account and then making an internal transfer to yet another account, of a dead woman, where the money was then being withdrawn in cash."

"How'd she do that without a supervisor override?" Sadie asked. "She didn't appear to be that smart to me."

"I gave her my supervisor number to run a transaction one time. She wasn't supposed to use it again without my permission." Tom shuffled his feet and looked at the floor. "I'm screwed."

Sadie shifted her weight off of her sore knee. "I'm sorry Tom, but I'm still angry at you for leaving me to deal with that ditsy woman. What she did at your branch is your problem, not mine. And for what it's worth, I don't care. Is that clear enough? I need to get back to work." Sadie started walking toward the door.

"You'll care when I tell you the name of the dead woman."

Sadie stopped and looked at Tom. "Goldie?"

"Nope."

"Pearl?"

"Nope."

"Like I said, I don't care."

"George Stump's mother."

Sadie froze, the wheels in her head began to fly. "Are you sure?"

"Positive."

"Who's been making the cash withdrawals?"

"I'm not sure, but based on the cozy relationship between Polly and Stump . . . " Tom stopped for a moment and then continued. "I haven't even called anybody at the home office yet. I was so freaked out, I just left and came here to talk to you."

"Tom, who is running the branch?"

"Oh, that's all under control. They sent two women down from Sycamore Springs to fill in until I hire someone. I just told them I had to run an errand. This is really going to look bad on my record."

Sadie found a dusty chair and sat down.

"This could cost me my job—" Tom stopped in midsentence. "You're not even listening to me, are you?"

"Tom, why don't you have any video cameras set up in this branch? I thought after all the robberies that took place last year, the main office made them mandatory."

"We're working on it. Evidently the wiring in that old building is a nightmare. We've got someone scheduled to work on it in a few days. They put one in the ATM last week before I left."

"The ATM?" she asked. "Does it run all the time?"

"It's supposed to."

"Where's the tape? I didn't see a monitor anywhere when I was in your office."

"It's locked up in my credenza. On the bottom shelf. You have to practically stand on your head to get to it. They're supposed to install the monitor when they finish putting the cameras inside. Why? You won't be able to tell anything from that as far as Polly is concerned."

Sadie stood. "Because if we're lucky and the camera angle is wide enough, we just might be able to see who left the bank after they shoved me into the vault." She took a deep breath and let it out. "And if I'm right," she paused and then continued, "he might even be wearing a uniform."

Tom's mouth dropped open in disbelief.

"It all makes sense now, Tom. Our infamous Deputy Dawg was afraid I was getting too close to uncovering his and Polly's shenanigans." She started toward the door. "And I'll bet you a ten-dollar bill, she'll cop to it all."

"Polly? Why?"

"What's that old saying? Something about a woman scorned . . . "

Rosalee watched as Sadie and Tom emerged from the kitchen.

"I'll be back shortly, Rosalee," said Sadie. "Can you handle everything while I'm gone?"

"Sure." Rosalee said, as the two hurried out the door.

This was the first time in her life Rosalee actually felt like someone trusted her, and the new responsibility felt good. She noticed Red was almost through eating and got up to refresh his coffee.

He wiped his mouth with a napkin and allowed Rosalee to pick up his plate. She filled his coffee cup about half full before he held up his hand signaling her to stop. She replaced the coffeepot and began to talk to him.

"Why do people call you Red?"

Red studied her face. "Why do you ask?"

"Well, I was wondering if it was short for redskin."

Red chuckled. "No. My name is not short for redskin."

"I heard Sadie talking about it. She says redskin is a bad word . . . for mascots, I mean."

"Do you know why?"

"Not really."

"Do you want to know?"

Rosalee propped her elbow on the counter and rested her chin on her hand. "Yeah, I would."

Red rubbed his chin. "I'll give you an abbreviated version. Okay?"

Rosalee nodded. "Okay."

"When the white man came to America, they wanted to own all of our land. The best way to do that was to kill off all of the Indians. So bounty hunters would kill as many Indians as they could, then cut off the Indians' scalps for proof of how many kills they should get paid for. They called those bloody scalps "redskins." So you can see where it's not very palatable to Indian people to be referred to as redskins."

Rosalee's eyes widened. "Oh, wow. I didn't know that."

"Most people don't. They think they are honoring us by using that term for their mascots."

Rosalee chewed on her fingernail as she contemplated Red's story.

"In the end," Red added, "the joke is on them, not us."

"Why is that?"

"Because we can laugh at them in their ignorance. We know that two hundred years ago, they thought they could kill us all off, but it's the twenty-first century and we're still here."

"Do you have any brothers or sisters?" she asked.

Red looked at her for a moment before answering. "Why do you ask?"

"I found out not long ago that I was adopted. I grew up with two adoptive siblings, but now I'm wondering if I have any real brothers or sisters."

"Hmmm." Red slurped coffee.

"So, do you?" she insisted. "Have any brothers or sisters?"

"One brother. He's dead."

"Oh." Rosalee backed away. "I'm sorry."

"It's okay. It was a long time ago."

Rosalee stepped forward and began again. "Have you lived around here for very long?"

"Long enough."

"Do you know John Mobley?"

"Yes."

Rosalee leaned closer and whispered. "I think Pearl Mobley was my mother."

Red searched Rosalee's face. "Oh, yeah?"

"I read an article about a rape that took place in Liberty in 1966, behind this very restaurant. Pearl told Sadie someone had their way with her. And the article said someone identified the victim as Pearl Mobley."

"I see."

"And if you do the math, calculate forward nine months, you land right next to my date of birth."

Red smiled. "You've got quite an imagination, don't you?"

"It's all possible, isn't it?"

"You may have been conceived in Liberty, but I doubt it was behind this café." Red finished his coffee, placed the cup on the saucer, and pushed them both toward Rosalee. "However, if Pearl Mobley did turn out to be your mother, then I guess you would have a brother and his name would be John Mobley."

"That's what I'm afraid of, and I don't know how to go about finding out for sure."

"It should be relatively easy in this day and time."

Rosalee's eyes twinkled. "How?"

"Run a blood test. That should tell you if you two are related."

"Oh, I thought about that, but that would take money and then I'd have to convince John Mobley to give me a blood sample and, well, he's just plain scary."

"Hmmm." Red pursed his lips and nodded. "How about a DNA sample? Wouldn't that be easier?"

"That's sounds more expensive than a blood test."

"I tell you what. I have a friend who works in a forensic lab in Oklahoma City. I'll make arrangements for him to run the DNA test if you can get me something to test."

"Oh, wow, such as?"

"Hair, saliva, skin, blood, urine—"

"Yuck." Rosalee scrunched her face.

The front door opened and Rosalee looked up. Three customers entered the café and took one of the booths near the front door.

"Okay, I'll work on it." She grabbed his dirty cup and saucer and hurried back to work.

Red laughed silently, so hard his shoulders shook.

Sadie waited in front of Tom's desk and tried to look uninterested while Tom, on hands and knees, retrieved the tape from the video recorder hidden in the bowels of his credenza. He placed the tape on his desk and inserted a new one into the machine, brushing off the knees of his pants as he stood. Sadie wanted to grab it but refrained.

"Are you going to label it?" she asked.

"Hold on." Tom pulled a label out of his top desk drawer, checked his calendar, and carefully recorded the beginning and ending dates on it. Then he looked at Sadie with a blank face. "Now what?"

Sadie lowered her voice and directed her speech toward Tom, so neither of the other employees would hear what she said. "Well, my guess would be if you don't have a monitor, we take it somewhere so we can see who is on it."

"I shouldn't leave again until after we close."

"Then give it to me."

Tom looked at Sadie. "I can't do that. What if something happens to it. I'm already in hot water as it is."

Sadie chose one of Tom's chairs and sat poised as if she were discussing business. "Please don't flake out on me, Tom. If you don't trust me, why did you come and tell me all of this?"

"I didn't think about the tape. It's bank property."

"Would you turn it over to a police officer?"

"Sadie, we don't even know what's on this tape yet."

"Okay, just chill out." Sadie pulled out her cell phone, retrieved Charlie McCord's number, selected it and pressed the send button. He answered on the second ring. Sadie quickly retreated out the front door and down the sidewalk in an effort to keep her conversation private.

"Charlie, I need your help. When is Lance coming back to Liberty?"

"As a matter of fact, I'm delivering him home to Tahlequah as we speak."

"You're kidding. I didn't think he was going to be released until tomorrow."

"That was the plan until our friend Lance turned out to be an unsavory and uncooperative patient. He made the head nurse mad, and before she got glad again he checked himself out." Charlie chuckled. "Don't worry, he'll be all right. But it's going to be a few days before he's up and running at full speed. Do you want to talk to him?"

"No, not right now. Can you stop by Liberty on your way to Tahlequah? I'm at the bank, and I think I may know who attacked me. The only problem is if there is any proof, it is on a videotape from the ATM. But the manager is reluctant to give it to me. He might give it to you or Lance."

"I thought all you bankers were buddies."

"Don't call me a banker. Are you going to help me or not?"

"Okay, no problem. We should be in your area in less than an hour."

"Something else, Charlie. It might be a good idea if George Stump doesn't know about this for right now. I think he may be helping Polly embezzle money."

"We'll meet you there and see what we can do."

Sadie hung up, returned to Tom's desk, and almost panicked. Both Tom and the videotape had disappeared. She rounded his desk, pulled out the top drawer, and found the tape. When Tom returned, she planted herself in his chair, unwilling to let the tape out of her sight again. Forty minutes later Charlie McCord and Lance Smith walked in.

When Sadie saw Lance and his bandaged shoulder, her heart jumped. She wanted to run to him, make sure he was all right, and ask him if he remembered seeing her at the hospital. But she could never do that.

"Lance." She stood but remained by her chair. "How are you? Are you still in a lot of pain?"

"Nah, I'm okay."

"And you don't think it's a little soon to be running around with this guy?" She looked at Charlie and winked.

Lance smiled. "You'd think I'd learn my lesson about hanging out with him, wouldn't you?"

Tom Duncan cleared his throat and Sadie immediately started making introductions. It took Charlie less than five minutes, with Lance looking on, to convince Tom it was in the bank's best interest to give the videotape to him and Lance. Otherwise, Charlie promised, they would simply wait for the county sheriff to deliver a search warrant, which he was sure would create an undesirable scene for the bank, not to mention the chance they would be taking that someone might tip off the chief of police that Tom had caught on to his money making scheme. Tom agreed.

Charlie signed a receipt for the tape, then he and Lance took it and left.

29

The next morning, Tom Duncan stormed into the café just as Sadie emerged from the kitchen. "I need to talk to you again," he blurted.

"Can it wait, Tom? Rosalee doesn't work on Tuesday mornings, and I'm kind of busy." She picked up the coffeepot and refilled coffee cups up and down the counter. Virgil Wilson and his son, Junior, held their cups in midair as she poured. One of the other sawmill workers jumped up to make another pot for her.

Tom stood for a moment and then sat on the last empty stool at the end of the counter. "Okay, I'll wait."

Sadie automatically filled a glass with water and slid it in front of him. "Want something to eat or drink?"

He took a sip of water. "Thanks to you my office is going to be crawling with auditors tomorrow."

"That's not my fault."

"Was you-know-who on the you-know-what?" he asked hoping to disguise the content of his question to anyone listening.

"I don't know." Sadie turned away to take a customer's money, then returned to clear dishes from a nearby table.

Tom swiveled on his seat as she walked past him carrying dishes toward the kitchen. "What do you mean you don't know? Didn't you see it?"

"Nope."

"Why not? What happened?"

Two plates appeared in the pass-through window. Sadie stacked them on her left hand and wrist like a pro, picked up the coffeepot, and delivered all of it to a man and woman seated in the corner booth, then returned the coffeepot to its burner behind the counter.

"They took it with them, Tom," she said. "I didn't get to see it. It's in their hands now. They'll take care of it, I promise."

"You know the auditors are going to ask for it."

"So?"

"I shouldn't have let you take it." Distress crept into Tom's voice.

"I didn't take it. Just tell them what happened, Tom. You didn't do anything wrong by giving it to the police."

Tom looked around quickly when she mentioned the police.

"Tom, try to think logically," she said. "If the home office is sending auditors, who do you think contacted them? It wasn't me."

Tom gulped down the rest of his water. "If I get fired, it's going to be your fault."

Sadie shook her head as Tom stomped out the front door.

It was the first time in a long while that Rosalee didn't want to go to her AA meeting. But then she thought about her dead friend, Logan, how he had helped her turn her life around, and about the promise she'd made to him to stay sober. She had made that same commitment to Sadie when she took the job at the café. With those reminders echoing in her head, she took a deep breath and turned her Jeep south toward Tahlequah. Her stomach growled and she wished she had taken time for breakfast. But her reluctance to see her mother had overridden her hunger pangs. Maybe she would stop and get something on the way.

Labor Day had come and gone, and the early autumn days were beginning to shorten. The road between Liberty and Tahlequah crawled with active wildlife enjoying the cool mornings. A herd of deer stood motionless near the road until her vehicle got close, then they darted in all directions. She shrieked and hit the brakes. White tails and hooves bounced over a nearby fence and disappeared into a line of trees.

She let out a long breath and resumed her normal speed, wondering if she would run into John Mobley at the meeting. What would she say to him? The idea of securing a DNA or blood sample from him seemed less feasible now that they were about to come face-to-face. It was at times like this she questioned her obsession to find out the truth about her past. What if she uncovered something she didn't really want to know? In the larger scope of things, she thought, maybe the identity of her birth mother wasn't that important.

When she parked in front of the church where the AA group met, she noticed John Mobley's motorcycle. A small towel lay on the ground next to the back wheel with an assortment of nuts, bolts, and other small parts placed on it in an orderly fashion. John appeared, dropped to the ground, and began to crank on the wheel with a funny-shaped tool.

Rosalee's mind and spirit moved toward the door, but her disobliging feet walked toward the bike. Fright seeped into her veins, but she spoke anyway. "Do you need some help?"

John's head popped up, but his grease-covered fingers continued to work. "Know anything about motorcycles?" His pronunciation of "cycles" sounded like he had taken the word "nickels" and replaced the *n* with an *s*.

"No, not really. But I can give you a ride somewhere if you need it."

About the time John stuck his nose back into his work, something snapped, and a piece of metal dropped into the grass below the bike. John cursed, then looked at Rosalee. "I guess I'll take you up on that ride. At least you know where I live."

"Oh, yes." Rosalee could feel the blood draining from her face. What was she thinking? It was as if her mouth was working and words were coming out, all independent of her brain. Suddenly she wished like hell she had a drink. She dismissed him and his motorcycle and headed for the meeting hall. He followed and sat on the opposite side of the room. When the meeting was over, he followed her outside and stood beside her Jeep.

Rosalee stopped and looked at the ailing motorcycle. "You're just going to leave it here?"

"It'll be all right."

"Did you know it's leaking oil everywhere?"

"If it didn't leak oil, it wouldn't be a Harley."

"Oh."

They both climbed into the Jeep. Rosalee started the engine and turned east toward the street that would take her back to Highway 82.

"I just need to get back to the house and pick up a couple of parts," he said, "then I'll catch a ride back down here and fix it."

"You act like this is a normal thing."

"It is." John sounded unemotional about the whole thing.

Rosalee decided to disregard any offer he might be fishing for to bring him back to Tahlequah. The two rode in silence for a few moments, then

Rosalee abruptly turned south back into the heart of Tahlequah, the opposite direction of home. "Are you hungry?" she asked.

"Are you kidding? I can always eat."

"Then if you don't mind, let's grab a bite. I'm starving."

He shrugged. "You're driving."

Rosalee drove east on Downing Street and pulled into the first slot available at the Sonic Drive-In. They scanned the menu and both ordered foot-long chili dogs with all the trimmings. John offered to buy, and Rosalee let him. Food, she thought, the eternal bonding mechanism.

They ate in silence until every morsel was gone, then John got out and deposited their trash in a nearby receptacle. Rosalee started to feel easier about her passenger. When he got back in, they headed north toward Liberty. Finally, Rosalee began to work her way into a conversation.

"I'm sorry about your mother." She could sense John's muscles tighten and regretted her words as soon as they came out of her mouth.

After a few moments, he seemed to relax. "I know you think my momma killed your friend, but she didn't."

"Goldie was my aunt," Rosalee corrected him.

"Whoever she was, Momma didn't kill her."

Rosalee couldn't stop herself now. "But they said she left a note."

"Yeah, but all it said was she was sorry for what she did. It didn't say she killed anyone."

"Oh."

John's voice began to rise in pitch. "My mother was a crazy old woman, but she never hurt anybody."

"How can you be sure about that if you say she was crazy? She threatened someone at the café, too, you know."

"You have no idea how many times my momma picked up a shotgun and pointed it at me. All I had to do was walk over and take it away from her. It was always empty."

"Damn, you are crazy," Rosalee muttered under her breath.

"What?"

She could feel his level of agitation building but decided to go for broke anyway. "Do you have any brothers or sisters?"

"Why do you care?"

"Because I'm adopted, and someone said your mother had twins when you were born, and—"

John turned in his seat and stared at her.

She gritted her teeth and punched the accelerator.

"Slow down," he barked. "You're going to kill us."

She hit the brake and slid to a stop. "Please, I have to know. How old are you?"

"I'm thirty-six."

Rosalee gasped.

"It is none of your business, but I did have a twin sister. She died at birth."

Rosalee's eyes widened. "Are you sure she died? I'm thirty-six, too."

John began to laugh. "You're the one that's crazy, lady. Who in their right mind would want to deliberately become part of the Mobley family?" He continued to laugh.

"Were you born in Liberty?" she asked.

"Somewhere around here, I guess. Out in the sticks, I think. I sure wasn't born in a hospital if that's what you're asking. I guess Grandma must have delivered me."

"Maybe we could ask your grandmother."

"You can." He tilted his head and stared at her. "If you can talk to the dead." Then he laughed again.

Rosalee felt weak and had no idea what to say. As she began to drive north again, a brown paper sack rolled across the highway in front of the Jeep. She ignored it and drove straight ahead. John screamed, covered his head with his arms, and dove toward the floorboard. "Watch out!"

Unnerved, Rosalee hit the brakes again and the Jeep slid to a stop on the shoulder of the road. "What's wrong with you?" Her voice climbed to a higher pitch. "It was just a paper sack!"

John moved his hands and raised his head. He blinked his eyes a couple of times as if trying to focus. Slowly, he sat back up. "Oh, man," he whispered. "I'm sorry."

"Are you okay?" Rosalee's voice trembled.

"I thought it was a bomb."

Damn, Rosalee thought, *he's having flashbacks. What did I get myself into this time?* "Are you sure you're all right? Do you want me to call someone for you?"

"You don't get it, do you?" he snapped. "Everyone's dead. They're all dead. I'm the only sucker left. Even my best buddy in the Marines bought the big one. And he did it while he was standing two feet from me. Do you have any idea what it feels like to have a friend's brains splattered all over your face?"

Rosalee pulled the car back onto the road and drove as fast as she could toward Liberty. She thought about stopping and asking him to get out, but then he would probably hunt her down and kill her. She would just keep quiet, get to town as soon as possible, and never speak to him again.

"Do you want to know why he did it?" John's voice calmed.

Rosalee ignored him and continued to drive.

"Do you know how hot it is in the Iraqi desert?" he asked. "Do you have any idea what it's like to have sand fleas crawling all over you?" He pulled his lips into a snarl. "They crawl in and out of your eyes . . . and your ears . . . and your—" He stopped in midsentence. "Forget it." After a few minutes, he spoke in a normal voice. "I'm sorry. You don't have anything to drink stashed in here, do you?"

She ignored his questions and they rode in silence until they reached the edge of town. "Do you want me to go ahead and take you out to your house?" she asked.

"Just let me out by Maynard Johnson's garage. I need to buy a part."

She parked in front of the service station and John started to get out.

"Wait," she said. "I'll pay you."

John leaned back into the vehicle. "You want me to pay you for your gas?"

"No, I'll pay you if you'll give me a blood sample so I can prove whether or not you're, uh, whether or not we're related."

His eyebrows shot up. "You want me to what?"

"Just a little sample. Maybe we can get Dr. Brown to do it. I already know where I can get the test done."

John looked as if he was sizing her up. "How much?"

Rosalee searched her brain for an amount. She couldn't pay very much, mainly because she didn't have any money, and whatever amount she did offer would have to come out of her wages as a waitress, which wasn't a lot. She turned the tables. "How much would you want?"

John started to get out of the vehicle again. "Well, when you decide, let me know."

"A hundred dollars," she blurted.

John smiled. "Just tell me where to line up, Sister, I'll give you all the blood you want."

"Can I call you?"

"It's listed in the phonebook under Pearl Mobley." He slammed the car door and disappeared into the garage.

30

Lance Smith leaned against the passenger-side door of his truck, dividing his attention equally between the front door of Polly Gibson's house and a set of computer printouts. "I don't know how anyone can make heads or tails out of all these numbers." He dropped the reports on the front seat beside him.

Charlie sat behind the steering wheel, complaining. "This is a waste of good vacation time. I'm using time that would have been better spent stalking game. Deer season is less than six weeks away, you know."

Lance smiled. He was thankful his friend was willing to take personal time to help him.

"Geez," groaned Charlie. "Grandma was slow, but she was old. How long does it take to ask a few questions? Are you sure they said they didn't need our help?"

"I don't think they used the word need. They said they didn't *want* our help."

Forty-five minutes earlier, two FBI agents had climbed out of the unmarked vehicle now parked in front of Charlie and Lance and entered the Gibson house. They were intent on collecting as much information as possible about the funny transactions the former teller had made at the bank and about what the connection might be between her and her friend, the illustrious George Stump.

Lance tightened and relaxed his fist over and over in an attempt to exercise the muscles in his left arm. Every squeeze hurt, but he would rather work through the painful sensation than tolerate the pills the doctor gave him. He planned to do whatever it took to regain full use of his left arm in record time, regardless of the pain. As far as today was concerned, there was no way he would miss this event. He would savor every word when he got the chance to recite to George Stump his Miranda rights. In the meantime, Lance hoped Stump wouldn't show up at Polly's house before the FBI guys finished.

"Those boys are slower than molasses," Charlie complained again.

Lance checked his watch, then glanced at the right rearview mirror. "I just hope they don't screw it up."

He knew the agents had gone in ready to make Polly an offer, armed with a stack of bank reports showing the illegal transactions she had made. She wouldn't know they mainly wanted information about the bigger fish in this scheme: George Stump. "Spill the beans and we'll let you go" was their MO. They would get what they needed, have her sign a statement, probably videotape the whole thing, then cart her off to jail, too. Lance didn't like the federal agents, but they were a necessary evil in this situation.

"Why would Stump risk his career on a penny ante embezzlement deal?" asked Lance. "It doesn't make any sense. He doesn't appear to need the money."

"Being the only nag in a one-horse town might've gone to his head," Charlie said. "Criminals rationalize all kinds of crap."

"Yeah, but he couldn't be so stupid as to think he could get away with it, especially pushing Sadie in the vault."

"Why not? It's a false sense of security. Some of these country law-dogs think they can get away with murder."

"I'm wondering if that isn't exactly what happened."

Charlie looked at Lance and frowned. "I can't imagine he would be *that* stupid."

"He took a cinnamon roll from a dead woman's house, Charlie."

"That doesn't mean he killed her."

"Yeah, but don't you think that's kind of sick?"

Charlie chuckled. "You need to grow a thicker skin." He stretched out his left leg as far as he could and dug around in his pocket for something. "Speaking of thick skin, I keep forgetting to give you this souvenir I saved for you." He pulled out the red shotgun shell and handed it to Lance. "You'd better save this for good luck. Luck's the only explanation I can think of for you to still be alive and kicking." Charlie looked into the distance. "Too bad about the girl. She was awful young to die."

Lance reached over and took the empty shell with his right hand. "I really hate what's happening to the young people around here. They get hooked on that junk, and it eats their brain cells. She could have killed her own kid."

"She damned near killed you."

"I know, but I took that chance when I signed up for a job wearing a badge. That kid didn't even ask to be born into a world like that."

"Don't start getting all soft on me. Because when you do, it's going to be time for you to start looking for another line of work."

Lance turned the red plastic shell around in his hand and examined it carefully. "You know, this looks exactly like the shell that Red brought in. He said he got it out of one of Goldie Ray's flower pots."

"What's the deal on that case? Wasn't it the prisoner who hung herself?"

"She made a confession of sorts in front of Stump and the preacher and implied in her suicide note that she had done something she was sorry for. But remember, the shell didn't match back to the shotgun she had. Stump closed the file, but I don't think she killed Goldie."

"You know, Sadie made a similar comment when I showed that shell casing to her."

Lance looked at Charlie. "What did she say?"

"I don't remember exactly. I think she asked if this shell could have come from the gun that killed Goldie, but I told her that chance was pretty remote."

"You should never question that woman's intuition." Lance bounced the shell in his hand, then shoved it into his pocket. "I might just check that out."

The front door of the house opened and Polly walked out in hand-cuffs. The agents flanked her, each one carrying a briefcase. After they secured their prisoner in the back seat of their vehicle, one man got behind the wheel and the other walked to Lance's side of the car. "We've got what we need," he said. "She rolled all over your police chief, including his little trick of locking the other employee in the vault. We're ready to pick him up now, but since you said you wanted the arrest, we'll defer to you. Bring him to Tulsa. That's where we're taking her."

Lance nodded and the agent left to join his partner. Charlie clicked on his seat belt and revved the engine. Both vehicles pulled away from the curb in tandem. At the end of the block, one headed out of town, the other toward downtown Liberty.

When George Stump arrived at the police station, Lance was already seated at his desk with his feet resting on the corner. Charlie sat across from him in a chair facing the doorway.

Stump dropped his keys on his own desk, picked up the phone and dialed. "Maggie, do you have any messages from Mrs. Gibson?" he asked. "We were supposed to have a meeting and she didn't show." After a few moments, he grunted and hung up. As if seeing Lance for the first time, Stump walked toward him and raised his chin. "What the hell are you doing here? Do you have a release from the doctor?"

Lance ignored the questions and lowered his feet to the floor. Charlie stood. "This is my friend, Charlie McCord," said Lance.

Stump plastered a smile across his face and shoved out his hand. "Nice to meet you. I hear you're quite a lawman."

Charlie ignored his hand. "Sorry I can't say the same about you."

Stump's smile faded to a frown about the time Lance pitched a videotape onto the center of his desk.

"What's that?" asked Stump.

"That's a tape that came out of the cash machine that sits in front of the Liberty branch of First Merc State Bank," said Lance.

Stump's face showed no emotion.

"They installed a camera in that machine just about a week ago, about the time someone pushed a woman into the vault and slammed the door. I'm sure you remember that, don't you?"

Stump continued to hold his stone face intact. "Oh, yeah, when your girlfriend locked herself in the vault. I do remember that. She caused a waste of law enforcement time as I recall."

"Well, the angle on the camera records everyone who enters and leaves the bank."

A bead of perspiration formed on Stump's forehead. "Well, that's great work, Lance, but I think you should still be nursing that gunshot wound of yours. Why don't you get out of here and get some rest? I'll have someone check out this tape."

"I can't. There won't be anyone to run this office."

Stump glared at Lance.

"You see," continued Lance, "the reason Polly Gibson didn't make your meeting is because she is on her way to Tulsa, with two men, in the back seat of an FBI car. And that's why I'm here without the permission of any doctor, and that's why my friend Charlie McCord is here to stand in for any physical limitations I might have due to a wounded shoulder. You see, George Stump, you are under arrest for obtaining money through fraudulent means, and assault and battery. You have the right to remain silent . . . "

As Lance finished advising Stump of his Miranda rights, Charlie reached over, removed Stump's gun, and motioned for him to remove his holster. The color drained from Stump's face.

"That bitch," muttered Stump.

Charlie handcuffed Stump and patted him down for any hidden weapons. "You can't go around pissing off women, man," snickered Charlie. "It'll get you in the doghouse every time."

Lance picked up the phone and dialed. "Maggie, this is Lance . . . Yes, I'm okay. . . . Yes, I'm sure. . . . Listen, you're going to have to forward any emergency calls to either the sheriff's office or the Cherokee Marshals. . . . Yes, we have an agreement with them. . . . I've already talked to them. They are expecting your call. . . . The chief? . . . Oh, the chief is going to be gone for a while, quite a long while as a matter of fact."

31

As Sadie drove toward Liberty in the early morning hours, she began to question how long she could keep it up. Driving back and forth to Liberty was beginning to take a toll on her. She never seemed to have extra time to spend with her aunt and uncle, not to mention Sonny and Joe. It was worse than the long hours she used to put in at the bank. She thought about Emma and how she had pitched in to help with the café and what a blessing it had turned out to be to have Rosalee to help, too. She thought maybe their mother-daughter relationship would improve the longer they worked together, and if it did maybe she could turn the café over to them to run. She hated to admit it, but trying to fulfill her childhood dream of owning a café may not have been one of her better ideas.

When she got to Liberty, she pulled into Johnson's garage, filled her car with gas, and bought a copy of the two-day-old weekly Liberty paper. By the time she got to the café, the regulars were already there, so she parked behind the café and entered through the kitchen. Emma had already arrived.

"Good morning, Emma. What do you need me to do?"

"I've got everything under control, honey. Get yourself some coffee and visit with the people. They like to talk to you." Emma opened the oven and peeked inside. "You know, honey, I've been trying to clean out some of Goldie's things, and she had a bunch of Indian baskets and some other stuff I have absolutely no use for. You want to take a look at it? There's a beaded purse I thought you might want, you being Indian and all."

Sadie stared at Emma. She had made an extra effort to accept Emma just the way she was but she was growing tired of her racist innuendos. Emma's attitude toward Indian people in general seemed to be so deeply embedded, Sadie doubted she even knew how offensive she sounded.

"Sure, when's a good time?" Sadie asked.

"I tell you what, after we close today, why don't you give me a ride home? Then you can take a look at all of her junk and take what you want."

"Okay." Sadie continued through the kitchen and entered the café with her newspaper under her arm just as one of the regulars returned the coffeepot back to its burner. He hurried to fetch a cup for her.

She took the coffee and sat down at her favorite table near the kitchen door, thinking how unusual it was for her to be comfortable with other people helping themselves to her space. But it seemed to be working.

She flattened out the paper and began to read as she stirred cream and sugar into the hot liquid. An article about halfway down on the right-hand side of the paper caught her attention: "MIA Soldier Laid to Rest." She began to read:

> "The remains of an Oklahoma soldier killed in Cambodia thirty-six years ago finally came home last week and were buried at the Fort Gibson National Cemetery. U.S. Army Staff Sgt. McIntosh Yahola died when his unit's Huey assault helicopter took enemy fire in the Cambodian jungle west of the South Vietnamese border. Three other soldiers were able to exit and escape. Although it is believed Yahola died instantly, he was declared missing in action. The Cambodian government allowed American search teams into the jungles to search for missing comrades in the 1990s, and they eventually found a mass grave containing Yahola's helmet and some bone fragments. Recent DNA testing linked the bones to his only living relative, a brother, Eto Catuce Yahola. More than 1,800 Americans are still listed as missing in action from the Vietnam War, according to officials. Related story and picture on page 8."

Sadie could feel someone reading over her shoulder. She put the paper down and quickly turned around. When she looked up, Lance Smith smiled at her. His left arm rested in a sling wrapped around his neck.

"Oh, wow, Lance. You look terrible. How are you?"

"Thanks a lot," he said, eyes twinkling.

Realizing how her comment must have sounded, she tried to elaborate. "It's barely been a week. Are you sure you should be out and about?" She blew across the top of her coffee and sipped.

"I had to suck it up and get back to work. Charlie and I delivered Deputy Dawg to the Tulsa County Jail last night."

Sadie almost spit out her coffee. "What happened? Here, sit down." She jumped up and retrieved a cup of coffee for him.

He waited until she returned before sitting. "The bank called the FBI and asked them to arrest Polly Gibson for embezzling. She managed to siphon off about fifteen thousand dollars before they caught her."

"It was from a dormant account, wasn't it?"

"Yep. Evidently, she thought since the chief of police was involved, she would never get caught. Then you came along and turned over her applecart."

"Me? I didn't do anything. The internal auditors already knew there was something funny going on, and Tom knew she was stealing money out of her cash drawer. But that was just piddly amounts. I had no idea she was in that deep."

"Well, she and Stump thought you were on to them. That's why Stump pushed you in the vault."

"*Suli*," she muttered and then translated, "the old buzzard."

"I guess he thought killing you that way would look like an accident."

"Killing me? He was trying to kill me?"

"Yeah, Polly said he thought you would run out of air and suffocate. He really isn't very bright."

"Oh, he didn't know about the air vent." Sadie frowned. "Come to think of it, I didn't know about it either until I found the lights. That was scary. What about charges?"

"They've already charged him, but there will be more."

"Like what?"

"Charlie had already sent your radiator hose in to see if there were any identifiable prints on it. The lab found one good print but couldn't match it back to anyone in the crime record database. When all this came up about Stump, Charlie called and had them check it against Stump's CLEET records, and sure enough they found a match."

"Oh, my." Sadie shook her head.

"I can't believe he was that dumb. Anyway, we'll have to find out what the charges will be on that."

Sadie's eyebrows shot up. "The tape. He was on the tape, wasn't he?"

Lance leaned back in his chair. "The tape was very useful."

"Can I see it?"

"Nothing to see."

"What do you mean?"

"The camera was out of focus." Lance laughed. "All you could see were shadowy figures. We never could identify anyone on it."

Sadie wrinkled her forehead. "I thought you said it was useful."

"It was. The FBI told Polly they had a tape from the cash machine and she spilled her guts."

Sadie took a deep breath. "Wow."

"I also came to thank you for coming to the hospital."

Sadie tried to hide her face behind her cup. "You remember?"

"Actually, I don't remember a thing."

"Then how do you know I was there?"

"I'm psychic."

"Yeah, right," Sadie laughed. "Charlie McCord told you."

Rosalee came through the front door with a smile on her face. A man at the counter flirted with her as she grabbed a white apron and tied it around her waist, a signal to the regulars that normal café business was about to begin. She approached Sadie and Lance. "You all want anything to eat?"

Lance nodded. "Yes, ma'am. I'll take a ham and cheese omelet with biscuits and gravy."

Rosalee took notes on a small green pad and looked at Sadie. "You want anything Sadie?"

"No, I'll fix myself something in a little while. How are you doing, Rosalee? Did you make your meeting yesterday?"

"Yes, I did and the trip there and back turned out to be very interesting. I gave John Mobley a ride."

Sadie gave her a questioning look. "Oh, really?"

"Yeah, I'll tell you about it later. And I want to talk to you about something else, too," she added.

"What?"

Rosalee looked at Lance and hesitated.

"What?" Sadie repeated. "He won't bite."

"I need a hundred dollars," she whispered. "Do you think I could get an advance? John Mobley has agreed to give me a blood sample so I can get it tested to see if we are brother and sister."

"Ooh, your mom's not going to like that. Does she know?"

"Not yet. I'm going to tell her this afternoon after I make sure I have the money and he's really going to do it. I'm afraid if I tell her here, she'll take a butcher knife after me."

"She's definitely not going to be very happy about it." Sadie sipped coffee and thought for a moment. "I'll loan you the money and you can pay me back."

"Thanks." Rosalee disappeared into the kitchen.

"What's that all about?" asked Lance.

Sadie explained Rosalee's dilemma of being adopted and how she thought Pearl Mobley might have been her mother.

Lance rolled his eyes. "That's pretty far-fetched."

"Yes," agreed Sadie. "But it's her journey to make."

Rosalee delivered Lance's breakfast to him and then rushed to wait on other customers.

Lance peppered his eggs and began to eat. "You know, Sadie, Emma's a pretty good cook. Is she going to stay around?"

"I hope so. She seems to really enjoy working here and I don't think I could ever handle this place on my own the way Goldie did."

Lance began to eat as Sadie turned the paper over and continued reading the article she had started earlier.

The last paragraph read:

"The ceremony for Yahola was punctuated by an unusual display of Native pride. When the honor guard folded the U.S. flag and presented it to Yahola's brother, he took it, laid it on his chair, handed them back another flag, and asked them to drape it on the casket. While they unfolded the flag of the Muscogee Creek Nation, a Native drummer could be heard singing in the distance. Members of the Creek Nation Red Stick Warriors Group gathered nearby to honor Yahola."

"What's a Red Stick Warrior?" asked Sadie.

"Creeks." Lance took a bite of food.

She waited for a better explanation.

"Haven't you ever heard of the Battle of Horseshoe Bend?"

"Yeah, that's when we should have killed Andrew Jackson and we didn't."

Lance laid down his fork and wiped his mouth with a napkin. "I think if you study history you'll find that some of the Cherokees were fighting on Jackson's side that day. We, meaning us Cherokees, were trying to protect him. Bad move on our part. Our ancestors were naive enough to believe Jackson would stand behind his word. He'd promised if we'd fight for him he wouldn't take any more Cherokee land. So, in all our wisdom, we nearly wiped out the Red Sticks."

"What's that got to do with it?" Sadie sounded perplexed.

"The Creek warriors were fighting against Jackson and the Cherokees. If the Red Sticks had been successful and killed Jackson, there might not have been a Trail of Tears for any of the five tribes." Lance grinned mischievously. "We ought to apologize to the Red Sticks."

Sadie rolled her eyes. "I don't believe that, but I'm going to let it slide. So why are they called Red Sticks?"

"I'm not exactly an expert on Creek history, but I know they had upper towns and lower towns—white towns and red towns—white for peace, red for war. Supposedly, the warriors from the red towns carried sticks dipped in red paint. When they sent a bundle of sticks to the War Chief, the number of sticks determined how many days were left until they went to war. I'm sure it's a lot more complicated than that. Red should be able to tell you."

Sadie took the paper and studied the adjoining photo. "Oh, my gosh. This is Red." She handed him the newspaper. "Lance, look."

"Let's see." Lance skimmed the article. "Hmmm, I wish I'd known about this. I heard they'd found this guy's remains, but I didn't know they had already been returned." Lance shook his head. "That war sucked." He continued to read for a moment, then looked at the picture. "Yeah, that looks like Red. Must have been his brother. Look at this member of the honor guard." He handed the paper back to Sadie and continued to eat. "That's Mobley all decked out in his dress blues."

Sadie squinted and looked at the photo again. "Are you sure?"

"Looks like him. I know he's a Marine. Must be part of the local honor guard around here."

"Rosalee, come here," Sadie said.

Rosalee brought the coffeepot to warm Lance's coffee.

"Look at this picture," Sadie said.

Rosalee set the pot down on the edge of the table and stared at the photo.

"Remember when you went to see John Mobley and he was all dressed up in his military uniform? Looks like he's part of the honor guard."

Rosalee's eyes got big. "Good grief. He scares me to death." She picked up the coffee and walked off.

Lance finished eating and Sadie cleared his dishes.

"Where's my check?" he asked, as he pulled out his money clip.

Sadie returned to the table and wiped it off with a clean cloth. "Forget it, Smith. Your money is no good here."

"You know in some circles that could be deemed a bribe of sorts."

"Well, in my circle it's just good business to keep the local lawman happy."

Lance dropped several dollar bills on the table. "Here's a donation toward Rosalee's pursuit of finding out who she is."

"Thanks, Lance." Sadie walked with him to the door and out onto the sidewalk. "When you feel like you're up to it, why don't we go for another horseback ride?"

Lance nodded. "We'll have to wait for this shoulder to heal."

A man and two boys came out of the café, and the youngest one almost collided with Sadie. It was Matthew Littledave and his sons.

"Oh, hi," exclaimed Sadie. "I'm so sorry, I didn't see you inside. I told you I would buy your meal."

"Oh, don't worry about that, ma'am," the father replied.

Sadie introduced the Littledaves to Lance, and he shook hands with all three.

"It's nice to meet you," the father said to Lance, "and nice to see you again, ma'am. We're on our way to Tahlequah to pick up some parts, and we've got to get going." They climbed into their truck and started to pull away when little Matt pushed his elbow out the open window. "Tell Mrs. Ray the food was as good as she said it would be." And then they were gone.

Lance wrinkled his forehead. "Mrs. Ray?"

"Evidently, Goldie had done some business there in the past and invited them to the café. He doesn't know she's dead."

Lance nodded, then he climbed into his police car and drove off.

32

That afternoon, Sadie and Emma closed the café, climbed into the Explorer, and drove toward Emma's. Sadie looked forward to seeing more of Goldie's collection of Indian artwork and baskets.

Emma leaned back and rested her head on the headrest. "Whew, this has been a long day."

"Emma, I should help you more in the kitchen since Rosalee has been doing so well managing the front by herself."

"It's a habit I have, liking to do everything myself. I guess I just want to prove to myself and everyone else that I can run that place as well as Goldie did. And, you know, I think I could have if she'd have just given me a chance." A look of satisfaction appeared on her face. "Besides that, it feels good to be tired. I sleep better when I'm tired."

"Well, we haven't had much of a chance to talk today. Did you hear what happened to George Stump?"

"Land o' living, I guess. I don't know why people can't figure out that having an illicit sexual affair like that is going to get them in trouble. Always has, always will."

"It's hard to believe the chief of police was in on an embezzlement scheme, though. Not to mention, they proved he's the one who pushed me in the vault and then a few days later sabotaged my car. I think they are actually looking into the possibility he may have had something to do with Goldie's murder."

A look of surprise covered Emma's face. "I thought they said Pearl killed Goldie."

"I don't think they were ever able to prove anything."

Anger swelled in Emma's voice. "I thought she confessed. I thought it was over."

"I think I may have spoken out of turn, Emma. I'm sorry. I'm sure if something else comes up about—I'm sure Lance will let you know if anything changes about that."

Sadie parked in front of the house and the two women got out and went inside. Sadie could see where Emma had been boxing up many of Goldie's things.

"Just make yourself at home, honey," said Emma. "Some of the baskets are piled up in that corner. The beaded bag is in that box with the pictures." She pointed at a cardboard box on the sofa. "I'll get the rest for you."

The framed photos once displayed on top of the piano had been stacked haphazardly in another box on a nearby table. Sadie picked up the top picture, a very old photo of Goldie and her boyfriend. She dusted it off with the palm of her hand and looked closely. An envelope that had been taped to the back of the frame came loose in her hand. The outside of the envelope was addressed to someone named Skye. She turned the picture back over and stared at the young man.

"Emma?" Sadie raised her voice hoping Emma could hear her.

"I'll be right there," she called from a back room.

"Do you know what Goldie's boyfriend's name was? The one that went off to the army?"

Emma carried a beaded gun sheath into the living room, dropped it on the floor, and wiped her forehead with the back of her wrist.

"Oh, Emma. This is awesome." Sadie placed the picture and envelope on the table and hurried to retrieve the suede cover. "Let me help you."

"No, this is it, for now. What did you say?"

"Oh, nothing." Sadie fingered the beadwork and noticed the initials. "I just wondered what Goldie's boyfriend's name was. He looks familiar."

"Nick, or Mick . . . Mickey, I think. He was Indian."

The tone of Emma's last three words washed over Sadie, and she instantly shot back before she could stop herself.

"Did you not like him just because he was Indian, Emma?" Sadie asked.

"He was okay, I guess. Goldie could have done better."

Sadie bristled. "You seem to have forgotten that I'm Cherokee."

"It's one thing to work with an Indian, but I'd never marry one."

"With your attitude I doubt an Indian would be interested in marrying you, either."

Emma glared. "Well at least I don't live off the government like they do. It's our tax dollars they get in those checks every month."

Sadie's anger flared. "Let's just nip that lie in the bud right here. I know a lot of Indians, and the only one who gets a check from the Bureau of Indian Affairs gets it because there is a gas well on his restricted land. The BIA manages it for him because he's Indian. Haven't you heard about the lawsuit where the Indians are suing the Federal government for losing billions of their dollars? That's Indian money they lost, Emma, not government money."

Emma blinked wildly at Sadie. "I thought they all lived on welfare."

"No, we don't all live on welfare. Where do you get that stuff? We work and pay taxes in this country like everyone else does. It's a lot harder for Indians to get jobs around here because of attitudes like yours. Believe it or not, Emma, we're not going away anytime soon."

"Well, I'm sorry." Emma's eyes began to water and her face turned sour.

"That's okay. I don't think we're going to cure the ills of centuries of Indian-white history here." Sadie turned, picked up the picture again and quickly moved the conversation forward. "What did you say happened to Goldie's boyfriend?"

"He ran off," snorted Emma, "and never came back for Goldie. Served her right."

Sadie looked at the initials on the beadwork and suddenly remembered the grainy photo in the newspaper article about Red's brother. "Was his name Yahola?"

Emma frowned. "I don't know. It was more than thirty years ago. It doesn't matter anymore."

The front door opened and Rosalee rushed in. With a radiant smile, she held up a pink invoice and waved it in the air. "This is going to tell us for sure." Rosalee sounded excited. "I don't know how to thank you, Sadie."

Emma wiped her eyes with the back of her hand. "What's this all about, Rosalee? What do we need to thank Sadie for?"

"She lent me a hundred dollars so I could pay John Mobley to give me a blood sample."

"A hundred dollars?" gasped Emma.

"We just met at Dr. Brown's office and he drew the blood. Red's going to get it tested for us."

"Oh." Emma's face fell. "I can't believe this. I don't know why you and Goldie want to hurt me like this after everything I've done for you." She turned on her heels and stormed into the bedroom.

Sadie looked at Rosalee. "Why did she say 'you and Goldie'?"

Rosalee shrugged. "I don't know and I don't care. I'm tired of her trying to make me feel guilty. It isn't going to work anymore."

"Do you know anyone named Skye?"

Rosalee smiled and her face softened. "The last time I saw Aunt Goldie, she called me that. She said I was like the sky on a cloudless day."

Sadie picked up the envelope and handed it to Rosalee. "Then I guess this is for you."

Rosalee sat down on the edge of the sofa and ran her finger under the flap of the envelope and unfolded a legal document. After she looked at it for a moment her eyes widened and her face lit up. "Oh, my gosh. Mother's really going to be pissed off about this."

"What is it?" asked Sadie.

Rosalee hurriedly stuffed the paper back in the envelope. "It's a deed to Aunt Goldie's house, and it's made out to me." She stood and wiggled her behind. "My mother is going to croak." She stopped dancing and faced Sadie. "Please don't tell her about this just yet. Okay?"

Sadie smiled at Rosalee's antics and nodded. "Okay."

"I'm going to wait outside for John," continued Rosalee. "He should be here any minute." She walked to the door. "He wants to talk. Can you believe it? He's acting like a normal human being." She held the envelope in the air. "This is going to change everything."

As Rosalee left the room, Sadie returned to the box of pictures and dug out the beaded bag from under several pictures. When she tugged the drawstring open and looked inside, she saw two yellowed pieces of paper, each folded many times to fit inside the small purse. She gingerly removed them and carefully unfolded two handwritten notes. She read the one that appeared to be the oldest first.

My dearest Goldie,
Tomorrow I leave for a place on the other side of the world. I made this

purse for you so when you look at it you will know that my heart is here with you. I will think of you every day and when I return we will make a home and a family together. I pledge my love to you forever and ever.

Love, Mickey

Sadie swallowed hard and unfolded the second piece of paper. She read it and took a deep breath. "I'm afraid this is going to change more than anyone ever dreamed," she muttered to herself as she refolded both notes and returned them to the bag. As she replaced the purse in the box with the pictures, her cell phone rang. It was Lance.

"Oh, Lance, wait 'til you hear what I just found out. Goldie had a beaded bag and inside—"

Sadie could hear alarm in Lance's voice through the tinny speaker of her cell phone. "Sadie, I did some checking with Matthew Littledave in Siloam Springs. According to his records, Goldie Ray rented a red Geo Tracker on July 22 and returned it on July 24."

"So?" she asked and switched the phone to her other ear, hoping to hear better.

"Goldie was murdered on the morning of July 23." He paused for a moment for that fact to sink in. "She paid in cash. One of the boys took her money and failed to get a credit card or a picture I.D."

"Oh, no."

"The kid recognized Emma in the café this morning as Goldie Ray because that was the name she used when she rented the car. And that's not all. The shotgun that Gertie used on me was traced back to a gun dealer, also in Siloam Springs. It was sold to Emily Singer. Sadie, you were right. It's the same gun that killed Goldie Ray."

Sadie gasped. "Emma bought the gun?" Her heart dropped like a rock as she realized what that must mean. She turned toward the kitchen, hoping to make a quick exit out the back door. Suddenly, she felt something very cold and hard in the middle of her back.

Sadie twirled around and her knees buckled. All she could see was the barrel of a .410 shotgun.

"Emma! No!" yelled Sadie.

"Sadie, where are you?" Lance's voice squawked through the phone.

Emma struck Sadie's hand with the end of the gun barrel and the phone flew onto the floor. Sadie eased backward in an attempt to increase the distance between her and the shotgun. Emma stood her ground.

"Where's the money?" asked Emma, as she poked at Sadie with the gun.

"What money?"

"Don't play innocent with me. I know Goldie had some cash money from selling the café. You bought it, so where is it?"

"I don't know anything about Goldie's money, Emma. But I know she had a lot of doctor bills."

"I don't believe you. She always hid her money under her mattress. I turned her bed upside down, and all I found was five hundred dollars. That ain't squat and you know it. You cheated her out of that café, didn't you?" She jabbed at Sadie with the end of the gun again. "Never mind. I'm going to kill you anyway. The café is going to be mine. I've already proved I can run it without help from anyone, including you and Rosalee. She's nothing but a drunk. I heard you in here asking her who Skye was. This is all going to stop right here."

"Think, Emma." Sadie tried to stay calm. "You will never get away with this."

"I got away with it last time, didn't I? And I'll get away with it again."

"You're not thinking straight. Rosalee's right outside."

"I don't care. You've turned her against me. I worked my hands to the bone to support that girl, and she turned out to be a drunk. She's done nothing but cause me heartache for thirty-six years. Nothing!"

Sadie looked at the phone on the floor and wondered if Lance heard enough to realize what was going on. But where was he? If he was still at Littledave's car lot in Siloam Springs, he would never make it in time. Emma's eyes looked like they belonged to a rabid dog, totally void of any emotion. I've got to keep talking, thought Sadie.

"She just wants to know who her birth mother was," said Sadie. "That's not so bad, is it? Tell her, Emma. You know who her mother was. It's not the end of the world for her to know Goldie was her mother. She's going to find out anyway and this way you can work through it together. This is not worth ruining your life over."

"My life is already ruined. You ruined it."

"No, Emma. I didn't do anything to hurt you."

"You took the café. It should have been mine. I could have run it all these years just as good as she did. Mom and Daddy gave her that café because they loved her more than they loved me. And she was the one having an illegitimate baby. She was a slut. I had to take her baby and raise it, and she got to keep the café. What kind of deal was that?"

"Emma, just put the gun down and we can work it out." Keep talking, keep talking, Sadie reminded herself. "We'll talk about it. I promise it'll be okay. You can have the café. I'll give it to you."

"It's too late for you." Emma blinked wildly. "Do you have any idea how hard it was for me to act like I actually cared about Goldie and stay in a town where everyone thought she was the best thing that ever stirred up a pot of beans? I had to kill her. She was going to tell Rosalee the truth, that she was her mother. God knows who the father is. Probably that Indian boy who ran off and left her. You see, Goldie always got everything she wanted. She screwed up and gave away her baby. Then she wanted it back. I just couldn't let that happen." Emma's chin began to quiver. "It's not fair."

The front door opened and John Mobley walked in with Rosalee close behind.

"Mother!" screamed Rosalee.

"Get out!" yelled Emma, as she swung the .410 toward the door.

"You crazy old woman. You're as bad as my mother." Without a hint of hesitation, John marched straight toward Emma with the confidence of a seasoned Marine. He grabbed the shotgun, jerked the barrel toward him, and ripped the stock from Emma's hands just as she pulled the trigger. The power of the deafening blast knocked Emma backward onto the floor. John Mobley crumpled, holding his chest.

"No!" screamed Rosalee as she fell to John's side. "John, John, please don't die," she cried, as she tried to stop the bleeding with her hand. "He's not breathing!" she yelled. "Someone help me! He's not breathing!"

Sadie ran to the phone, dialed 9-1-1, and begged Maggie to send help immediately. Emma rolled onto her stomach and crawled slowly toward the bedroom.

"Stay put, Emma!" Sadie yelled as she dropped the phone. She kicked the shotgun out of reach and placed her knee in the small of Emma's back to keep her from moving.

Rosalee, covered in blood, cradled John's head and rocked back and forth. Tears streamed down her face. "Why? Why?" she repeated.

Emma began to cry as the sound of a siren sang in the distance.

33

Sadie and Rosalee sat cross-legged on a blanket of grass in the shade of a tall blackgum tree. They took turns tossing pebbles into the rippling water of a nearby stream and watching as, periodically, the tree surrendered a fiery red leaf to the late September breeze. Some leaves floated slowly to the ground, while others landed in the water and rode the current until they disappeared downstream.

"I didn't even know this park was here," Rosalee said.

"It's kind of nice, isn't it? It's peaceful."

Red walked down a slope covered in crimson sumac on the opposite side of the stream. He wore his black hat with an unusually large feather secured under a beaded band and carried a bundle under his arm. He hopped across a makeshift bridge of large rocks and joined the two women.

"Thank you for coming," he said. "I couldn't think of a nicer place to talk."

Sadie started to stand.

"No," he said. "Stay seated." He chose a spot in front of them, placed the bundle on the grass, and sat down next to it. He looked at Rosalee and winked. "We have the test results back."

"Oh, Red, I should have told you. We don't need that test any more. I know Goldie was my mother, not Pearl."

Red ignored her. "And the results were positive," he said.

"Positive?" Sadie asked.

Red nodded once. "Positive," he repeated.

"But I know John Mobley was not my brother," Rosalee said. "You're wrong."

"I always knew John Mobley, may he rest in peace, was not your brother," he said.

Rosalee stared at him. "If you knew that, why did you let me go through all of that with the stupid blood test?"

"I knew John wasn't your brother because I buried his twin sister."

Both women looked stunned.

"When Pearl was raped," he continued, "and yes, you were right about the article, she was raped behind the café, her folks were so embarrassed about Pearl's predicament that they took her to a little shack in the woods behind their place. They left her there with food and supplies and checked on her about once a week."

"Oh, my." Sadie shook her head.

"I came upon Pearl not long after she had given birth to twins, a boy and a girl. She had wrapped John in a towel and propped him against a tree. He was screaming his head off. She was holding the little girl under the water in the creek. I rushed over to her, but the baby was dead. Pearl was delirious. I don't really know if she drowned the poor thing, or if it died during childbirth. I put Pearl and John back in the cabin and buried the baby. Then I walked to her folks' place and told them they needed to get up there and take care of their daughter."

"That's why Pearl kept saying someone took her baby girl." Sadie hugged her knees to her chest.

"Did you tell anyone about the other baby?" Rosalee asked.

"No, not until now. I don't know if that was right or wrong, but that was the decision I made and I've lived with it all these years."

"I don't understand." Rosalee shrugged her shoulders. "Then how can the test results be positive? You just said Pearl was John's mother, and I know Goldie was mine."

Red untied the string around the bundle and unrolled the piece of suede holding the contents together. He uncovered an old envelope, opened it, removed the letter inside, and held it in his hand. "This is the last letter I received from my brother before his helicopter was shot down in Vietnam. I never really understood what he was talking about. Now I know." He unfolded the letter and began to read:

Dear Brother,

Keep the fire burning for me. Soon there will be another baby Red Stick warrior born to carry on our legacy. And, brother, we are going to eat

very well for the rest of our lives.
Mickey

Rosalee looked around. "I don't get it," she said.

Tears streamed down Sadie's cheeks as she looked into Red's face and felt the impact of his brother's words.

"How can you tell anything from that letter?" Rosalee sounded irritated. "This doesn't make any sense to me."

Red pulled another envelope out, this time from his shirt pocket. "I asked the lab to check your blood against mine. They had a DNA sample from me, because they had to have it to identify Mickey's remains."

Rosalee stared at Red.

"Mickey was my twin brother. Our DNA is identical. You are Mickey's daughter. I am your uncle. I knew it the first time I saw you, but I wouldn't let myself believe it. But it's true. And here is the proof." He dug in the contents of the bundle again and pulled out a photograph of his brother. "You have his smile," he said, "and his laugh. Yes, you are his. I told you one time that you were conceived in Liberty. To tell you the truth, I don't know where conception took place. But I can tell you one thing. You were conceived in love. Your daddy and your momma loved you."

Tears glazed Rosalee's eyes. She took the photograph and held it carefully in her hand. "Why did he refer to me as a Red Stick?"

Red laughed. "When we were born, my father looked at my brother and deemed him to be a great leader and named him McIntosh after a Creek chief. We called him Mickey. He looked at me and decided I should be a great warrior and named me *Eto Catuce*, which means Red Stick, so they called me Red. But my brother didn't want to be a leader. He wanted to be a warrior."

"I went to Vietnam and fought in a senseless war. I came home and, as a combat veteran, became a member of the Creek Red Stick Society. Mickey was so proud of me he wanted to go, too. I begged him not to go. I knew how bad it was. But he joined the army anyway and shipped off to be just like his brother. Only he didn't make it home, not for thirty-six years anyway. But now you are here, and that is good."

Rosalee swallowed hard. "I can't believe this." She looked at Sadie. "Did you know about this?"

"No, not for sure, but I suspected that was the case. When I approached Red about it, he asked me to allow him to take care of it in his own time. And I did."

Rosalee took a deep breath. "I don't know what to say."

"You don't have to say anything." Red pulled a small beaded purse from his shirt. "Mickey made this for you. It matches the one he gave your mother, Goldie." He rewrapped the bundle and placed the bag on top. "These things are for you. Take them, and when you are ready we will talk."

Rosalee reached for the items and he held her hand in his.

"I am so sorry." Red dropped his chin to his chest. "As Mickey's brother, it was my responsibility to take care of Goldie. I had no idea she was in danger. I am so sorry. Maybe I can do a better job taking care of their daughter."

Sadie wiped her face. "It's okay, Red."

The following month faded into shades of burnt copper and golden red across the October countryside. Before long, the winter rains would arrive and wash away the leaves, revealing the bare bones of the oak and maple and the pale bark of the birch. But for now, the warmth of the afternoon sun had temporarily returned.

Sadie and Lance waited in Sadie's Explorer in front of the Cherokee County Courthouse. Sonny sat in the backseat, trying to force his head and shoulders between the front bucket seats.

"I still don't understand how the shotgun that killed Goldie ended up in a meth house in Delaware County," Sadie said.

"According to the Campbell boy, he found it somewhere below Powderhorn on Lake Eucha, which is exactly where Charlie lost his lure. The boy saw something shiny in the water, climbed down on the rocks to see what it was, and found the gun wedged between a couple of large boulders. Emma confessed to throwing it in the lake on her way back to Siloam Springs. She thought it would fall into the water, but it didn't make it that far."

"That was kind of out of her way, wasn't it?"

"Yeah, but she needed to kill some time anyway. Remember, she didn't show up in Liberty until the day after Goldie was killed."

Sadie thought for a moment. "What happened to Gertie's kid?"

"His Kiowa grandparents have him. I met them and they seem to be good people. They'll remember the good things about his mother and pass them on to him. Hopefully, he won't fall prey to drugs and alcohol the way Gertie did. I think he'll be all right. Kids are pretty resilient."

Sadie could see Rosalee and Red walking up the sidewalk. Sadie got out and waited, then handed Rosalee an envelope. "Hi, Rosalee. I have the deed to the café for you. Red asked me to put the café in your name when he gave me the money." They both looked at Red who stood staring at the ground. Sadie returned her attention to Rosalee. "I know it hasn't been very long, but I think you've proven you've got what it takes to persevere. It's a trait you must have inherited from your real mother and father. And I think Goldie would be proud to know that her daughter is the one who will carry on for her. And I won't mind if you change the name back to the Liberty Diner."

"Oh, I could never do that," Rosalee said.

"I think we should name it the Indian Café." Red smiled and adjusted his hat.

Sadie laughed. "I know the regulars are anxious for the café to reopen, and I'm thrilled to be getting back to life in Eucha."

"I will never be able to thank you enough, Sadie."

"I'm sorry about Goldie," said Sadie, "and Emma."

Rosalee looked down. "It's kind of funny isn't it? I knew my mother all along. I just thought she was my aunt, a very special aunt. I wish I knew why she gave me away."

"You know," Red interrupted. "Your mother would have never given you up for adoption if Mickey hadn't been killed. She thought she was doing what was best for you. Nowadays, single women raise kids on their own all the time. But not back then. It was a different time, Rosalee."

Rosalee held the envelope to her chest and smiled. Sadie pulled a small camera from her pocket, snapped a picture, and stepped back by Lance.

"I think everything worked out the way it was supposed to," said Rosalee. "I have a wonderful new family. It's awesome. And that includes you, Sadie. I feel like we are family, too." She looked at Red, then rummaged in her purse and pulled out a Creek tribal card. "Look, I'm a Creek citizen."

Sadie took the card and read out loud. "Rosalee Skye Yahola. That's got a nice ring to it, Rosalee. You're not keeping Singer as your name?"

"No. I'm starting a new life. Red got my birth certificate unsealed and he's helping me with the legal work to change my name. That's what my name should have been all along, anyway. And besides that, I'm learning so much about my ancestors." She smiled. "I am so happy."

Red grinned and repositioned his hat. "*Cehecakares,*" he said, then walked away.

Sadie and Lance looked at each other with blank faces.

"It means, See you all later," said Rosalee over her shoulder as she hurried to catch her uncle.

Sadie looked at Lance. "I think they're going to be just fine."

"Yes, I agree." He opened the car door and waited for Sadie to get in. "Let's see," he said. "I think you owe me a horseback ride."

"Let's go," beamed Sadie, as Sonny barked his approval.

About the Author

Sara Sue Hoklotubbe is a Cherokee tribal citizen who loves to write about her people and transport readers into modern-day Cherokee life. She grew up on the banks of Lake Eucha in northeastern Oklahoma and uses that location as the setting for her mystery novels.

As author of *Deception on All Accounts* (The University of Arizona Press, 2003), Sara was named "Writer of the Year" by the Wordcraft Circle of Native Writers and Storytellers. She and her husband divide their time between Oklahoma and Colorado.